Pride of the Sioux

Karen Dee Musson

ISBN: 979-8-89397-661-8

Published by EliteScribes Book Writing

This book is dedicated to my angels, Kimberly Musson Vergonet, Liz (Medicine Moon) Martinez, Kailyn Hope, Ruth Dennis, and my Lord Jesus Christ.

Special thanks to Millie Musson and Millie Van Gundy Walker for your time and dedication. I could not have done this without you.

Table of Contents

CHAPTER ONE 8

Prospector Earl 8

CHAPTER TWO 17

The Necklace 17

CHAPTER THREE 26

The New Arrivals 26

CHAPTER FOUR 38

Dream Catcher 38

CHAPTER FIVE 50

The Enigma 50

CHAPTER SIX 64

The Iron Horse 64

CHAPTER SEVEN 78

The Scouts 78

CHAPTER EIGHT 90

The Great Healer 90

CHAPTER NINE 105

A Boy's Demise 105

CHAPTER TEN 117

The Underground Fortress 117

CHAPTER ELEVEN 125

A Doctor's Rage 125

CHAPTER TWELVE 139

The Sweet One 139

CHAPTER THIRTEEN 150

A Big Dilemma 150

CHAPTER FOURTEEN 160

Spirit Dog...160

CHAPTER FIFTEEN 168

Suspicions..168

CHAPTER SIXTEEN 179

The Yellow Rock...179

CHAPTER SEVENTEEN 190

Medicine Moon 190

CHAPTER EIGHTEEN..200

A Leap of Courage 200

CHAPTER NINETEEN..213

The Tracks..213

CHAPTER TWENTY 222

The Slaughtering 222

CHAPTER TWENTY-ONE 231

The Healers 231

CHAPTER TWENTY-TWO 240

The Lost Souls 240

CHAPTER TWENTY-THREE...256

The Stranger in the Trees 256

CHAPTER TWENTY-FOUR..266

The Dark Man...266

CHAPTER TWENTY-FIVE..274

The Betrayal 274

CHAPTER TWENTY-SIX..284

The Warning..284

CHAPTER TWENTY-SEVEN 293

A Chief's Frustration...293

CHAPTER TWENTY-EIGHT 304

The Cabin in the Woods 304

CHAPTER TWENTY-NINE..311

The Yuletides 311

CHAPTER THIRTY..324

The Indian Scout 324

CHAPTER THIRTY-ONE 333

The Diversion 333

CHAPTER THIRTY-TWO 343

The Fabricated Plan...343

CHAPTER THIRTY-THREE 352

The Closure 352

EPILOGUE 365

About the Author 368

CHAPTER ONE
Prospector Earl

Rose sits next to her husband, Roger, gazing out at the landscape in front of her. She is holding her parasol over her head to shield herself from the blazing sun. Her mind is deep in thought of her sister-in-law Carrie and the Lakota band that she left behind early this morning. She is relieved to know that Koawa is going to be alright from the stab wounds that he received from his wicked stepbrother Red Hawk, when he and Prairie Dawn were saving her life when Dog Soldiers kidnapped her. She owes Koawa her life and is feeling very sheepish for not trusting him and giving him such a hard time when they were on the run. She is certain that she would not be here today if it were not for him and Prairie Dawn.

She deeply sighs as she remembers the warm welcome that she and Roger received when they arrived back at camp with White Horse and the others, and the joyous love that they showed Roger when they received word of how he saved Koawa's life. A huge celebration around the center fire was held. She and Roger were entertained with music, dancing, and a big feast in honor of Roger, whom the Lakota call the Great Healer. She remembers how much she enjoyed listening to White Horse, as he was praising his people for how Roger not only saved Koawa's life, but his own as well. She saw the love that the Lakota people have for each other and was taken aback a little at the welcome that she received from them as well. Her insides turn angry when she realizes how foolish she was about her belief that the Sioux were bad people. After just spending a short night with them, she quickly saw the injustice they were given and was horrified at herself for believing the lies she was always told about them. She has never met any other people who show so much love and have so much compassion for one another. She understands now why her husband is so good to them.

She found herself quickly falling in love with these people, and she dried a tear when she and Roger rode away from them this morning. She vows to herself that she will never turn her back on them again, and she will always open her heart up to any of them, especially Koawa, to whom she owes her life. She is aware that White Horse has only one small band of Sioux, and not all Indians will welcome white people. She saw that firsthand when the Dog Soldiers kidnapped her, but she will look at them differently now, and she will treat them with the utmost respect that they deserve. Her thoughts are interrupted when she hears Roger calling her name.

"Rose," he says. He smiles over at her when she turns her eyes to him.

"Where did you go?" he says. "I called your name several times."

"I am sorry, dear. My mind was wandering," she blushes.

"You were thinking about them, weren't you?"

"Yes, oh, Roger, I was so wrong about them. They are such good people and so humble."

"Yes. I can see how my sister fell in love with White Horse. He is a good man. He is very proud and very wise."

"Yes, and he welcomed me with open arms, despite how mean and cruel I was to him and Koawa."

"He understands, and unfortunately, I think they are both used to it."

There is a moment of silence in the air, except for the wagon wheels rolling across the prairie, as Rose once again thinks back on how mean she was to Koawa. Roger sees the sadness in his wife's eyes and reaches across to squeeze her hand.

"I have an idea," he tells her, as he changes the subject with hopes of putting a smile back on his wife's face.

His heart goes out to her, as these last few weeks have been a nightmare for her. He is certain that when they return home and her adrenaline has died down, she will break down when the reality of everything that has transpired sinks in. He thinks to himself how they have not spent one night together in nearly six months, because of a series of events that have been out of their control. He decides that she is overdue for some pampering.

"How would you like to spend the evening in a nice hotel that caters to hot water? We can bathe in a hot tub, and then I can take you out to a nice dinner. We can take a moonlight stroll down the walkway, and then we can spend a nice evening in a comfortable bed beside each other." He lifts her hand up to his lips and gently kisses it. "I have missed you, my darling, more than you can imagine."

Rose blushes just thinking about how much she wants to lie with her husband and wrap her body around his. Roger does not appear to be the type of man who would be good in bed, but on their wedding night, she was proven wrong. It was the first time for both, and she was not disappointed and was surprised at how well he performed for being a virgin. They do not connect every night, but when they do, it is like their wedding night all over again. Her insides tingle just thinking about it.

"Darling, I would love to," she says.

"There is a town not far from here. I have been there before, and they have a very nice hotel and restaurant. Max can sleep in the stable with the horses."

Rose's twinkle in her eyes assures Roger that she agrees to his idea, and he quickly nudges his team further ahead and into the town. "But first, dear, if it is not a bother to you, I would like to check on prospector Earl. We are very close to his place, and I haven't checked on him since last fall, just before White Horse came."

"Earl?" she questions. "Isn't he the one we met in Hedge Brook last spring when the town had an influenza outbreak, and you were called on to help?"

"Yes," he answers. Rose crinkles up her bottom lip as she remembers the prospector very well. She rarely ever accompanies Roger when he is called upon, but there were so many people who had fallen ill that she went along with him to help him out. It was then that she met the rude and vulgar man. He claimed he was there to cash in a few nuggets from a gold mine. When Roger questioned him where it was, he refused to say. His reasoning was that he feared that if he said that, Roger would come and steal his claim. As crazy as it sounded, Roger just ignored it and was thankful that the ornery man was willing to help, as nearly two-thirds of the town had fallen ill, and the death rate from it was the most that Roger had ever had to deal with at one time.

After the influenza outbreak was contained, Earl had fallen ill with it. Most of Rogers's medicine had been used, and he had very little left to help Earl with. Earl was persistent in returning home and telling Roger that if he was going to die, he wanted to die with his claim. Earl had just enough strength in him to tell Roger where he lived. Rose remembers very well sitting in the back of the wagon beside Earl, fearing that he would die before he got home. Roger and Rose stayed with Earl for almost a week, bringing him back to health. Miraculously, Earl survived. It may have been because of his near-death experience, but almost immediately upon his recovery, Earl's heart turned soft and Roger and he have been friends ever since.

"No, I do not mind at all," she smiles.

Although she is not really thrilled about the idea of seeing the man again, she completely understands why her husband would, and being that they were so close to his place, it would be foolish not to stop and check in on him. In a little less than an hour, the small little cabin tucked down in a valley is seen.

"I forgot how beautiful it is here," Rose says, gazing out at the valley around her.

"Yes, a virgin of nature," Roger agrees.

"It is so quiet here. Are you sure he is here?" Rose asks.

"I see his mule. He must be around here." Roger then calls. "Hello there!"

After a few moments of stillness, Roger hands Rose the reins and jumps down, making his way to the house. He gazes out at the stream that is just to the edge of the house and watches his dog Max as he starts to run around. He knocks on the door. He waits a few seconds for Earl to answer. He notices the door is partially ajar. He nudges it open and calls out again.

Rose is waiting patiently, holding onto the reins of the team, as she too looks around. Roger steps inside the cabin to see that it is empty. He then hears Rose yell out his name. He runs outside just as Rose jumps out of the wagon and takes off running up a hill to the outhouse. She comes down on her knees in front of Earl.

"I must be dead, and my angel has come," Earl gasps.

"Shh," she says, just as Roger has made it up the hill.

"Doc," he hears Earl whisper.

Roger can tell that Earl is having problems breathing and has broken out in a sweat.

"Rose, go get my bag off the wagon," he says before turning his attention back to Earl. "What has happened?" he asks him.

"I crossed paths with a rattlesnake when I was returning from the outhouse."

"You need to save your strength," Roger tells him.

Rose has returned with Rogers's bag. He opens it up to remove what he will need.

"There is no time, Doc," Earl mumbles. "Too much time has gone by. No medicine can help me now."

"Where did it bite you?"

"On my leg, but Doc, listen to me. Please."

Roger lifts Earl's pant leg, revealing the gruesome bite. Roger is worried that the venom in the bite is too great and is concerned about the amount of time that has gone by, and fears he is too late. He can tell that Earl is fading fast. He has dealt with only two other venous bites from rattlesnakes in his career, and both died before Roger could help them. He fears the same fate is going to happen to Earl.

"Rose darling, wait for me down at the wagon. And watch your step, the snake could still be nearby."

Rose is certain as to why her husband wants her to leave. He realizes that there is nothing that he can do to help Earl. She remembers Roger telling her how sometimes the victim of a snake bite will go into convulsions and foam at the mouth just before they die. He said that the sight of it can turn your stomach or give you nightmares from the image for a long time. She is certain that he is shielding her from this in the event it does happen, so for that reason, she quietly does as she is asked and makes her way down the hill, watching the ground for the snake as she goes. Roger takes his friend's hand into his and squeezes it.

"Have you made good with your Maker, Earl?" he asks.

"Don't worry about me. I need you to promise me."

"Shh, it's alright," Roger says. "I will stay with you until the end."

"My claim, keep my claim. Don't let anyone take it."

Roger can see that Earl's breathing is getting shallower and he is fighting to hold on.

"Just let yourself go. It will not hurt as much if you just relax."

Earl faintly shook his head. He is determined to tell the only friend that he has ever had what his dying wish is.

"Fireplace, mattress, map."

"Shh! It's alright."

"Take it."

Roger is not certain as to what Earl is trying to tell him, but he can tell that it is important to him. He lowers his ear closer to Earl's lips to hear him faintly speaking.

"Gold, a lot of it. Take it."

"Earl, I will do whatever you wish, but I do not want your gold."

"You take it. Where I am going, I don't need it." Earl tried to laugh but is unable and closes his eyes.

"You rest in peace, my friend," Roger says. "I will keep it."

Roger then begins to recite the Lord's Prayer. As Earl takes his final few breaths, a faint smile appears on his face. He can die in peace now, as he knows his gold is in safe hands. Just when Roger says amen, Earl passes away.

CHAPTER TWO
The Necklace

Life at the Lakota camp is back to normal. Rose and Roger left at first light this morning. It was hard to see them go, and I only hope that very soon I will see them again. White Horse has made a remarkable recovery and has full use of his leg. Although his mind is still a little sketchy from his accident, he is back to himself. Little Foot's stitches are healing well in his head, but I still insist on him wearing the bandage around it to keep it clean from any prairie dust. Rising Sun is doing well despite Red Hawk's absence. Minoke has taken her in and become her mother figure and shares her lodge with her. Rising Sun is still unaware that White Horse is her real father, and he is planning on keeping it that way. I do not totally agree with this, but I have been sworn to secrecy.

No one has seen or heard from Red Hawk. This pleases White Horse and gives him no concern. I, on the other hand, cannot shake the feeling that we haven't seen the last of him. Koawa is slowly getting better. It has been nearly a week since he was stabbed by Red Hawk, and Roger had to go in and stop the bleeding. It took Roger many hours to stitch Koawa back up, and several days passed before Koawa was stable enough to come home. We are all so fortunate that Roger was able to stop the bleeding, and Koawa was so determined to hang on.

I have just finished feeding my family their afternoon meal, and I am on my way to give Koawa his. I find him resting on his pelt when I step in.

"I thought you might be hungry," I tell him, coming down on my knees beside him.

"I am afraid I still do not have much of an appetite," he tells me.

"If you want to get out of this bed, then you need to eat something."

"You are impossible," he groans as he struggles to sit up.

"I have been called worse," I tease him, giving him my arm for support as he comes to a sit. When he is as comfortable as he is going to get, I place the bowl of food on his lap.

"I will be more than happy to sit with you while you eat if you wish." He faintly grins.

"I would like that." I watch him pick up a berry and bite into it. Like his daughter, Koawa loves any kind of berry.

"Morning Dove picked the berries fresh this morning."

"Yes, she came in and saw me a few hours ago when you were tending to Little Foot. She brought me a bowl then. Of course, she ate almost all of them." I chuckle, as I know Morning Dove loves her berries. Every time she and I are picking them, she will end up putting more in her mouth than in her basket.

"Blue Thunder was telling me that there is still no sign of Red Hawk."

"Yes, that is what I hear as well," I agree.

"He will be back," Koawa growls.

"White Horse doesn't seem to think so. He says that he is not ignorant enough to return because he knows that our warriors will kill him for what he did to you and White Horse. I can't help but wonder that White Horse is hoping that he doesn't because, for some reason, White Horse wants him alive."

"That is because he is kin, and White Horse has a sense of loyalty to him."

"He is your kin too," I argue.

"I have no love for him. Red Hawk is a bad seed. I have no room for him in my life. If I ever see him again, I will not hesitate to kill him."

"He nearly killed you."

"That was ignorance on my part. I guarantee you it will not happen again."

"I have never been more fearful for your life than I was then." He looks up at me from his bowl of food, resting his hand on top of mine.

"Prairie Dawn, when I was lying on the boulder, I believed I was going to die. I did not want to go without telling you how I felt about you."

I interrupt him and place my hand over his. I know Koawa is not a man who expresses his feelings to anyone, especially a woman. Even in the years that he was married to Running Water, he rarely ever told her that he loved her, unlike White Horse, who tells me every day. But Running Water always knew, by the way, Koawa treated her, that he loved her. For Koawa to even faintly acknowledge his feelings for me, despite thinking that he was going to die, means a lot to me.

"You don't need to tell me, Koawa, as I already know. You have always been there for me and have given me the love and protection when White Horse couldn't. I will always treasure what we have, and I will always love you."

He faintly grins and squeezes my hand. He quickly takes it away upon seeing White Horse walk in. I know by the look on White Horse's face that he overheard the conversation. His eyes are thick on Koawa's.

"Darling," I say, coming to my feet. "I was just giving Koawa something to eat."

White Horse fails to look my way when I come up in front of him. His eyes never leave Koawa's. I am uncertain as to what thoughts are going through his mind or just what conclusion he has jumped to. I glance back at Koawa, and by the glance, he returns to me, I know I need to leave. I look up at White Horse, whose eyes are still pierced on Koawa's. I gently pat his well-formed chest and leave the lodge.

I am in our lodge. I find on the pelt that I share with my husband his necklace that he removed from around my neck the day I left to go get Rose from the Dog Soldiers. I place it over my head, allowing it to fall free. It is then that it dawns on me that Koawa's necklace is gone as well. I start looking for it. I looked everywhere, and it was nowhere to be found. I can only assume that White Horse must still have it. I am certain that he was not happy that I still had it on, but with everything transpiring with him being found alive and the news of my miscarriage, he said nothing about it.

I am continuing in my search when I see White Horse step into our lodge. I watch him come down on the pelt, resting his arm across his bent leg. His eyes become fixed on mine. White Horse is a man who is extremely hard to read, unlike me, who you can read like a book. His eyes are very dark and mysterious. He shows no emotion on his face; however, I know my husband well enough, and I am certain that the wheels in his head are turning regarding the conversation that I am certain he overheard.

"Looking for something?" he finally says.

"Koawa's necklace. It was taken off the day I left with Blue Thunder to get Rose, and I haven't seen it since?"

"Your marriage to my brother is no more. Therefore, the meaning of it no longer exists. Why would you want it?"

"Koawa is dear to me, and he saw me through a very difficult time," I answer him.

"The necklace represents a bond of unity between a husband and a wife, just as a white man would wear a ring. I am your husband. It is my necklace you are to wear, not Koawa's."

It then came clear to me that White Horse took it upon himself and did something to the necklace. This angers me, as I feel he had no right.

"You are jealous?" I huff.

"Jealousy is for the weak at heart," he calmly says. "It will turn a wise man into a fool. I am not jealous of Koawa or anyone for that matter."

"Then where is it?"

"I burnt it the night that I ate the turkey with Roger and Little Foot," he confesses.

"If you are not jealous, then why did you burn it?" I snap.

"It is simple: what it symbolizes no longer exists. The marriage officially is no more, so, therefore, the necklace must be destroyed."

I am not certain if there is any belief behind what White Horse is telling me or if maybe he really is jealous of the strong connection that I share with his brother. I start to calm myself down. Although I am not convinced that he didn't destroy the necklace out of jealousy or spite, I try to see it from his point of view. I am his wife, and I can see how it would look to him if I was wearing another man's necklace.

"I love you, White Horse. You do believe that, right?"

"I have never questioned your love for me," he answers.

"Good, because without your love, I am nothing."

I watch White Horse slightly tilt his head and faintly chuckle.

"What is so funny?" I questioned him.

"You say that you are nothing without me, but when you thought I was dead, you quickly ran to my brother's arms."

"That is not true, White Horse," I argue. "Koawa and I had to marry fast because of Red Hawk." I can tell by the look he gave me that he is not completely convinced by my words.

"Are you in love with him?" he asks.

"Not the kind of love that I have for you," I answer.

"But if I had not returned, you would still be married to him and sharing his pelt and not giving me a second thought."

"What was I supposed to do, White Horse? You yourself wanted him to take me in upon your death."

"Take you in. I never said to marry you. Carrie, you are the wife of a Chief. It is not custom that you would remarry. Koawa knows this."

"I will not live with a man and share his lodge unless I am married to him," I argue.

"There were ways for him to take you in and protect you that would not involve you in sharing a lodge with him. Carrie, I was not even gone for six months, and you remarried. In our custom, we grieve for years, and, being the chief's wife, you would be expected to grieve longer than most. I am blown away that not only Koawa allowed this, but Flying Hawk went along with it."

"You make it sound like Koawa took advantage of me and my ignorance of your culture. But White Horse, I assure you that it was not like that. Koawa showed me great love. When I lost you and then our child, I wanted to die. I had never felt so alone and scared in all my life. Koawa gave me a reason to live. He showed me the love in Little Foot that is carried on from you from our love for each other. I grieved for you. It destroyed me leaving your scaffold behind and joining the others in our winter home. I have never loved anyone more than I love you. Koawa was there not only to protect me from Red Hawk but also to show me how important it was to move on so your memory could live on. I married Koawa because I had to. There was no way I was going to allow Red Hawk to get anywhere near me. If he knew that I was married, then he would leave me alone."

For several moments, White Horse is still, gazing thickly into my eyes. I have never known White Horse to be the type of man who would be jealous of anything. He is the wealthiest and most prestigious man in our band, with the most horses, the biggest lodge, and the most coups. The only other warrior that would be even remotely close to White Horse in wealth is Koawa, and it is only because White Horse is chief that he is over him. There is no reason, except for me, for White Horse to be jealous of Koawa. After a few seconds, I watch White Horse extend out his hand. I come down on my knees in front of him and take it.

"I know you grieved, and I am grateful that my brother was there for you and the boys," he says, stroking my cheek. "As kind and generous as my brother can be, I think his feelings for you are stronger than what he makes it appear. I cannot blame him for this, as you are easy to love, and you're right; I brought this on myself."

My thought is interrupted when we hear Blue Thunder at the flap announcing to his chief that we have company. Before anything else can be said, White Horse is quick to step out of the flap to see who it is.

CHAPTER THREE
The New Arrivals

Roger dug a hole and buried Earl on top of a hill that overlooks his claim. Rose watches him pound the cross into the ground that she made when Roger was digging. Together, they give Earl a burial that would make Roger's father proud. Earl's mule is packed up with food from the cabin that Roger doesn't want to go to waste. Both he and Rose agree that neither one of them is in the mood for any pampering and decides to just head home. Roger squats down in front of Earl's grave and places the wildflowers that his wife freshly picked on top of it. "I will return, my friend. I promise." He then secures the house the best he can and heads his team for home.

White Horse and I step outside our lodge just as we see a small group of eight men, women, and children walking into camp. They all look tired, hungry, and distraught. It does not take us long to realize that our guests are from another band of Sioux who have escaped death when their camp was attacked by Blue Coats. White Horse is quick at greeting one of the warriors who is standing next to a woman close to my age.

"My friend," he says in his tongue as he extends out his hand. "I am Chief White Horse. Welcome."

"Thank you, Chief. My name is Crow Dog, and this is my sister Dancing Bear. Our camp was attacked by Pony soldiers a few days ago. We are all that remains. Our horses were slaughtered, and we have been walking for days. I ask of you if you can spare any food, as all we had to eat was a few berries along the way. Our children are growing weak and could use some nourishment before we move on. If you can spare anything, we would be most grateful."

"You are more than welcome to help yourself to whatever we have," White Horse says. "After you are fed, I will provide you with a horse and a few of my warriors. You can take them to your camp, and they will help you with collecting your dead, and you will travel no more, my friend, as you are home."

"You are most gracious," Crow Dog says.

"Come," White Horse says. "My wife will show you where you can lodge and rest until you are able to put up your own. Plenty of food will be brought to you all."

White Horse walks his guest up to me and orders Songbird and Minoke to bring them some food. Our guests are warmly welcomed, and quickly, we make every one of them feel like they are home. Unbeknownst to the Lakota camp, a figure is crouched down deeply in the tall grass and watches the Chief and the others as they greet their guests.

Roger and Rose make it home. They rode as far as they could during the night, only stopping briefly when neither one could keep their eyes open any longer and it was too dark to proceed. They are both extremely tired and relieved to finally be home. As Roger is bringing the wagon to a stop in front of the house, Rose looks over at the flower garden that is in full bloom.

"Oh, Roger," she says, widely grinning. "You are such a doll. You fixed the gate when I was gone and surprised me by planting flowers. They are so beautiful."

Roger faintly grins to himself as to why the garden looks the way it does and is a little surprised by how well it has grown despite the weeds pushing up and the lack of water that it has received due to their unsuspected absence. He still feels guilty that he had to discreetly bury Clarence there, and that is the reason as to why he planted the flowers, and it had nothing to do with his wife coming home. His conscience still bothers him that he must keep quiet about Clarence's death and that he did not receive a proper burial. He was given no choice in the matter and felt it was necessary to protect the Sioux from retaliation from the army if word got out on how Clarence died.

"I have been pestering you for months to fix the gate and plant the flowers," Rose says. "What made you decide to finally do it?"

"Oh, I reckon I was just missing you," he says.

She sweetly smiles at him as he applies the brake on the wagon and jumps down. He comes around to her side, reaching up to take her hand and helping her down. Max is quick at running off to the barn to find his bone.

"Oh, it feels so good to be home," Rose says.

"Yes, it does," he agrees. Roger begins to remove the supplies from the back of the wagon. "Darling," Rose says. "Can't that wait?"

"I suppose, but there is a lot to unload, and I would like to get it done before it gets dark."

"It is not going to get dark for hours," she says. She comes over and places her hands on his chest. "I think we can find something else to do that would be much more entertaining than unloading a wagon."

He watches her smirk as she walks one of her fingers up his chest. He softly chuckles with her flirting. He has missed the unity with his wife and was planning on uniting with her tonight, but she is giving him an invitation that he cannot refuse. He gently gives her a kiss while reaching for her hands.

"I think you're right," he smirks.

She felt like a newlywed when Roger was leading her into the house and over to their bed. The candles that he lit prior to her being taken by the Dog Soldiers have since gone out, but the covers on the bed are still pulled back. In a matter of minutes, both had each other undressed, and their lovemaking began.

When they are finished, Roger rolls over and lies down next to his wife to catch his breath. He curls her body into his chest as he gazes up at the ceiling. He feels so in love with her and so blessed that the Lord sent her to him. He never imagined that he would ever fall in love or even marry. His devotion to his work always took top priority and never allowed him time to even think about a mate. He is so grateful that the Lord had different plans for him and sent him the love of his life. His thought is interrupted when he hears her sniff. He lifts his head and looks down at her.

"Rose?" he asks. She comes out from his chest and wipes her nose. "Why, my precious darling, are you crying?" he asks her.

She fails to respond to his question as she wipes her nose again. He comes up to sit in front of her. He gently lifts her chin to see her eyes drenched with tears. He knows that Rose is not a crier and has only seen her cry once. He is puzzled as to what has gotten her so upset just out of the blue. They have not been together for many months, and their recent lovemaking was very hard. He does not consider himself a large man by any means, but he is wondering if perhaps the intensity and the deepness of his thrusting have hurt her in some way.

"Did I hurt you?" he asks her.

"No," she says. "You were wonderful."

"Then why the tears, my love?"

"When I was taken away by the Dog Soldiers, I never thought I would see you again. I was so scared that you were dead. I thought that God was punishing me for being so spoiled and selfish because I was furious that you did not go with me to Boston for the holidays, and instead, you stayed back to tend to White Horse. I could have cared less whether he had lived or died because he was an Indian. I prayed to God when I was kidnapped that the Lord would forgive my selfish ways and please get me out of there. I bargained with him that if he got me out, I would change my ways and that I would

31

stop being so self-centered. He brought your sister and Koawa to me, and they got me out of there, but once again, I failed in my bargaining, and I was rude to Koawa because he was an Indian and a savage. I realized how foolish I was when your sister pointed out to me everything that Koawa had done for me. When he got stabbed, I blamed myself. I thought because of my behavior that God was punishing me, and Koawa got hurt because of it. Oh, Roger, I have been such a fool all these years. You tried to tell me, but I refused to listen to you. I love you, Roger, with all my heart, and please forgive me for my ignorance."

"Rose, I love you with every ounce of my blood. You are who you are because that is how our good Lord wanted you to be. Everyone has regrets about things that they have done or said. The important thing is, is that you learn from them. I am a firm believer that everything happens for a reason and that God put Koawa in front of you for a reason. Don't ever stop being who you are. I married you because I love you, and I love every little spoiled thing about you."

"Oh, Roger," he hears her cry out. He takes her into his arms and embraces her tightly. She welcomes his embrace and clings onto him as a flood of emotions overcomes her. He remains there, holding his wife tightly in his arms as she weeps.

Three days have passed. Our new guests are adapting well. Crow Dog has been accepted by all the other warriors and rides alongside them when they leave camp to scout, hunt, or fight. He has taken a great liking to Minoke and is hunting for her, as well as bringing her gifts.

Koawa is up and moving slowly. He keeps himself close to camp and has yet to be on his horse. White Horse and Kikimo are doing his hunting, and I am making sure that both he and Morning Dove have everything they need. Koawa is an extremely active man and is frustrated at how slow he is recovering. Everyone is trying to keep him entertained. Blue Thunder has started up a game of dice, a form of gambling, and a crowd of warriors has gathered around them. There is much laughter being heard. White Horse has now joined them, and I am certain that the laughter is going to get louder, as never has White Horse ever lost against Koawa. Koawa is convinced that his brother is cheating, but he has never in all these years been able to figure out how White Horse is doing it. It is the center of the laughter amongst the other warriors as White Horse plays against Koawa.

I am sitting on my knees next to Morning Dove and our newest member, Dancing Bear, getting ready to prepare the berries that I will use for tonight's dinner. I catch Dancing Bear gazing over at Koawa, a short distance away. I smile to myself as I feel she is smitten by him, and I cannot say that I blame her. Koawa is a very attractive man who many women find irresistible.

"After dinner, Koawa usually walks to the lake and watches the sunset. The shore is wide enough for two people to casually bump into each other," I comment.

She looks my way and blushes. I am certain that I embarrassed her. "Oh, I couldn't," she says in her tongue.

"Why not?"

"It is not proper for a woman to be so direct to a warrior." I chuckle. She doesn't know Koawa like I do.

"I have known that man for many years. His wife was my best friend until she died. We were even married briefly."

"You were married to him?" she asks wide-eyed.

"Yes, a few months ago. Our Chief had gone missing and was presumed dead. Many months went by, and he never returned. Another man was after me, and Koawa stepped in and took me and my boys in. We married. The night of our honeymoon, we got word that our Chief was alive."

"Wow, how noble of him," she gasps.

"Koawa is a good man. Any woman would be lucky to have him."

"So why is he without one?"

"His wife died a little over a year ago. He had a great amount of love for her. His grief was very heavy in his heart. I believe it will take a great woman like his Running Water was, to rekindle his heart."

"But he married you?"

"He married me because of a promise he made to your Chief, his brother. Koawa is very dear to me, and there is nothing I wouldn't do for him."

I do not know very much about Dancing Bear, but from what I see, she appears to have a good heart and is strong both mentally and physically. This is a good quality to have if she wants to capture the heart of Koawa. I feel like I need to protect Koawa, as he protects me, so I want to get to know more about the woman who is so curious about my best friend.

"You arrived at our camp with no husband or child," I say. "Did they perish in your attack?"

"No," she answers. "Crow Dog is very protective of me and has not allowed very many men near me. There was one that would come into camp occasionally and stay for a few days. Crow Dog liked him. Many times, together, they would recruit some warriors and attack homesteads and wagon trains. When he stayed the night in our camp, Crow Dog would allow him to stay in our lodge and insist that he share my pelt. I did not like him, but Crow Dog persisted that I go with him, as he was not as bad as he appeared, and that I owed it to the band. He was alright with me, and every time he came, he would bring me gifts and say kind words to me. I lay with him a few times, but I always drank the baby tea afterward so no child would grow inside me."

I am not surprised that she was forced to be with this warrior despite her feelings towards him. Arranged marriages and the sharing of a pelt are customs, and in some bands, it is routinely done. In most cases, it is done to help the growth of the band because the more children that are made, especially boys, the stronger in the future the band will be. In other cases, it may be arranged as a return favor or a gift. I personally have never seen this done, but I do know that is how Songbird met Yellow Hawk many years ago. I am a little surprised, however, that she was allowed to drink the baby tea, and I am wondering if she did this behind her brother's back.

"Where are your parents?" I ask her.

"My mother died of fever a few years back, and my father died in battle. When my father died, Crow Dog became my protector. He is a good brother. He provides very well for me, but sometimes I wish he was not so protective of me."

"You are fortunate," I tell her. "That you survived your Blue Coat attack and found us."

She just looks over at me, failing to say a word. I wasn't sure if I had said something wrong. I then remember White Horse telling me in detail about their attack and how gruesome it was. He was telling me how some of the women were bludgeoned to death or cut up from their genitals to their stomachs for the army to save on ammunition. I think that perhaps the mention of the attack brought back memories.

"I must go prepare Crow Dog his meal," she says. "Excuse me."

"Dancing Bear, I am sorry," I tell her as she quickly walks off.

I deeply sigh to myself, feeling like such a heel. Once again, my mouth got ahead of my brain. "Carrie," I tell myself. "When are you ever going to learn to think before you speak?"

CHAPTER FOUR
Dream Catcher

Kikimo is enjoying a beautiful day with his best friend, Eagle Scout. He considers him a brother, and there is nothing in the world that he would not do for him, but he is growing tired of his best friend always competing against him and somehow or another always managing to come out ahead of him. The only thing so far he has been able to beat Eagle Scout in is running, and he only beat him by a hair. They always seem to be dead even on just about everything they do, and he has yet been able to be called the clear winner at anything. This is really starting to annoy him. He digs deep inside and allows the competitor in him to come out as he wrestles his best friend in the prairie grass. He hears the occasional teaching of his father and uncle as they, as well as several other warriors, are watching on.

His friend is on the top, prohibiting Kikimo from moving. He is refusing to allow Eagle Scout another win and is determined to finally beat him. He thinks back to the time when he wrestled the Blue Coat that raped his mother last spring. He was so enraged with him that if his uncle had not come between them, he most likely would have killed him.

Surely, if he can bring a soldier down, then he should be able to bring Eagle Scout down.

His frustration has won, and Kikimo is getting the upper hand. He rolls his friend over and pins him down. He smirks down at him as he is holding down his wrists. He is confident that he has the upper hand and has finally defeated his mouthy friend. He suddenly bellows in pain when Eagle Scout gives him a low blow, and Kikimo surrenders, allowing Eagle Scout to win.

Chuckles are heard throughout, and Yellow Hawk praises his son for winning. The small group of warriors slowly starts to walk away, still chuckling to themselves. Kikimo is so embarrassed by his loss that he lowers his head. White Horse, who is trying not to chuckle as he can see the humiliation on his son's face, reaches down to help him to his feet. Kikimo stands in front of his uncle and father in total humiliation.

"I almost had him," he whines.

"You got overconfident," Koawa says, "and he saw right through it."

"I am never going to beat him," Kikimo says.

"Not with that attitude, you won't," White Horse scolds.

"He has beaten me in everything. I just barely beat him in running. He even rides better than me."

"Son, there is more to becoming a good warrior than who can run the fastest or who is better on their pony. You want to beat Eagle Scout, then you are going to have to think like him. It is just like fighting the White Man. If you want to defeat them, you must think like them. This is no different. A good warrior is not based solely on strength. It is also based on the mind. You must allow yourself to get into your enemy's mind if you want to beat them. Do not become frustrated and remain patient, and I guarantee you; you will win."

Kikimo is still embarrassed by the way he lost, and he is certain that his arrogant, mouthy friend, Eagle Scout, will never let him live this down. He has learned his lesson, and his father's teaching has sunk in. Next time, he is confident that he will beat him.

Two days pass on the Great Plains. Rose has spent most of it cleaning up the place, tending to her garden, and doing the mounds of laundry that have accumulated from all the time that they were away. She is hanging the clothes on the line when her mind starts to wander. She starts to think about her childhood.

Growing up on the rich side of Boston, Rose's mother always had servants to do all the menial labor. Rose rarely ever had to do anything for herself. She is an only child and was her father's pride and joy. Her mother was extremely high maintenance and enjoyed flaunting her wealth. She rarely ever took Rose anywhere with her, nor did she ever spend much time with her. Rose can remember how much she would look forward to Sunday mass every week because that was the only day that she would spend time with her mother. When they were together, they always had a good time. She knew that her mother loved her but felt at times that she loved her money more.

Although Rose had everything that any little girl could imagine growing up, she was very lonely. She had very few friends and was never allowed to go to school with the other children because her mother felt that she would not fit in with them. She was educated by her father and her nanny. It was her nanny who taught Rose how to cook, maintain a home, and mend, all of it being done behind her mother's back. Her nanny and father have both passed on, but their legacy still lives on to this day, and there is not a moment that she does not think or miss them both. Her mother is still alive and still living in the big house in Boston that she grew up in. She visits her when she can, and routinely, they write. She loves her mother tremendously but has no desire to return to Boston. She is grateful to this day to her nanny, who taught her how to be a wife and one day, she hopes, a mother. Her thoughts are interrupted when she hears her husband riding up the path. She removes the last of the clothes from the line, putting them in her basket when Roger brings his wagon to a stop. She watches Max jump out from the back and happily run off just as Roger greets her.

"You have been gone nearly all day. I was getting worried about you," she tells him.

"Yes, I am afraid it took me longer at the Fort than I thought. My absence was missed, and I had a lot to catch up on."

Rose can see by the look on her husband's face that something heavy is on his mind. She notices the stack of mail that he is holding in his hand and wonders if there is something in it that has got him bothered.

"What is it, Roger?" she asks him.

"I received a telegram from Fort Laramie. There is a new Fort under construction about forty miles from here."

"Oh no," Rose gasps.

At one time Rose would have been delighted that another Fort was going up, but since she has met her new family and has grown to love them, she is less than enthusiastic by the news.

"The Fort is being built on the trail and is being established to prevent Indian attacks on folks traveling through and for the Union Pacific to start surveying and laying tracks across the land. I have been asked to provide my services at this Fort to train a new doctor fresh out of school. I have been offered a permanent position with them after the Fort is established outside of the perimeter for anyone who may need doctoring along the way."

"What does all this mean? Do we have to move?"

"If I accept the position, yes." Roger can tell by his wife's look that she is not thrilled about the idea of moving.

"Sweetheart, hear me out. I have an idea that I think you will like."

"What is it?" she wonders.

"I was looking at the map of where the Fort is going up, and it is roughly ten miles from Earl's place. We can fix up his place and live there. We will be closer to the Sioux and White Horse."

"That is a good idea," she says. "Oh, Roger, yes, let's do it."

Just then, before anything else can be said, both Rose and Roger look down at Max, who has plopped himself down at Roger's feet. He is chewing on a rather large and unusually shaped bone. Roger's heart drops to his knees as he immediately looks over at the flower bed, noticing that the gate is open. He is certain that the dog got in and found the grave of Clarence and dug it up. His hunch is proven correct when he hears his wife screaming in horror when she realizes that it is the bones of a hand and it is missing one finger. Rose drops the basket of clothes on the ground and screams a little louder when she sees that Max is gnawing on the finger.

"Where did he get that!" she yells.

Roger is quick at coming to his wife's side.

"Sweetheart, I have something to tell you, and you are not going to like it." He wasn't sure how to tell her how he buried Clarence's body in her flower garden and is certain that she is not going to take this well. "When you were gone, I buried Clarence's body in the flower garden."

"What! Why is Clarence in our flower garden?"

"When you were gone, White Horse had regained his memory and wanted to get home. The pass was too deep with snow, and we could not get through. He came up with the idea of a big fire in the hopes of the Dog Soldiers seeing it and coming. Clarence saw the smoke in the sky, and along with the amount of supplies I purchased, he concluded that I must be hiding out Indians. Come spring, the Dog Soldiers helped get White Horse home by sending word to the Sioux that he was here. Koawa and several other warriors came to get him. That was when I saw Carrie. I guess somehow Clarence was watching on, and one of White Horse's warriors killed him. To protect White Horse and myself from the Army, I buried Clarence in the flower garden and planted the flowers around him so it didn't look so obvious."

"Are you nuts? Why in the world would you do something like that?"

"Come," he calmly says, taking her hand into his. "Let us go inside, and I will try to explain further, and then maybe you will understand why I made the decision that I did."

"You better hope I do," she snaps. "Or you will be sleeping in the barn."

Further down the prairie, it is late afternoon, and I am in the woods along with Rising Sun, Minoke, Morning Dove, and Dancing Bear, picking wild berries off the bushes. Our baskets are nearly full, and we will be heading back into camp very shortly. Rising Sun steps further out into the trees to collect the berries off the last bushes before meeting up with us and heading back to camp. She gathers the berries off the bushes, one by one, and puts them in her basket. As she approaches the last bush, she notices something hanging from it. She becomes puzzled when she notices that it is a small dream catcher. She removes it from the branch and gazes at its beauty.

She believes in the magic that it holds and has always held it close to her heart. She runs her fingers down the beadwork and allows the feathers to dangle through them. She finds it odd that it was left on a branch off the main path where anyone would be walking by. By the freshness of it, she concludes that it has not been here long and appears as if it was placed here on purpose, not too long ago. The beadwork consists of all her favorite colors, and the feathers are her father's favorite bird, a hawk. She remembers him making her one after her mother died by army guns to keep her bad dreams away that kept reoccurring after her mother's death. She remembers how, almost immediately after her father hung it over her pelt, her bad dreams went away. She then gasps as it suddenly becomes perfectly clear.

"Papa," she whispers to herself. It is then that she hears the rustling in the trees. She looks to where it is coming from and sees her father standing on a hill. She is quick at running to him and embracing him hard. He returns the embrace along with a gentle kiss on her forehead.

"Papa, I have missed you," she cries.

"As have I," Red Hawk says. "You must be quiet. No one must know that I am here."

"Oh, Papa, I have been so worried about you. Is it true that you tried to kill our Chief and his brother?"

"You need not worry your beautiful mind about that. I have come to make sure that you are alright."

"Oh, yes, Papa," she answers. "Minoke and Prairie Dawn are taking very good care of me."

"Is the Chief leaving you alone?"

"Yes, he rarely even looks my way or says a word to me."

This burns Red Hawk to the core, but he does not let on to Rising Sun how he feels. He does not have much time and is taking a huge risk of being seen. He is quick at getting to his point. He briefly glances out at the trees in front of him to make sure that they are still alone. He can hear the other woman conversing back and forth, and knows that if he does not want to be seen or heard, then he must move his daughter further out into the woods before he can talk to her any further. He takes her hand and motions for her to be quiet as he walks her further into the trees.

"Where is your pony, Papa?" she asks.

"I left my pony behind, as I did not want it to be seen grazing."

"Where are you staying?"

"Oh, my precious, do not worry for your father, for I am fine. I have come to make sure that you were taken care of."

"I am sleeping in Minoke's lodge. She is very good to me," she says.

"Good. If you have any problems, I want you to go to Crow Dog. He will come for me."

"He scares me, Papa."

She hears her father chuckle. He places his hand through her hair and smiles down at her. "You have nothing to fear from him. I have known him all my life. He is a very good friend of mine. I am the reason that he and his family did not perish in that attack."

"You need not worry for me, Papa. Our Chief will keep me safe, as he does everyone else." Red Hawk arrogantly smirks at his daughter's comment, and again, he keeps his thoughts to himself. "When will you be back, Papa?" she asks him.

"Oh, my precious, I know you miss me as I do you, but I cannot return to your Chief's camp just yet."

"But why?" Red Hawk consoles his daughter by putting his hands on her shoulders.

He loves Rising Sun with all his heart and worries about her every day, but he knows that he cannot return, for if he does, he will be killed. He is grateful that his friend and his family were not near the camp when it was attacked, or for certain they, too, would have been killed. He despises White Horse but knows that if his friend came here with his family, they would be safe. Luck is on his side, and with Crow Dog watching the Chief from a distance, he is certain that within a few months, he can put his plan into action and finally get his revenge.

"I do not want you to worry your beautiful mind as to why I have chosen not to return. I need you to promise me that you will tell no one that you have seen me. I will come for you or send for you when I can. Crow Dog knows that you are my daughter, and he will keep you safe. You are to listen to him, and you are to go to him if you need anything." He lifts her chin with his long fingers. "Do you understand my daughter?"

"Yes, Papa. I understand."

Their tender moment ends when Red Hawk hears Minoke calling nearby for Rising Sun.

"Go, hurry," he tells her. "Before anyone gets suspicious as to why you have gone so far from the others."

He brings Rising Sun into his arms and tightly embraces her before rushing her off.

"I'm coming," she calls out as she rushes off into the trees towards Minoke.

She quickly hides the dream catcher in her basket as her guardian comes into view.

"There you are," she says. "You gave me a start. You must not journey out so far from the safety of the others, as there may be danger lurking around."

"I am sorry," she tells her. "I needed to relieve myself."

"It is alright, dear," Minoke smiles. "But next time, tell one of us that you are leaving, for we have been looking for you."

"Yes, ma'am."

Red Hawk watches from the thickness of the trees as his daughter leaves with Minoke to join the others. It pains him to leave her behind, but he knows he has no choice. He is confident now that she is being well taken care of and that he can concentrate without any further distractions on planning his revenge.

CHAPTER FIVE
The Enigma

The sun sets on the Great Plains. Roger is sitting up in bed reading the last of his mail. He is grateful that his wife is not too upset with him over Clarence and he will be enjoying a peaceful sleep in a warm bed and not in a stall beside his horses. His beloved wife is reading a book beside him, as she enjoys a bowl of popcorn. She glances up from her reading when she hears Roger softly curse under his breath from frustration. This is unusual behavior for him, as Roger is one of the most patient men that she has ever met and rarely does he ever lose his temper.

"What is in the letter that has you so upset, my darling?" she asks him.

"It is from Stella." She now understands his actions.

She has never personally ever met her, but by what Roger tells her about Stella, she does not care for her. She remembers when Roger first mentioned her when they were courting and at one time how, at first, Stella and her sister-in-law, Carrie, were the best of friends. She understands that at one time, Roger and Stella had courted very briefly after his sister left to go with the Sioux. He had gone through a period of very deep depression and loneliness due to the death of his father and his sister leaving. Stella was there for him, and for that, Rose is grateful. However, after just a few weeks of their courtship, Roger saw her true colors and did not agree with the lifestyle she was setting herself up for and called it off. Roger and Stella have been in consistent contact with each other over the years and for reasons that she has never figured out, Roger is always there to bail her out of trouble.

"What does she want from you now?" she asks him.

"What does she always want," he huffs, "money."

"Roger, I know you mean well, but you need to stop sending her money."

"I know, but I just keep thinking about Matthew."

"He is not your responsibility."

"I know, but I cannot see a child suffer because of a mother's poor judgment."

"Where is she now?"

"Nebraska territory. She is camping out in a railroad town."

"A railroad town?" she says in disgust. "With a six-year-old boy? You know as well as I do what she is doing."

"Yes, she even admits it in this letter. She says that she does not want this life for Matthew and wants to get into an honest trade and become a seamstress but can't do it without money and that is why she has had to return to her old ways."

"Poor Matthew," she says. "That boy needs a positive foundation in his life. It is going to be hard enough for him as he gets older being a half-breed, especially the way times are now. It angers me that Stella is so careless when it comes to that child's feelings."

"I know, sweetheart, but what can you do?

"The child is not yours."

"The boy would be better off in my father's Orphanage," he huffs, "At least there I can guarantee his well-being."

Rose couldn't believe what she was hearing. Of all the people to say that Matthew would be better off in an Orphanage is Roger, who at one time was an orphan himself.

"I can't believe what I am hearing," she says. "You, of all people, would think he would be better off in an Orphanage."

"It is not just any Orphanage, Rose. It is my father's, which I inherited. I can make sure that he is taken care of. It has moved out of Cedar Brook and has relocated to a better area out in the country. Matthew can be around children his own age. He can go to school and learn there. When Stella gets her life together, she can then return to him. I would be willing to help her become a seamstress if that is really what she wants. I think it is for the best."

"Stella will never agree to that."

"She would if I threatened the law on her. Besides, Matthew has more than one parent." Rose nearly drops her jaw. "Are you telling me that you are going back on your word to Stella?" Roger looks over at her and nods his head yes. "Oh Roger, you could be starting up something that could really get ugly if Matthew's father goes after him. You realize that right?"

"Yes, but things have changed, and I do not believe that Stella has anything to fear from him. I realized that when you were taken by the Dog Soldiers. He had a major role in your escape. I spent some time with him when White Horse and I were camped out near the canyon. He seems sincere. I think I owe it to him to tell him the truth. My mind is made up. It is time I paid Koawa a visit anyway and get Earl's home ready for the move. I will send a post tomorrow to Fort Laramie to accept the position. We will leave at first light the day after tomorrow." Rose knows Roger's mind is made up and there is no changing it.

"Alright. I will say my goodbyes tomorrow."

There is a beautiful moonlight glistening across the water. White Horse and I decide to take a late-night walk and have some time to ourselves before turning in for the night, but first, I take a moment to take Koawa his evening meal. I find him sitting by the fire in his lodge. "I wasn't certain if you had been fed, so I brought you some food."

"Thank you," he says. "Morning Dove and Minoke fed me a few hours ago, but it looks good, and you were kind to bring it in, so I will eat again," he smiles.

He removes the bowl from my hand, and I stand up to leave.

"What?" he smiles. "You won't sit with me while I eat?"

"As much as I enjoy your company, I can't, White Horse is waiting for me. The night is beautiful, so we are going for a walk by the lake, before turning in for the night."

"Hmm," he says. "Perhaps later I will go too. I am feeling restless, and the fresh air would do me some good."

"Just be careful," I caution. "You still have not fully healed. Perhaps you should take someone with you in case you need help back."

"I need no help," he barks. "I am a man, and I can do it myself."

"I wasn't implying that you could not handle it yourself, I was just saying that the night is so beautiful it would be a shame that you don't enjoy it with someone."

He quizzically looks up at me as he swallows. "Prairie Dawn, you just told me that you and White Horse were going for a walk before turning in for the night. I know your husband well. After your walk is finished and you take refuge in your lodge, you will not turn in, as he will want something else from you before his eyes close."

I chuckled to myself as I knew he was right. Seldom does a night pass that White Horse and I do not unite before going to sleep.

"I was not thinking of me," I tell him.

"Then who?"

"Dancing Bear." I see him just roll his eyes and focus back on his meal. "I see the way she looks at you," I tell him. "She is smitten with you."

"Many women turn their eyes to me. It is not my fault that I am irresistible," he arrogantly says. "You tell me nothing that I do not already know."

"Koawa, she is really nice and very pretty."

"Yes, I agree she is very nice on the eyes, but I have not seen her heart yet."

"Well, go find it. Ask her to walk with you."

He faintly smiles and chuckles under his breath. I know he is thinking that I am deliberately trying to set him up, and he would be right. Koawa is a beautiful person inside and out and it pains me to see him alone. It has been over a year since Running Water died. I know it is custom to grieve a loss for a very long time, but I feel Koawa is ready to move on, and although he would never admit it to me, I think he wants a woman in his life.

"Your husband awaits you," he says. He shakes his head chuckling, turning his attention back to his food, making it clear to me that the conversation is over.

"Good night," I smile.

"Good night, impossible," he grins. Koawa glances up at me as I leave the lodge, wondering if, indeed, he should ask Dancing Bear for a walk.

Two days later Roger and Rose pull their covered wagon, stuffed with all their belongings, up to Earl's old house.

"Welcome home dear," he tells his wife.

"Home," she says. "It has not sunk in yet that this place is ours."

"It will as soon as you put your magic touch to the place and make it feel like home."

"I can't wait."

"We will get the wagon unloaded and start moving in today. Tomorrow, I want to go see Koawa. I promised him I would return before his stitches were due to come out. I also need to make sure that my nephew has not received any other symptoms from his fall. I would like to leave at first light."

"Well then, I reckon we better get busy."

The heat of the day is upon us. With my chores completed and boredom setting in with the children, I decided to take them for a swim in the river nearby. I am joined by Minoke and Dancing Bear. It does not take long for Eagle Scout to jump in and challenge Kikimo in a swim. Rising Sun steps into the ankle-deep water, holding onto Morning Dove's hand. Minoke is soon behind her, followed by Little Foot. I, in return, am following in behind him, stopping just above my knees. I look back at Dancing Bear, who is still on the bank.

"Are you going to join us?" I ask her in her tongue.

"I do not know how to swim," she says.

"Do you want me to teach you?" I ask her.

"No, I am enjoying just watching."

"The water is clear and shallow here," I tell her. "You will be alright."

"No, thank you, Prairie Dawn. I can watch just fine from here."

"Alright," I shrug.

Kikimo has swum a good distance out, I hear him call me. "Ma, we are going to race to you. See who touches you first."

"Alright," I yell at him.

The race is on and both are dead even. The younger children are cheering Kikimo on.

"Come on, Kikimo," Little Foot yells.

"Go Kikimo Go!" Morning Dove hollers.

I felt bad for Eagle Scout, as no one was cheering him on. I love Kikimo to death, but I thought Eagle Scout needed some encouragement as well.

"Push it, Eagle Scout," I tell him.

"Mama," Little Foot says. "Don't say that he might win."

"I am not picking favorites, son. This is all in fun."

We turn our attention back to the swimmers. Kikimo is a good arm's length ahead. I am not surprised by this, as Kikimo, like his father, is a fish in the water. The cheering continues as the race approaches the finishing line. It is obvious to me who is going to come out ahead, and it will be closer than I originally thought. With only a few more strokes to go, Eagle Scout is gaining in but will fall short by one stroke behind Kikimo when he touches my hand first.

Cheers are heard, mostly from Little Foot when Kikimo is declared the winner. Kikimo boasts by pushing his chest out and pumping it. Eagle Scout is disappointed in himself, and it is seen clearly on his face. I rub the top of his wet head.

"You have nothing to be ashamed of," I tell him in his tongue. "You are both fine swimmers."

"But I beat you," Kikimo boasts.

Out of frustration, Eagle Scout splashes water at Kikimo. I turn my attention to the shore and see that Dancing Bear is gone. I am puzzled as to why she left and where she went. The children would swim for a little while longer before we call it a day and make our way back into camp. I am still unsure as to where Dancing Bear is and am assuming I will find her back at camp.

I glance back and see that Morning Dove is lagging behind everyone else. I stop to wait for her to catch up, as everyone else continues. Unaware of the others, a figure pushes a branch back and watches the woman with the golden hair wait for the younger child to catch up.

"Are you alright, sunshine?" I ask her as she finally catches up.

"My stomach hurts," she whines.

"Oh, I am sorry, sweetheart. Perhaps you drank too much river water when you were swimming. I will make you some Merigold tea when we get back."

"Alright," she softly says tucking her head into my waist, as we make our way back to camp.

Upon entering our camp, I see Dancing Bear sneaking in from the other side of the camp from the woods. She is holding something in her hand that she quickly tucks into her dress when she comes into view of the camp. I thought this was odd and was asking myself where she had been and what is she hiding? I know my curiosity will get the best of me, and I will ask her where she went later on, but my first priority was getting Morning Dove her Merigiold tea.

The great moon shines high in the sky. Roger and Rose are exhausted from their busy day of moving in. The place that they now call home is nearly completed, and within a few days, everything should be in its place. Their new home is about the same size as their old house, with the exception that there is a bedroom that is closed off by its own private door. There is a small loft at the back end of the home that is just large enough to hold a small bed. There are no windows in it, nor is it open to the ground below. A twisting staircase runs on the edge of the fireplace that leads up to the loft.

Roger is unclear as to why Earl would have built it, as it is obvious to him that it was an afterthought after the home had already been built. As a doctor, he has visited many homes and has lived in several different ones himself, and never has he seen one so unusually built. There are no windows at the back of the house and it is tucked in snugly against the bluff. The fireplace is the biggest that he has ever seen and the oddest in shape. The fireplace itself is normal-looking and functions well, but the surrounding wall on one side of it protrudes out by several inches. Although it does look odd, it gives the home a flattering design with the twisting staircase accenting around it. The interior of the home has been well taken care of, but the exterior needs desperate repair. This has him curious, as well, as to why Earl would be so meticulous about the interior of the home but allow the exterior to get so neglected.

Roger is sitting in his chair near the lit fireplace, reading the map that he found earlier in the day under the mattress. He has little faith that Earl has struck it rich or that there is any gold anywhere near here, but he feels that he owes it to his old friend to see what the map reveals. Upon reading the map, he is once again surprised to learn that Earl was an educated man and brilliant when it came to figures. Roger himself feels he is smarter than most others, but he is having a difficult time figuring out what these numbers mean.

"Oh, Roger," Rose says as she sits down on the arm of the chair beside him. "You have been reading that map for hours."

"I know, I have been trying to figure out what all these numbers mean. I have a feeling that they are markings for something that may be buried, but I can't figure it out."

"You mean like a treasure?" She asks him.

"I cannot imagine Earl having much to his name, but he was determined before he died to tell me about this map."

"What did he tell you?" she wonders.

"He said, mattress, map, fireplace, and then he proceeded to tell me that he had a claim and that I was to keep it. He did not want anyone else to claim it. He was adamant about it."

"Earl was a crazy man who didn't have a penny to his name. No one has ever found any gold around these hills. If Earl did find gold, why didn't he claim it?"

"Maybe he didn't want a repeat of California," Roger comments.

"I was at the creek today, and I didn't see any gold," Rose says.

"Maybe it wasn't at the creek. Maybe he found it somewhere else and drew this map so he could remember where he found it."

"But why all the numbers? Why not just mark it out?"

"Earl was a very suspicious man," Roger says. "He didn't trust anyone. I would not put it past him to put the map in code."

"And the numbers break the code?" Rose concludes.

"Exactly."

"Well, if there is any truth in what Earl told you and there is a claim, it is now yours."

"Sweetheart, I don't want his gold. If there is a claim, it will stay buried. I just wish I could figure out what all these numbers mean."

"Darling," Rose smiles, wrapping her fingers through a lock of his hair. "We have a long ride ahead of us tomorrow. We need to get some sleep."

"You go ahead, darling," he says, stroking her cheek. "I will be there shortly."

"You promise?"

"Yes, I promise," he says. She leans down and kisses him before turning in for the night. Roger turns his attention back to the map, determined to figure it out.

CHAPTER SIX
The Iron Horse

Another day arrives on the Great Plains. Morning Dove awakes with stomach pain and has not left her pelt except to void by a nearby stream. I am not too alarmed, as she does not seem to be running a fever or have any other symptoms. Flying Hawk has been taking care of her, and she is sleeping in her lodge. I am assuming by this time tomorrow or later this evening that she will be back to herself and just needs time for it to run its course.

Koawa is growing extremely restless and is taking short walks around camp. He is anxious to get back on his horse, and I am certain that within a few days, he will be strong enough to do it. As he is taking his walk, he spots Dancing Bear near the water. She turns her attention to him when he comes into her view. He stops in front of her and, for a few seconds, gazes into her eyes. Then, in his tongue, he tells her.

"We will walk."

Together, they walk along the path until they get to a log, and Koawa tells her to sit down. He comes down beside her, and a conversation starts.

I am on the ground in front of our lodge, making moccasins as White Horse sits under his favorite tree. I glance over at the water and spot Koawa and Dancing Bear talking among themselves.

"I am glad he took my advice," I say out loud.

White Horse looks over at where his brother and Dancing Bear are sitting.

"Am I to assume that you had something to do with that?" he says.

"I mentioned to him how she looked at him and that he should give it a try."

"My brother does not need help finding a woman. The camp is filled with many maidens that would love to call Koawa theirs."

"I know that. I am just giving him a little boast."

White Horse smiles over at me. "You are beautiful, my wife, and I love you tremendously, but I do not think Dancing Bear is Koawa's type."

"Why not? She is young, nice, pretty, and able to provide him with a son. What more could he want?"

"Koawa is content with Morning Dove."

"All men want a son, White Horse. You just don't see it because you have two."

"When Little Foot was growing inside you, I did not pray for a son, I prayed for a healthy and strong child. I was blessed double that he was a boy."

I know that White Horse would have been happy with me no matter what gender I had given birth to, but he is not fooling me at all. Having a son who will grow up to be a warrior is very important to all our men, including White Horse. I glance back over to the water and watch the two conversing.

Their conversation is casual, and Dancing Bear is very nervous. They remain there in conversation for a good length of time. She slowly starts to become comfortable with him and starts to enjoy his company. She glances down at Koawa's bandages across his stomach.

"What happened?" she asks him.

"I was stabbed," he answers.

"I heard that you nearly died."

"Yes, I did."

"Who stabbed you?" she wonders.

"A man by the name of Red Hawk."

Suddenly, Dancing Bear became very still and had a desire to quickly leave but did not want to insult Koawa with a haste getaway, so she made up a lie.

"I have to get back," she tells him. "I have chores to do."

Koawa gave her no objection and was ready to head back himself. He sits on the log as he watches Dancing Bear scamper away. His thoughts are interrupted when he sees

Night Owl and Grey Wolf riding into camp, escorting some visitors.

White Horse and I see our visitors at the same time and are making our way from our lodge just as Koawa stops next to us.

"Great Healer," he says.

I smile across at him as I wait for Roger and Rose to ride in, with Max trailing close behind them.

"It has been almost two weeks," I say. "He has come for you."

Kikimo and Eagle Scout greet our guests as they dismount off their horses. Each boy grabs their lead and walks the horses off to be with the others. I greet my brother with a hug. I then turn to Rose and embrace her.

"It is good to see you, brother," White Horse says as the two shake hands.

"I hope we are not intruding," Roger says. "I wanted to check on Koawa."

"You are never intruding," White Horse says. "You and your wife are always welcome here. Come! Let us go inside, and you can tend to Koawa, and then we can visit."

"Carrie," Rose says as we are walking up to our lodge. "I brought you some jam."

"Oh, thank you," I smile. "That was very thoughtful of you."

Koawa is behind Rose and will be the last to step into the lodge. She appears a little timid around him, and I expect it was due to her behavior toward him when we were on the run. I am grateful when Koawa breaks the ice by smiling at her as he holds the flap open for her to step in.

Several hours will pass. Roger removes Koawa's stitches and gives him a good bill of health. Little Foot would receive one as well. Morning Dove is still not feeling well, and Koawa asked Roger if he would mind looking at her. Morning Dove, who is only seven, was terrified of Roger, but with Koawa's coaxing, she held still enough for Roger to examine her. He gave me some powder that I am to mix with water and give to her several times a day. He is confident that because she is showing no other symptoms, within a few days, she will be back to herself.

With the sunset and everyone's bellies full, including Max's, we all sit around the fire in our lodge and talk. Little Foot has become very close to Uncle Roger and is tucked close to his side between us. White Horse is next to me, then Koawa, then Rose, who is on the other side of Roger. Max is resting his head comfortably on White Horse's knee.

"It is good that you stay for the night," White Horse tells Roger. "You bring all of us great joy when you are here."

"As it does us," Roger says. "But I am afraid, my brother, that I did not only come to visit and check on Koawa."

"What else is there?" White Horse asks. "Many things have come up since I was last here that you need to be aware of." White Horse lifts a brow in curiosity.

"Please do not be afraid to tell me what is on your mind."

"Rose and I have moved."

"What!" I gasp. "Oh no."

"Oh, do not worry, Carrie, for we are closer."

"Then what is the problem?" White Horse asks.

"There is a new Fort going up not far from here."

"I am aware of that," White Horse says. I was not surprised that White Horse knew this. "What does that have to do with you?"

"They offered me a position outside of the Fort for the wagon trains and surveyors that are crossing the land. I stumbled across a homestead of a former patient of mine, and that is where we are living."

"Tell me what this surveyor is?"

I can tell that White Horse is unfamiliar with the word. "A surveyor measures the most accurate position of the land to lay an object. In this case, it is for tracks that will carry a train that will cross this land."

I am very familiar with the English language and have grown up with many of the white man's ways, but like White Horse, I am confused about what a train is. White Horse is the first to ask what it is.

"What is this train?" he asks confused.

"Oh, it is really remarkable; it can take you from one ocean to the next in just a few days." I see a look of disgust on White Horse's face.

"I never have liked the White Man's words. They have no meaning. No spirit. I never wanted to learn it. Our father made both Koawa and I learn the language when we were very young. While other boys our age went out playing or hunting, my brother and I were confined to our lodge until we learned."

"You both speak it very well," Rose says.

"Thank you," he tells Rose before putting his attention back on Roger. "Tell me, my brother, what does this train mean for us?"

"Well, I am not real sure. It is going to be a while before any tracks will be laid this far. But they are nearing completion and have almost connected to the east coast." White Horse now knows what it is.

"The Iron Horse," he says.

"Yes," Roger says. "I have heard that term before being used to describe it."

"Our brothers from the south of us have warned us about it. They tell us that it is like a big angry ghost that breathes out hot air and floats across the prairie on iron wheels."

"That is a good analogy for it," Roger admits. "The army is afraid of another Indian uprising because of it, and that is why they are building the Fort."

White Horse just shook his head. "You know I did not start this war. Bad White Men started this war. The White Men are like locusts. We kill one, and hundreds more come."

Roger faintly grins. "They say the same thing about you."

"I do not want to fight. I want our two worlds to be as one, but your men in Washington do not want to talk about peace. Their ears are closed to listening. Their words mean nothing to me. They repeatedly tell lies. I do not know what else to do but to fight because I refuse to be told how to live or how my children will live."

"I understand, White Horse, and I wish I knew what to do to help you. But I don't."

"Brother, they will listen to you. You understand the White Man's ways, and you hear their thoughts. You can teach me, and then I can teach my people, and then maybe we will find peace."

"I will do what I can, White Horse. I truly will, but I can only go so far."

"I have confidence in you," White Horse says. "You have brought much luck to this band. Many lives you have touched. Great love you have shown. You are a good man, Roger. I am proud to call you brother."

I can tell that Roger is touched. I always knew that Roger had a huge heart, and I am certain that Rose sees it too, but it must mean the world to him that this powerful Indian Chief sees it too. I glance over at Max, who is enjoying being pet on his head by White Horse. It is obvious that the dog has taken a great liking to White Horse and has not forgotten the bond that was formed between them last winter when he was recovering from his bad fall at Roger's house.

"Look at him," I smile. "I think you lost your companion, Roger."

"That's alright, he has me," Rose grins.

Max lifts his head when White Horse stops petting him. "He was a good friend to me when Roger would leave and get supplies. He even warned me when the soldiers were coming. I have never seen a dog do that."

"I do not have any problem with him," Rose says. "Until he brought that hand to me."

"What?" I ask.

Rose then tells us a story that left all of us dumbfounded. None of us could believe that Roger had hidden a body.

"I didn't see any other way. I was not going to let the army come after you because of Clarence."

A puzzled White Horse just looks at Roger. "Why would they come after us?" he asks.

"Because one of your warriors had to have killed him."

White Horse looks over at Koawa. During his absence, Koawa was Chief, and if one of his warriors had killed a man when they were there, Koawa would have heard about it. He shakes his head no at White Horse.

"No, they didn't," he says.

"Forgive me for arguing with you Koawa, but they had to have, you were the only ones there." White Horse grins.

"My brother, just because you cannot see us does not mean that we are not there. I suspect another warrior from another band killed this man. I assure you it was not us."

Roger just sighs. He buried Clarence for nothing.

"Oh well, he was a pain in the ass anyways," Roger says.

Everyone laughs at Roger's comment. Just then, we see Rose nudge Roger.

"Go on," she whispers. "Tell him."

"There is more on my brother's mind that needs to be shared," White Horse says.

"Yes, and on the ride up here, I was determined to tell you, but for some reason, I can't find the right words."

"Perhaps because what you must tell me is hard to speak of. My brother, there is nothing that you cannot tell me. My ears are always open to your words. Do not ever fear me, for I would never do you harm."

"I guess you are right. Alright, I will just say it."

He looks over at Rose and squeezes her hand. It brings a smile to my face when I see the love that they have for each other. I never thought that Roger would ever marry, but I am glad he did, and I am glad that he is so happy.

"Do you remember Stella?" he asks. Both White Horse and I shook our heads yes.

"She was my best friend in Willow Creek," I add.

"Yes, shortly after you left to join the Sioux, Stella became pregnant. Everyone thought that the baby was Hanks's."

"And it wasn't?" I wonder.

"No. Stella knew that it wasn't Hanks, and she came to me in a panic. She told me that the child was Blue Thunder's."

Both White Horse and I nearly dropped our teeth.

"Whatever happened to the child?" White Horse asks.

After you left Carrie, I became very depressed, and I took comfort in Stella. I was going to help her with the baby, but soon afterward, I realized that she was not going to change her ways, and I worried about the child. So, I sent her away to the Orphanage to live there until the child was born. I delivered the child. It was a boy. I begged Stella not to leave with the boy, but she wouldn't listen to me. She begged me not to tell anyone who the father was and that if she was asked that, she was going to pass the child off as Mexican because they are more accepted than an Indian is."

I could tell that White Horse was burned by this. "Where is this child now?" he asks.

"He is in Nebraska. Stella is staying in a railroad town, prostituting."

White Horse sits straight up. I can tell that he is fuming. It is one thing to deny the child his culture, but to allow him to be surrounded by, in White Horse's opinion, by trash is a total disrespect to Sioux culture.

"I know what you are thinking, White Horse, and I agree. The child needs to get out of there, and I believe I know of a way, but that is not why I am telling you this. I have given it a great deal of thought, and I feel that Blue Thunder deserves to know that he has a beautiful son who is smart and brave. But I fear that by telling him this, he may go looking for the child and that he may take it, and by doing that, he could get him or Matthew killed."

"Blue Thunder will be told, but first, you need to tell me what your idea is on his son."

Roger spent the next hour explaining to White Horse about the orphanage and how he thought that Matthew being there would benefit him. It took some doing because White Horse wanted the child to be here and raised a Sioux alongside his best friend, Blue Thunder. Finally, White Horse agreed but made it very clear to Roger that the decision not to go after Matthew was up to Blue Thunder and that he would not do anything to stop him. He assured Roger that he would talk to Blue Thunder in the morning and he would do whatever he could to convince him not to go after Matthew and to wait to see him until after he got to the Orphanage. I only pray that not only for Matthew's well-being but for Blue Thunder's, too, he will listen to the advice of his Chief and allow Roger to work with Stella on willingly allowing Matthew to live at the orphanage.

The evening comes to a close. I make room for Roger and Rose to sleep on their own pelt close to White Horse and me. I also provide a privacy blanket that I hang up between us so they can freely undress without feeling awkward about being seen by everyone else.

The boys and our guests are sound asleep, and very soon, I will be right behind them.

I snuggle myself into White Horse. He is deep in thought, gazing out at the fire.

"Are you alright, sweetheart?" I ask him.

"I am just thinking," he says.

"If it is about Blue Thunder, he will be alright with the news."

"Oh, I know he will. That is not what I was thinking about."

"Then what?"

"I worry about the Iron Horse. So many of our people are dying because of it. I have always stood firm in what I believe in. But what I see in my vision is not good."

I know that visions are common among the Sioux, and many receive them. Some may wait their entire life and never get one, while others will receive many. White Horse is one of these.

"What do you see?" I ask.

"I did not completely understand the meaning until just recently when Koawa was brought home in the back of Roger's wagon. I looked down at the wheels, and it reminded me of our medicine wheel. In my dream, these wheels collided. I see much bloodshed on both sides."

He looks down at me as he squeezes my hand. I can see in his eyes that he is really disturbed by this. "It is not good, Carrie. It is not good at all."

I lay my head down on his chest and held him.

On the other side of the blanket, Roger is still awake and overhears White Horse's vision. He, too, is alarmed by it and fears the same thing. He must think of something to help the people that he loves before it is too late.

CHAPTER SEVEN
The Scouts

White Horse awakes to shouts from one of his warriors outdoors. He is quick to the flap as everyone else stirs awake. He sees Grey Wolf running fast on his pony. Several other warriors are alarmed by the rush and start emerging from their lodges. Grey Wolf is heard yelling in his tongue.

"Blue Coats!"

"How far away?" White Horse asks him.

"There is a small group of them camped a few miles away."

I am in an immediate panic upon hearing his warning through the hides of the lodge.

Roger is up and becomes alarmed when he sees Kikimo and Little Foot bolt off their pelts and quickly put on their moccasins.

"What's wrong?" he asks me. I hear White Horse yelling in his tongue.

"Men mount up and prepare for war. Women quickly move the camp!"

"Roger, we must move. Now!" I tell him as I rush to get dressed and push my boys out the door.

Kikimo pushes Rose awake. Roger is panicking because he knows that something is wrong.

"Soldiers have been spotted close to camp. We have to move."

"What do I have to do?" he asks me in a rush.

"Grab your wife. Take your horses and ride hard out of here," I tell him.

"I am not leaving you," he says. Rose is starting to cry out of fear.

"Roger, I know you mean well, but you have a wife to think of. I am not sure how fast they are moving."

Just then, White Horse comes in, grabbing his rifle. Roger is quick at approaching

him.

"I want to help," he says. White Horse looks over at a shaking Rose.

"Normally, I would not chance you any harm. It is unclear how fast the soldiers are moving or if we are even their target, but they are too close to camp, and we are going to have to back them off. It is not safe for you to take off on your own. You will have to go with us. Keep your wife calm and listen to Carrie."

"I will," he says. "White Horse, on my horse in the gun boot is my rife. Take it with you."

"You take it. You may need it to protect the women if the soldiers get too close."

White Horse then looks over at me. "Go to the ravine and wait for us. If we do not return before the sun is at its highest, you are to take the others and move to the next camp. We will meet you there."

I only nodded my head in agreement. This is not the first time that we have had to quickly pack up everything and move on while our warriors fight. As Chief, White Horse does not have to fight, and there are many chiefs who do not, but White Horse has always fought right alongside his men. This scares me to death, and my heart is pounding with fear for his safe return.

"Be careful," I say. He faintly grins at me.

"Always," he says before rushing off.

"What do we do?" Roger asks.

I can tell that Rose is still terrified, but at least she has stopped crying and is eager to help in any way she can.

"Get Rose on her horse along with Little Foot and wait for us at the edge of camp." Roger is fast at obeying. "Kikimo, start packing up what you can and get it ready for travel."

"Yes, Ma."

I have never seen Roger so scared or so out of his element. He remains calm for Rose's sake, but I am certain that he is terrified. "Come on Uncle."

We all rush and take what we can before heading outside. Kikimo grabs his aunt's hand and takes her to a horse.

"You stay here," Kikimo says. "I will be back for you."

"I am scared, Kikimo," she cries. He lifts Little Foot up and puts him in front of her.

"You will be alright. If you hear gunfire, you take him, and you run. We will catch up to you."

Just then, Roger rides up beside her with Morning Dove in front of him and Max following behind him. He can clearly see all over his wife's face that she is terrified.

"It's alright, Love," he says, trying to calm her down when he himself is just as scared as she is.

He looks at all the haste around him and watches as the warriors prepare themselves for battle. Although he feels that Koawa is not ready to fight, he does not say a word as he watches Koawa circling his horse, speaking his tongue in authority to several other warriors. He sees White Horse approach his warriors on his horse.

As with many other warriors, he, too, is covered with paint that is specifically designed for his marking of rank. He overhears him telling his warriors, as they are leaving out for battle, "Be brave, my warriors, fight with courage." He then watches them ride off.

Alongside Rose, Roger watches in awe as the camp is carefully and quickly taken down. He is in complete astonishment as he watches all the women carefully orchestrate everything that they own, lodges and all behind the horses, in less time than it would take him to eat a meal. Every person knows exactly what needs to be done, and everyone is making sure that nothing is left behind. He sees his sister riding up beside him, dragging her family's belongings behind her.

"You should come to the place where we will wait for our warriors with us. I do not know in which direction the Blue Coats are in, and I fear if you leave, you may head right into the battle."

"You may need me. I am not leaving you." I look over at Rose. The fear is obvious on her face. I wasn't sure that she felt the same way until she spoke.

"There is no way we are leaving you now. We are here for as long as you need."

I slightly nodded at her, and we started off. We hear no gunshots as we are leaving. I take this as a good sign that the Blue Coats are not as close as I thought, and White Horse is keeping them from advancing any closer. We are riding in complete silence, with only the dragging of the travois' being pulled by the horses being heard. The safety of the remote ravine is a short ride away, and we should be there soon. There is fear in everyone as we worry for our men who are out there fighting. No matter how mentally I can prepare myself for the unknown, I cannot help but be worried for not only the warriors but us as well, as the only one who is carrying any decent protection is Roger. All of us women routinely carry knives on us, mostly used for cooking or carving, but none of us are physically trained for one-on-one combat should Blue Coats find us.

White Horse stops his men on top of a hill, looking out at the Blue Coats in the valley below. He is pleased to see that there are only a few of them and thinks that because there are so few, they have not found his camp. He can see a Crow scout and is wondering if this small group is Army scouts out looking for him. He is making a point at allowing the Blue Coats to see him and his warriors on top of the hill. This is a tactic that he uses to tell his enemy that they do not fear them. He now has their attention, and they are staring them down. Koawa looks over at White Horse.

"What do you want to do?" he asks.

"Take me a scout. The rest kill."

Then, on his command, the warriors charge in. With only a small group of soldiers and scouts, White Horse is certain that his warriors can easily take them down, so he decides to stay back and watch.

We have made it to the remote ravine without incident. All anyone can do now is wait for our warriors to return. We all try to make ourselves as comfortable as possible. The older boys, who are too young to fight, start gathering what we will need to start a fire in the event we are here overnight. Depending on how our men do and how close the Blue Coats are will depend on how long we stay here. It could be just a few hours, or it could be up to a few days. So, for that reason, we will gather what we need but will not start a fire until we are certain that the enemy cannot see or smell it. Rose is holding up very well. She is sitting on the ground next to me and the children. Morning Dove is curled up on my lap. She is still complaining that her stomach hurts, and she is not acting herself. I am giving her a sip of water when Roger comes down beside me.

"How is she doing?" he asks. "She is alright," I reassure. "She just needs to sleep."

Roger glances out at everyone around him. Although no words are spoken, he can see the fear of the unknown on everyone's face. He is in total amazement at how brave these women and children are and how not once has he heard anyone complain or any tears shed. He finds these people to be the most humble and proudest that he has ever witnessed.

"I don't know how you remain so calm," he says to me.

"You get used to it after a while. I remember the first time that I had to move camp quickly. I was a nervous wreck. White Fawn was still alive, and she guided me through it. She stayed right by my side until White Horse returned."

"Does this happen a lot?" he wonders.

"It can. White Horse is pretty good at staying ahead of the soldiers. There was only one time when they found us, and that was the day that Running Water died. Ever since that day, White Horse has scouts out all day and night watching."

"That has to be hard."

"Sometimes it is."

Before anything else can be said, I hear Minoke becoming very alarmed. Of all us women, she is the calmest, so for her to become alarmed makes all of us come on edge.

"Something is wrong," I say.

I get Morning Dove off my lap and stand to find out what is going on. Just then, Kikimo comes running up.

"Rising Sun and Dancing Bear are gone."

"Gone," I gasp. "Are you sure? I am positive I saw them both leave with us."

"Yes, Minoke says they both left together to void and haven't returned."

"They can't be far. Did you check the water?"

"Yes, Ma. There is no trace of either one of them."

I am in a dilemma about what to do. I am uncertain as to what sort of danger is out there or where the Blue Coats are. White Horse would be furious with me if I left the safety of the ravine to go out to look for them. Especially since it is Rising Sun and his animosity towards her, but I sure in hell cannot make light of the fact that she is missing and could be hurt. I know Minoke is not going to sit back and do nothing, and my assumption is correct when I see her get on a horse. I deeply sigh.

"I will go look for her," Roger says.

Considering the circumstances of not knowing where the Blue Coats are, I knew Roger leaving to go and find them was the most logical thing to do. If he did run into any Blue Coats, he would have a better chance of bluffing his way by them than any of us would.

"Take your rifle," I tell him.

"Be careful, Darling," Rose says.

Roger then races to get on his horse and leaves when Rising Sun is seen exiting the woods. Minoke is quick at approaching her. I see her grab hold of Rising Sun's shoulders and gently shake them. Although I am too far away to hear what she is telling her, it is apparent to all who are watching that Minoke is furious with Rising Sun for taking off. We are still missing Dancing Bear, and although I would never interfere with Minoke's discipline, I needed to know if Rising Sun knew where she was. I approach them just as Minoke lets go of Rising Sun's shoulders, the anger is still clearly seen on her face.

"Rising Sun, where is Dancing Bear?" I ask her in her tongue.

"We left together to find a bush. When I was ready to come back, she was gone. I went looking for her. When I realized how far I had gone, I turned around and came back. I am sorry I worried you all. I really am."

Her story sounded reasonable if it wasn't for the fact that not once did she look at me in the eyes. This is unusual for her, and although Minoke does not say anything, I do not think that she believes her either. The remaining question is, why would she lie to us?

"Next time you have the urgency to void, we go together," Minoke tells her. She then takes her by the and whisks her back to the others. It was not until I saw Rising Sun being rushed away that I caught a glimpse of a hawk's feather that she has tied around her waist. I have never seen this before, and I am curious about where she got it. My thoughts are interrupted when Roger and Rose come up beside me.

"Where was she?" Roger asks.

"She said she had to find a bush, and when she was ready to come back, that Dancing Bear was gone. She left to go search for her and realized that she had been gone too long and needed to return."

"You sound like you don't believe her?"

"I don't."

"Where is Dancing Bear?" Rose asks.

"I do not know."

"Do you want me to go search for her?" Roger asks.

"No," I answer. "Leave her be. My only concern is for the ones that are here. White Horse should be back soon. He will send his men to go look for her."

The ambush of Lakota warriors charging in has taken the small group of army scouts, along with a few soldiers, off guard. With only a few seconds to prepare themselves for the battle, they rush for cover underneath the wagons. Many shots are taken by both sides. Koawa is quick at taking hold of a young scout who is hiding under a wagon. He grabs ahold of his foot and drags him out. Another soldier tries to fight Koawa off the young lad but is quickly succumbed to Koawa's tomahawk. The battle is near completion, with only a few soldiers still fighting for their lives. Blue Thunder has taken several down and is riding off to help the others when he is shot by a soldier as he is retreating. He manages to stay on his horse and continue riding as he painfully holds his side, which is dripping his blood. White Horse, who is still on top of the hill, is watching his warriors fight and is pleased that his warriors so easily took the soldiers and scouts down. He becomes alarmed when he sees that Blue Thunder has been hit and is struggling to stay on his pony. He rushes down the hill as Grey Wolf kills the soldier who shot Blue Thunder.

White Horse is quick at coming up to Blue Thunder, who is leaning on his horse. He reaches his hand across to support his warrior from falling off. Grey Wolf comes beside his chief and reaches to help Blue Thunder get off his pony and lay him down on the ground. White Horse is immediately at his side. He has a reason for concern when he sees the depth of the wound. He looks up at Grey Wolf.

"Go back and spread the word to our wives that we are fine and we will be camping out near the ridge. Tell Flying Hawk to move them on, and we will catch up with them. Bring Great Healer and my wife back with you."

Although White Horse does not usually allow his wife outside of camp for her own protection, he is going to allow it because he knows that his wife has the power to heal as well and may be of assistance to the Great Healer.

"Yes, Chief," he says.

White Horse turns his attention back onto his fallen warrior. "Hang in there, my friend," he tells Blue Thunder. "Hang in there."

CHAPTER EIGHT
The Great Healer

There is heavy breathing heard between the trees as Red Hawk takes his final thrusts into the woman that he married just a few weeks ago. He married his Dancing Bear in a secret ceremony next to a river overlooking a beautiful valley. Crow Dog did the honors, and Dancing Bear's sister and nieces were there as well. It was the day that her camp was raided by Blue Coats. He is so fortunate that he chose to marry her on that day, or she and her loved ones would surely have perished as well. He never imagined that he would ever marry until he met Dancing Bear. She is a woman who stands very strong and proud. He passionately kisses her as he empties himself inside of her. He continues locking his lips to her as he pushes his manhood as far in as he can in her, making certain that every drop of him enters inside her womb.

"I love you, my husband," she says when their lips part.

"As do I," he says.

"Why must we keep our love a secret from the others? For I am your wife, and we have done nothing wrong."

"My beautiful, I have told you why I cannot return."

"Then I want to stay with you."

"I know, and you will soon. I promise, but until then, you must remain at my brother's camp."

"You do not need Prairie Dawn anymore," she snaps. "You have me to fulfill your desires. I will provide you with many children, not her."

"My precious," he says, stroking her hair. "My revenge goes much deeper than Prairie Dawn. She is only a toy that I will use to get what I want."

"Then you must take her quickly because I do not like playing Koawa. He is no fool. I know it will not take him long to figure me out."

"You are safe. Crow Dog will see to it. You just do as we discussed, and everything will be fine."

"Prairie Dawn told me that Koawa lost a wife not too long ago. He may not be too eager to take another one."

"He took you for a walk by the lake. He is ready. You just keep doing what you are doing, and you will win his trust. You do whatever you have to do to get him to trust you."

He turns her chin to him when she looks away, shaking her head no. "I mean anything."

"I will not lay with him," she spats.

"If that is what it takes to win his trust, then you need to do it. I know your heart is with me."

"So, you would take Prairie Dawn as well, even though it is me that you love?"

"If I must, then yes, I will."

He hears her huff as she turns her head from his. He turns her chin to him again.

"My precious, there is no need to be jealous," he says. "I know that my seed was planted in you today. You have nothing to fear, for all my love is for you. Prairie Dawn will be a captive only until her husband is dead. He will come for her and try to rescue her, and he will bring Koawa with him. They will both die, and then I will have my justice. It is then that you can do whatever you want with Prairie Dawn, as she will be no use to me any longer."

"What about Rising Sun?"

"You were wise to bring her to me today, for now, she knows who you are and that you are now her mother and not Minoke. She will play her part well. Minoke will never see it coming. You do not need to worry about this, for she has her father's wickedness in her."

Dancing Bear does not like the idea of what her husband is doing, but she is so full of love for him that she will do whatever he wants without a word.

"Just hold me a little longer before I have to return," she whines. Red Hawk smiles down at her as he takes his wife into his arms.

White Horse and his warriors have made camp further up the plains and deep in the trees. White Horse has moved Blue

Thunder under a tree and is applying pressure to the wound as he waits for his wife and Roger to arrive. He glances over at Koawa, who is still healing himself, to see that he has his prisoner by his arm and is pushing him to an entrance of a cave. He motions to Yellow Hawk to take over his place before making his way to his captive. He stares down at the young lad, who cannot be any more than eighteen years of age. He admires the boy's courage, as he doesn't flinch when Koawa is tying his hands together so tight that his fingers are turning blue. He feels bad that he is going to have to be so hard on him, but he is left with no choice. He made a promise to himself after his last army attack that he would never allow the men in blue to get so close to his camp again, and for the foolish ones that do, he would make them an example of what he is capable of doing if they cross his path.

The scared lad looks up at the warrior who is standing in front of him. He can tell by what he is wearing that he is up in rank or even perhaps a chief. He made an oath of silence to the army when he joined, and he had no intention of breaking it. He has only been in the army for a short time, and this is his first encounter with Indians. He is trying to remain brave when his stomach is doing circles. He gulps on his own saliva as he looks into the menacing eyes of the warrior, who he is certain has his fate in his hands. Suddenly, to his amazement, he hears the man speak in perfectly clear English.

"Where are the others?" White Horse asks him.

The boy refuses to say a word. White Horse is not playing games and will not chance keeping this boy alive for much longer. He is hoping after some torture, the boy will break his silence and reveal to him what he wants to know. When he gets no response from the boy, White Horse is quick to grab the boy around his neck and lift him to his feet. The young lad's eyes grow huge at the strength of this man.

"We can do it the easy way or the hard way. It makes no difference to me." White Horse growls. "Now, where are the others?" The lad is terrified and is certain that no matter what he tells him, he will not leave this place alive.

"What difference does it make," the boy says. "You are going to kill me anyway."

White Horse is not amused by the boy's comment and refuses to waste any more time in negotiations. He releases his grip on the boy and watches him land hard on the ground. He then looks over at Koawa and nods his head. That is all the incentive that Koawa needs. He squats down in front of the boy, making a point to meet his eyes. He then grabs the boy's finger and pushes it back until it breaks. The boy bellows in pain, but Koawa is not done. He squeezes the broken finger as hard as he can while ripping the nail off. The young boy sees stars in front of his eyes from the pain.

"I will have him take you piece by piece if I have to," White Horse tells him. "Or you can cooperate with me and walk away."

White Horse waits for a few seconds for the boy to come to his senses. When he sees that he is still refusing to talk, he motions for Koawa to continue. Koawa rips the nail from another finger before breaking it. Together, they watch the boy cry out in agony.

"If you still refuse to talk after all the other fingers are broken and your nails are gone, then he will work on your teeth." With that said, White Horse walks away, leaving Koawa to tend to the boy.

Horses are heard riding into the temporary camp as White Horse is making his way back over to Blue Thunder. He sees Great Healer, along with his wife and his Prairie Dawn, enter. He comes down beside Blue Thunder as Roger and the women come running over.

"What happened?" Roger asks as Yellow Hawk releases his hand from the wound, allowing Roger to see.

"When he was leaving, he was shot by a soldier," White Horse says.

"How bad is it?" I ask my husband.

I come down beside White Horse to look at Blue Thunder. He is perspiring and in obvious pain. This is not the first time that Blue Thunder has been shot. The first time was a few years back when he was involved in a scrimmage with Blue Coats. At that time, he was hit in the shoulder, and I had the honor of removing the bullet. The bullet had only grazed him, and he was riding the next day. Unlike then, this appears to be more serious, and I truly am concerned for his life. I can see the concern on White Horse's face. He loves all his warriors with all his heart equally and has never picked a favorite. Although White Horse will never admit it, I know that he and Blue Thunder have a very close brotherly connection, and if he lost Blue Thunder, it would hit him very hard.

"I have seen worse," Roger says.

"Will he be alright?" White Horse asks.

"I will have to remove the bullet, and then I will have a better idea just how extensive the damage is."

Just then, we all jumped when we heard a scream of what sounded like someone being tortured. The three of us looked over to see a few yards away, Koawa towering over a soldier. I look over at White Horse in disbelief.

"You took a prisoner?" I asked him wide-eyed.

"Yes," he admits.

I am in total disbelief. Only one time have I ever known White Horse to take a captive, and that was the time when he hunted down the two men who raped me and tortured them at our camp for three days before taking them back to the scene of the crime where he killed them.

"You never seize to surprise me," I say.

White Horse faintly grins and is relieved that his Prairie Dawn decided now isn't the time to question him.

"Rose," Roger says. She has been so quiet standing there that I almost forgot she was here. "My bag," he tells her.

Rose has been so caught up with her surroundings that she forgot that she was holding Roger's bag. She hands it to him and quickly returns to where she was standing.

"Carrie," Roger begins. "Hold pressure here while I get what I need."

I am quick at following directions, come to where Roger is, and begin applying pressure to the seeping wound. I look at Blue Thunder, who is deathly pale.

"Hang in there, brother," I tell him in his tongue. He attempts to speak to his chief, who is across from me.

"Keep your strength," White Horse tells him in his tongue.

Roger lays everything that he needs and comes back down beside me. He hands White Horse a stick. "Put this between his teeth," he instructs, "and tell him to hold completely still." White Horse does as he is told.

I reach to hold Blue Thunder's hand as Roger is ready to go in. He jumps when he hears the soldier scream out in agony. White Horse is heard speaking his tongue to Yellow Hawk, who is close behind him, watching on.

"Go tell Koawa to back off for a few minutes until Roger is done."

Yellow Hawk is quick at obeying his chief and is seen rushing off. White Horse looks across at Roger. "I don't want to chance you jumping again and slicing him," he tells Roger, almost as if he is trying to be funny.

"I appreciate that," Roger says.

I look up at Rose, who is very timid. I am certain that she is feeling a little intimidated by the torture that is going on by Koawa a few yards away. I chuckle inside as I think how she must feel, as she is already afraid of Koawa, and I am certain that this is not helping her.

"Sorry, my friend," I hear Roger say. I focus my attention back on the matter at hand.

"This is going to hurt." I translated to Blue Thunder what was said.

He nods his head, telling us that he is ready for whatever is coming. Roger starts digging into Blue Thunder's chest. I am glad that White Horse is here to help hold Blue Thunder still as Roger twists and turns his instrument in an attempt to pull the bullet out. Blue Thunder takes the pain like the true warrior that he is.

"I got it," Roger says.

"How bad is it?" I ask him.

"It missed his lung." I hear him deeply sigh in relief. "I think he is going to be alright. He just needs his rest."

White Horse and I are both relieved. He reaches across and squeezes my hand before he speaks his tongue to Blue Thunder about what Roger had said as he is removing the stick from Blue Thunder's mouth.

"We will remain here for the night so he can rest," White Horse says.

"I think that is for the best," Roger agrees. "I understand if you want to leave."

"No, I need to stay here just in case Blue Thunder needs something."

"Alright, but I must warn you, unless our prisoner decides to talk, he will be slowly tortured through the night and finished off in the morning," White Horse cautions.

"I understand, allow me to see him, perhaps he will talk to me."

"I will take you to him," White Horse says.

Roger steps just inside the cave. Koawa moves aside, allowing Roger to squat down in front of the soldier. He will stand and watch next to White Horse just outside the entrance. Roger sees a boy, tattered and torn, around the age of eighteen. He looks down at his bloody and swollen hands to see that every finger has been broken and every nail torn completely off. His stomach curls at the sight of what Koawa has done.

He quickly pulls himself together before introducing himself to the lad.

"I am Doctor Briggs, and what is your name?"

"Seth, Seth McGinnis."

"Nice to meet you, Seth. Let me look at your hand."

"They broke it, Doctor. Every finger is broken, and every nail is torn off."

Roger can tell by the two front teeth missing when Seth spoke and his bloody gums that Seth's fingernails are not the only thing that is missing and that Koawa has moved on to his teeth.

"I see that."

It is taking Roger everything to keep his composure and not vomit up his lunch.

"Are you their prisoner as well?" Seth wonders.

"No, I can come and go freely as I wish."

"Then why are you here?"

"I am here to persuade you to cooperate with them."

"No. I will not betray my country for the likes of them."

"Your loyalty is admirable but foolish," Roger says.

"That may be, but I will die as a hero to my country."

"And that is important to you?" Roger wonders.

"Of course, isn't that important to every man?"

"No, I know it is not to me," Roger adds.

"Then you are not a real man. Serving your country and killing the ones who are destroying it is what makes a real man."

"How do you figure they are destroying it?"

"By not allowing progress and refusing to live the life of a Christian."

"Are you a Christian, Seth?" Roger asks.

"Yes," he answers.

"Then how can you call yourself a Christian and believe that killing another man is correct?"

"These men are not human. They are made from the devil. It is my Christian duty to kill them."

These words really burn Roger, and it pains him to think that such a young boy, who appears to be intelligent, would believe this.

"Do you have family, Seth?" Roger asks.

"Yes."

"Where are they?"

"My mother lives in California."

"And your father?"

"He died on the wagon train going over there from Cholera."

"Why did you join the Army?"

"To help support my mother."

"Do you enjoy it?"

"It is very honorable work."

"Are you willing to die for it?"

"Of course, as did my uncle. He received the most honorable burial ever for his work at Sand Creek."

"How did your uncle die?"

"He was killed by Indians when his wagon was ambushed."

"I see, and so you are here to revenge his death?"

"And to take back what is ours."

"Ironic, I should say," Roger says.

"What do you mean?"

"Your uncle died by Indians, and so are you." Seth gives Roger a very sinister look.

"Who are you really?" he asks Roger.

"I told you. I am Doctor Roger Briggs, and I, too, work for the army."

"I don't believe you."

"I assure you that I am. I will be stationed at the new Fort, and I am training a new doctor. I can prove it."

"Then why are you here with them?"

"Like you, I took an oath when I became a doctor that I would tend to the sick and wounded no matter what their creed. I am also very firm on the Lord, and I believe that these men are not heathens and deserve to be left alone to live their lives as they see fit. I really wish that you would reconsider your silence and give the chief the answers that he wants."

"No, I will not help any heathens. If they kill me, then I will die a hero just like my uncle."

"How old are you, son?" Roger asks.

"Nineteen."

"Nineteen, you have your whole life ahead of you. Why prevent yourself from living it? Just give the man what he wants."

"No!" Seth barks.

"You are being foolish. Don't you understand that these men will torture you until you are dead? There will be nothing left of you to take home to your family to be buried alongside your uncle. No one will ever know what happened to you. I can help you. Come back with me to my home. Let me heal your wounds. Your scars will follow you. Everyone will see what you went through, and you will be made a hero. I will pay to put you on a train to take you home. Just tell them what they want to know."

For a moment, Roger thought that he was getting through to the boy. He could sense it in his eyes, but the boy's hatred for the people that he had been told about was too deep, and he refused to talk. Roger knows that there is nothing else that he can do. Although his heart goes out to the young lad, he comes to his feet and calls defeat.

"You will be a wolf's breakfast by morning. I truly hope that you will come to your senses before then. If not, may God be with you, son." He then walks outside, shaking his head no to White Hor.

CHAPTER NINE
A Boy's Demise

The day turns into evening. Rose and I are next to the fire preparing our evening meal that was hunted earlier in the day. Blue Thunder is doing very well and resting comfortably under a tree. White Horse has been sitting beside him for over an hour. By the body language that I am receiving from both men, I believe that White Horse is breaking the news to Blue Thunder about being a father. Koawa, along with a few other warriors, has taken Seth to a secluded place further away from camp. I can only assume that this is being done for our benefit, to prevent us from witnessing any violence that is being done to him by Koawa or any of the other warriors.

Crow Dog joined us a few hours back. I am extremely curious about Dancing Bear's absence. Being that Crow Dog is here and not out looking for her, can only make me assume that he knows her whereabouts. Although I rarely ever approach a warrior who is not my family, I make an exception this time. I leave Rose behind and approach him.

"Excuse me," I tell him. He stops in his tracks and looks my way.

This is the closest I have ever been to him. He is not the friendliest person and reminds me a great deal of Night Owl in his rough appearance. He is aware that I am White Horse's wife, and I am certain that the only reason he stopped and is allowing me to speak to him is because I am.

"I was wondering if Dancing Bear has returned to camp yet?" I ask him in his tongue.

"Yes," he answers me.

"Where was she?"

"She would not tell me."

"And you did not push the matter?"

"She is a not held with bounds," he says. "She is free to leave as she wishes."

I thought this was odd, as all the women in the camp are highly protected, and seldom do any of us leave the camp alone or without telling someone where we are. I know nothing about Crow Dog and thought that maybe this was just his normal rude behavior or perhaps that he is not as protective of Dancing Bear as she let me believe. The conversation is dropped when he walks away. I watch him disappear into the trees with White Horse as Roger comes up beside me.

"Is everything alright?" he asks me.

"Yes," I answer.

I cannot explain it, but something is not sitting right with me when it comes to Dancing Bear, and I am starting to think that I am wrong about her and she is not the person that I thought she was. I wish that I had followed my husband's advice and not pushed Koawa on her.

"Are you sure?" Roger questions. "You have a rather perplexed look on your face."

"I am fine," I smile.

I notice that he is holding a bowl of food. "I am going to offer some food to Blue Thunder and check his wound. I was wondering if you could come with me to translate?"

"Sure."

We both come down alongside Blue Thunder. When he feels our presence, he opens his eyes. I see him faintly grin. In his tongue, I tell him, "Roger wants to check your wound, and you need to eat something." He agrees and allows Roger to do what he needs to do.

His eyes are thick on Roger, and it is making him a little uneasy. I am certain that Blue Thunder knows the truth about Matthew, but I am unclear as to how he feels about it or if he is upset with Roger for not telling him sooner. I believe Roger is thinking the same way, and that is why he is showing a little bit of fear around Blue Thunder. I know for a fact that Blue Thunder would not do anything to Roger, not that he is not capable of snapping his neck, but Roger has gained a great deal of respect from our people. I still am not sure what Blue Thunder is thinking. I watch as Blue Thunder remains there with his eyes fixed on Roger as he works. For a few moments, no words are spoken. Just as Roger is finishing up, it is then that Blue Thunder speaks.

"Thank you," he tells him.

Upon hearing him speak, Roger looks up at him.

"He said thank you," I tell him.

"You are welcome." I translate. Blue Thunder then speaks again.

"He said not just for this, but for telling him about his son."

"He is welcome, and tell him that I will do whatever I can to help Matthew."

I translated it back. It was then that Blue Thunder opened up and told us something about himself that not even I knew. I translate to Roger as he speaks.

"I loved Rose Petal, and I was angry when she wouldn't leave with me. I could not speak her language and was never able to tell her just how much she meant to me. I believe that she loved me too, but she was too frightened to leave the life that she was accustomed to. I do not blame her for this, for our worlds are so different. By what my Chief has told me, she is living a life full of wickedness and deception. I do not want my son anywhere around it. I agree with you that he needs to be in a better place where he is safe. I want him here with me, but this is not about me. It is about what is best for my son. He does not understand our ways. He does not speak our language. It will be too hard for such a little boy to adapt. I will not go after him or take him away from his mother, for I do not want him to fear me. When he is at this place that you call an orphanage, then I will go and meet him and his mother."

"Blue Thunder, I cannot be certain if Stella will go as well," Roger says.

"You must do everything to convince her to go with him. Our son needs his mother. You tell her when she is there, I will come. With Prairie Dawn and you by our sides, we will talk, and I will tell her what I should have told her many years ago." Roger's face said everything. He is not certain that Stella will go as well. Although I have never asked him, I am convinced that there is more to this story than what Roger is telling.

"Roger," I say. "Is there a reason why you believe Stella will not go with her son?"

"Stella has told me many times that she fears Blue Thunder and fears what he will do if he ever found out about Matthew. I worry that if I tell her that he knows that she will never let him go and if I get the welfare department involved, not even I will have any control over Matthew's fate."

"Then don't tell her about him until after they are both here."

"I am a horrible liar," he says. "Roger, you must. Blue Thunder would never hurt his child, nor do I believe that he would hurt Stella. You need to convince her that her life at the

Orphanage will be better for both. I am certain if you tell Sister Ann about the situation, that she will find her work at the schoolhouse or as a cook or house cleaner. Then, after she is there, you take them out for the day, and we will meet you. I think once she saw that he was peaceful, she would not run. You must try Roger, please."

"I will do what I can," he says. "When I get home, I will send a post to Sister Ann. I promise I will do everything I can."

I take a few moments and translate to Blue Thunder all that has been said. He seems pleased that Roger is so eager to help him. I watch him faintly smile at him before reaching for his bowl of food and starting to eat.

White Horse joins his other warriors deep in the thickets. He arrives just when Koawa removes another tooth from Seth's mouth. The boy is in dire pain. The blood is aspirating from his mouth when he screams. Seth glares over to White Horse.

"They will hang you for this," he spats.

White Horse comes down in front of the boy. "Tell me what I want to know, and he will stop."

"Fuck you!" Seth roars.

White Horse is thick-skinned and is not fazed at being cursed at. Unfortunately, he feels that the boy does not understand just how rough he can be on him. He fixes his eyes on the boy, and then, with all his force, he grabs one of the boy's ankles and pushes it to the side until it breaks. The boy bellows in pain. Before the young lad can catch his breath, White Horse breaks the other one.

"Alright, alright," Seth tells him. "I will tell you."

"Wise decision," White Horse says. "The rest are camped out at Popular Bluff."

White Horse is not fooled. "You lie; there is no one there."

"Then they have moved on."

White Horse is not amused and growing tired of the boy's lies. He presses down on one of the broken ankles, giving the boy a great amount of pain.

"Alright, yes, I lied," Seth admits.

"I am growing tired of you, boy. You tell me the truth, or you are at the mercy of every one of these warriors."

"If I tell you, you will let me go?"

"Yes," White Horse answers.

"They are camped out at the Black Sands near the creek's bed."

White Horse looks up at Koawa. "I knew it."

The boy watches the Chief remove his knife from his sheath and cut him free. He grabs Seth by the arm, bringing him to his knees and dragging him a few inches away. He then tosses him to the ground.

"Go," he tells him.

"But I can't walk. You broke both my ankles."

"Then crawl."

"I want to see the doctor," he tells him. "He said that he would help me. I want to see him. Please, Chief."

"He is no longer any help to you."

"Why? What did you do to him?"

"Go!" White Horse yells.

Seth is terrified. He knows that he cannot walk out of here and crawling will be very painful and slow with all his fingers broken. Surely, he will die before he can make it to any camp.

"You promised that you would let me go," Seth pleads.

"And I have," White Horse assures.

"But I thought you would at least take me to the doctor."

White Horse towers over the lad. "You can either go out on your own and chance that you will make it past the wolves or bears, or you can stay here and be certain of a very slow and painful death. It is up to you."

"You Son of a Bitch," Seth roars. "I knew I couldn't trust you."

"That makes two of us. Now go!"

With that said, White Horse kicks the boy in his rump until he comes on all fours. He follows behind the boy by several feet. The boy is in agony with every crawl he makes. The young soldier makes up speed when he comes up on his knees and elbows. Koawa walks up alongside White Horse and hands him a small tree branch that has been sharpened at the end.

White Horse then takes the branch and charges up behind the boy, shoving it up his backside. The boy suffers the worst pain yet. He is in tears as he frantically tries to rush away. White Horse is certain that with the broken bones, the smell of blood in the air, and the stick hanging out his backside, the boy will be dead within a few hours. He will stay there with his warriors to make sure that the boy keeps crawling before heading back to his wife and the others. He will order his men to raid the soldier camp. It is a good distance away, and he knows that they will be gone for several days. He will only send his best warriors and leave the rest here with him to help protect the camp should it be attacked when his best warriors are gone. When he is certain that his people are safe, he will then escort Roger and his wife back home, taking a few of his warriors with him.

The sun sets across the great prairie. White Horse has everyone comfortable for the night. His selected warriors have already left to head to the Blue Coat's camp. I am a little surprised that Koawa was not one of them. When I asked Koawa why, he said that he needed to be here when they burned down the Fort. It is at that moment that I realize just how serious White Horse is taking this.

I am lying down on the ground under the blanket next to my husband. I have been in deep thought for some time. I feel

White Horse stroke my cheek. It is then that I come out of my thoughts and look over at him.

"Where did you go?" he asks.

"I was just thinking," I answer him.

"About what?"

"I am not happy that you are attacking the Fort, but I understand." He lifts my hand and kisses it. "Good," he says.

"How does Roger feel about it?" I wonder.

"He does not know."

"Do you think that is fair to him? This is going to affect him too."

"I would never do anything to harm your brother or his wife."

"Maybe not physically, but his work is there. What is that going to do to him if he cannot provide for his wife?"

White Horse rolls his eyes. He loves his Prairie Dawn to the core but sometimes wishes that she would not worry so much and put some faith in him.

"With the amount of talent and intelligence that your brother has, he will always be able to provide for his wife."

He watches her turn her eyes away and huff. He hates seeing his wife upset, especially with him. He understands her concern completely, but he must remain firm in his belief. He is not just doing this for himself. He is doing this for his people as well.

"You must understand why it has to be this way, and it has nothing to do with your brother." "I do, White Horse, I truly do, but I worry for you and our men. We have already lost so many." He faintly smiles as he looks over at her radiant beauty and the great amount of concern that is on her face.

He has always been good at reading people, especially ones as easy as his Prairie Dawn. He can see her sadness and her deep concern. Her caring heart is one of many reasons why he loves her so much. He rolls himself on top of her and strokes her hair.

"I do not want you to worry, for I have everything under control."

"White Horse, all I do now a day is worry, and I am tired of it." He is quick at consoling her when she allows a tear to escape and flows down her cheek.

"I know, sweetheart, and for this, I am sorry. If it was up to me, none of this fighting would be happening."

"I know White Horse. I know this is not your fault. I just feel so helpless."

"Your heart is so huge. That is one of the many reasons that I love you so, but you must understand why I must do this."

"I do, but that doesn't mean that I have to like it."

"I promise you that both your brother and his wife will be safe. I will not allow any harm to come to either one of them."

"Just hold me," I cry.

White Horse brings his wife into his arms and tightly embraces her, reassuring her that everything will be alright. When his Prairie Dawn is sound asleep, he rises to his feet one last time to join Koawa before turning in for the night himself. Together, they will follow Seth secretly a few yards behind him until he is dead, and then they will collect his body and place it at the entrance of the Fort for all to see what he is capable of doing if you cross his path.

CHAPTER TEN
The Underground Fortress

The light of a full moon reflects off the prairie grass and hills as Seth collapses out of exhaustion onto the grass beneath him. The howling of wolves nearby brings fear to his soul as he comes to terms with his impending death. Koawa and White Horse are crouched nearby, feeling certain that at any moment, the young boy will be dead. They hear the howling of the wolves as they move in closer to their kill. It is not going to be much longer, White Horse thinks to himself, which he is thankful for because maybe he will still be able to get some sleep in before the sun rises.

Tomorrow, he will escort his brother-in-law home, and then he will plan the attack on the Fort. But first, if he wants to take Seth's body and place it at the front gate of the Fort, he must hurry and get it before the wolves do. He looks out at the hills across from him and sees the wolves circling. He must do it now. Koawa will cover him in the event the wolves should charge in when he is carrying the body off. He makes a dash to the boy who is lying motionless on the ground. He is not certain if he is asleep or has already met his maker. He gives him a nudge on his side. He sees the boy move. He removes his knife and quickly finishes him off by scalping him. He then takes the boy with him, and with his brother riding alongside him, they head for the Fort.

The sun has barely peaked over the hills. Roger is up and is checking on Blue Thunder, who is strapped behind Grey Wolf's horse on a travois for his journey home. White Horse will move everyone on except for Koawa, who will join us, escorting Roger and Rose home. If all goes as planned, everyone should be resting in their own lodges before sundown. A lone soldier mounts himself on top of one of the Fort's walls to start his day. He notices something lying on the ground just outside the gate. He climbs down to get a better look and nearly vomits when he sees the remains of young Seth. He takes a moment to compose himself before running to his commander and announcing his find.

It is late morning when we reach the last few yards to Roger's new home. It appeals little to me from the outside compared to his old home, but I am sure with Rose's expensive taste that in no time it will look nice. Roger shares with White Horse and I the story of how he acquired this old place from an old prospector friend who died from a rattlesnake bite. White Horse is very familiar with this place and has had it scouted on numerous occasions. He even claims that he met the old prospector by chance when he and our warriors were tracking the buffalo. He said that he liked the old man, even though he found him rather odd and did not follow the traditional White Man ways. Rose and I listen as they exchange what memories they had of Earl as we finish our ride home. White Horse and I remain on our horses as we say our goodbyes. Although I would have loved to stay for a while longer, I know if we are going to make it home before sunset, we are going to have to turn right around and head back home. Roger assures me that we won't be a part of it for long and that he and Rose will come and visit us as soon as they can. With our goodbyes done, White Horse and I head for home.

It is midafternoon. Roger is sitting in the chair next to the fireplace. He is determined to figure out the meaning behind the map and concentrates heavily on Earl's last words, mattress, map, and fireplace. He is certain that the fireplace is the key to the meaning of the map. He focuses his attention on it. The odd shape of it at one end and how it protrudes out at the corner makes him wonder if there is something behind it. He comes out of his chair and steps up to the bottom of the stairs leading up to the loft. He then starts to feel around the rocks of the fireplace for anything that might move. After a few minutes of pushing and prying, he is unsuccessful. Frustrated, he looks at the map again. He starts to wonder about the numbers, and in his head, he starts to add them up. He thinks out loud.

"Twenty-five plus five is thirty," he moves to the next line. "Fifteen plus fifteen is thirty." he moves to the next line. "Seventeen plus thirteen is thirty as well."

He stops to think for a moment. "Everything adds up to thirty."

He is completely stumped. "Earl," he says to himself, "you were adamant that I find this map and protect your claim. Help me, my friend. What is it you want me to find?"

He sits himself down on the bottom step and thinks. He hears something moving upstairs in the loft. It sounds like something dragging. Roger looks up the staircase, baffled by what he hears. He is certain that Rose is outside doing laundry, and he is alone in the house. He wonders if, by chance, a raccoon or opossum has somehow managed to get in and is making his home in his loft. He goes up the stairs and into the loft. It is so dark that he cannot see anything. He heads back downstairs to grab his lantern. He hears the noise again as he is lighting the lantern. He is up the stairway once again and holds his lantern up, reflecting it into the loft.

The loft is empty except for an old chest in a far back corner. He walks over to the chest. He hesitates for a moment and stares at it. It is very old in appearance, and except for the handles that are dust-free, it appears as if it has been untouched for years. He decides to open it, only to find that it is empty.

"Why would he have an empty chest up here and nothing else?" he wonders to himself.

He starts to slide it away from the angled wall. It is then that Roger sees that the chest is covering a hole. He removes the big rock that is covering it. It is then that he discovers that this is not any ordinary hole, it is large enough for someone to crawl into. He takes the lantern, holds it up next to the hole, and looks in. He gets down on his stomach and starts to slide into it to get a better look. He keeps holding the lantern in front of him as he crawls further in. He is surprised at how far back he is going. He keeps scooting until he gets to a turn. He can see the bricks of the fireplace leading up to the roof, and through some cracks in the wood, he can see the living area below. He is certain that he is crawling directly alongside the fireplace. The crawl space makes a quick left. Roger follows it for several moments until he gets to a door that is on the ground.

"I was not expecting this," he mumbles to himself.

Confused as to why there would be a door here, he hesitates to open it. He cautiously turns the handle and opens the door, revealing a ladder that goes down to the earth below him. His curiosity has taken over, and he quickly climbs down the ladder. He hears water trickling and the smell of fresh air. As he holds his lantern out in front of him, he gazes out in total amazement at his surroundings. He has entered an underground cavern that sparkles with golden rocks.

"Oh my God," Roger says. "This is his claim. I will be damned."

Roger follows the narrow path that slithers around a babbling brook that shines with gold dust. He notices a shovel, a pick, a screen, and a pan near the brook. Now, things are starting to make sense to Roger as to why the home is built like it is and why Earl was so adamant that Roger held his claim.

Although Roger is no expert on how much this claim is worth, one thing he is certain of is that this much gold traded in would make him a very wealthy man. He now understands why Earl kept his find to himself and why he refused to draw attention to himself. He, too, is thinking that he needs to do the same thing.

He follows the path for a great amount of time. It is very steep and slippery at times, and there are several corridors that split off from the main path throughout. He is uncertain about which direction to take. He notices crates that are stacked in one of the entrances of one of the corridors. Finding these out of place, he wonders if it is marking a turn. He decides to check it out. Holding his lantern in front of him and shining its light ahead, he turns and heads down the corridor. He estimates that he has followed this path that is winding and uneven for nearly a quarter of a mile. Suddenly, he comes to an end. He looks for a way out and discovers a slit in between the rocks that is just barely large enough for him to slip through. He slides his way through and steps out into the light of the land. He allows his eyes to adjust to the brightness of the sun before gazing around at his surroundings. In front of him is the brook that flows into the cavern. He squats down in front of the brook and dips his hands into the cool water to clean himself of dust. He is amazed by his find and is uncertain if he should tell anyone what he has discovered.

He steps into a meadow looking around, he soon concludes that his home is about a half mile away. He is in an area that is well isolated and untouched by any humans. Unless you knew where you were looking, the crack leading into the cavern would be easily missed.

He starts the short walk home through the trees as he remains deep in thought of what he will do next.

"Where have you been?" Rose says as she sees her husband coming out of the woods. He is quick at taking her by the hand.

"I went for a walk," he tells her.

"I have never known you to just take a walk. Are you feeling alright?" she says.

"Yes," he tells her.

He has never kept a secret from his wife, and he vowed to himself that he never would.

"I have something to show you," he tells her.

Before any more can be said, Roger and Rose see a soldier riding in.

"Are you Doctor Briggs?" the man asks when he stops in front of them.

"Yes," Roger answers.

"Your assistance is being requested back at the Fort."

"Let me grab my bag," Roger says.

Further down the plains, White Horse is in council, and plans are being made to attack the Fort at first light. He sends his scouts out ahead of them to case out the Fort. The attack is meticulously planned out down to the last detail. At first light, everyone will be in position, and the decoy will be made. Feeling confident that he will prevail, he dismisses his council, and the preparations begin.

CHAPTER ELEVEN
A Doctor's Rage

Roger is tending to a sick soldier who has a very high fever. The man's wife is watching on as Roger packs his patient in ice.

"Is he going to be alright, Doctor?" he hears her ask.

"My main concern at this time is getting his fever down," Roger answers.

"He has been coughing for days," she begins. "I begged him to rest and not go with the other men in search of the Sioux."

Roger just looks up at her. "Curse those Sioux. Damn them to hell. They are nothing but savages."

Roger bites his tongue and turns his attention back to his patient. He hears a knock on the door. The woman leaves to open it.

"General Phillips," she says. "Please, come in."

Roger stands up when he sees the General walk into the room. The General extends his hand out to shake Roger's. "I am General Phillips," he greets.

"Doctor Briggs," Roger greets back, returning the handshake. "I have heard many good things about you," the General says. "It is a pleasure to finally get to meet you."

Roger is a very humble man and does not feel that he is anything more than just a doctor doing his job. "Thank you, but I am only here until your new doctor arrives. I am stationed a few miles outside the Fort."

"Yes, how unfortunate that you and your wife are not staying in the safety of the Fort."

"I see no reason for concern," Roger says. "But I thank you."

The General then turns his attention to the ailing soldier. "How is he, Doctor?" he asks.

"I was just telling his wife that my main concern is his temperature."

"Do you think that this is something that could cause an epidemic?"

"No," Roger answers. "This man has pneumonia."

"And you are absolutely certain that I have no reason to be concerned for the remainder of the people that are here?"

"Absolutely," Roger says. "However, I can wire for the new doctor to come earlier if you are requesting a second opinion."

"That will not be necessary, Doctor, for you are highly recommended. I am just looking out for the others."

"I understand."

Roger can clearly see that the General is genuinely concerned about his soldiers, as well as the others that are here.

He has been around many generals and high-ranking soldiers and finds most of them to be stuffy and callous. But there is something about this man that sets him off from the others and that Roger likes. He watches the General as he addresses the soldier's wife.

"If you need anything, you come find me," he tells her.

"Yes sir, and thank you," the woman says.

Roger is impressed at how loving this man is to a soldier's wife. He wonders if there is a relationship to her but then remembers when she answered the door that, she addressed him as General and would think that if the woman was somehow related to him, she would have addressed him differently and not be so formal. He can only assume that the General is like this to everyone. This makes Roger like the man even more. The General turns his attention back to Roger.

"I feel I must caution you again," he says. "I have reason to believe that the Sioux are planning another uprising, and I fear for you and your wife's safety alone on the prairie. I will be more than happy to set you up with your own cabin inside the walls of the Fort for you and your wife until the Sioux are caught and their leader is hung."

This puts a chill down Roger's spine with the thought of White Horse being captured and hung. He knows for a fact that White Horse would not go without a fight, nor would any of his warriors stand there and allow their chief to be captured. He will warn White Horse as soon as he can.

"I again thank you, but like I said before, I have no reason for concern. The Sioux have never been a bother to me."

"You really should reconsider, Doctor," the woman chimes in. "You should have seen what they did to that poor boy."

"Mrs. Sanders," the General says, "we need not to bother the doctor with that, as there is nothing he can do to help the boy now." The woman looks away and finds a seat next to her ill husband.

"If you should change your mind," the General says, "you know where to find me, but I must warn you that I cannot guarantee the safety of you or your wife if, by chance, the Sioux find you. They will kill you, Doctor, that I can promise you."

Roger knows differently but appreciates the General's concern and shakes his hand again when he leaves. Roger will remain here with his patient until his fever breaks.

Soon, the sun will be setting, and he fears that he will be in for a long night. He is certain that Rose will be fine alone, as this is not the first time that she has stayed home alone all night while he works. She will keep Max inside and safely secure the door. He is confident that she will be alright.

White Horse's scout has secretly been hiding deep in the tall grass. He is virtually right under the noses of the soldiers as they ride their ponies through the gate. He is amused at how close he can get to the Fort walls and how easily he is able to get by the soldiers. He has been slouched down in the tall grass for hours, casing out the Fort. Soon, he will leave and report to his chief, who is camping nearby with the other warriors, on what he has found out. Then, tomorrow morning, he will return with the war party and set the Fort on fire, killing everyone inside.

The sun shines its bright rays on the horizon. Roger was up most of the night, tending to the sick soldier. Very early in the morning, the soldier's temperature went down, and Roger was feeling more optimistic about his recovery. Confident that he can leave his patient in the hands of the soldier's wife, he steps outside to the morning air and makes his short walk to the telegraph office to send a wire to Stella and Sister Ann. Much of the Fort is still under construction. Tents are seen throughout that house the lower rank soldiers and their families while their permanent homes are being built. He is greeted by many as he walks down the dusty street. He fails to stop to converse with anyone and smiles politely as he passes by.

He opens the door to the telegraph office and stops at the counter. He waits patiently behind the counter for an older man to finish writing down a message that has just come in.

"May I help you?"

"I need to send two telegraphs out," Roger says.

"Write your messages out on that paper," the man grumbles.

Roger picks up the paper and the writing pen. He dips it into the ink and then writes out his message. He is just finishing up when the man behind the counter walks up.

"Both messages will write the same," he tells the man as he hands him the paper.

"Sign it, Doctor Roger Briggs."

The grumpy man's face suddenly lights up. "Doctor Briggs, we have been expecting you."

"Yes, so I have been told."

The man starts to shake Roger's hand. "My name is Oscar Mercer. It is so good to finally meet you. I have been told so much about you. All good, I assure you, all good." Oscar continues shaking his hand as he is rattling on. Roger smiles along so as not to appear rude. He is relieved when Oscar finally decides to release his grip.

" I do hope that you and your wife are being properly quartered," he tells Roger.

"My wife and I are staying in a cabin a few miles out of town."

"Forgive me, Doctor, as I beg to differ with a man of such high intelligence, but I believe that you are being misled if you feel you and your wife are safe outside of the protection of the Fort from the hostile Indians."

"My wife and I are fine. Thank you for your concern."

"Perhaps you are not familiar with the Sioux, being from Boston, sir. They are vicious, lying, dirty thieves who do not care for any human life. Why, just this morning, the body of Seth Mc Ginnis was found outside the gate. They mutilated him, poor boy was hardly recognizable."

"I am well aware of that," Roger grumbles.

"General Phillips is furious. I have just sent a wire to Fort Kearney. General Phillips is requesting that more men be sent here to help stop the Sioux." Roger's ears perk up.

"Did they say when they would arrive?" he asks.

"Within a month," the man answers.

"I see," Fearing that he will blow his cover, Roger asks no further questions.

"See that my messages are sent out urgently."

"Certainly, Doctor, I will attend to it right away. Do you wish to wait for a response?"

"No, that will not be necessary. By the way, my wife is from Boston, and I received my degree there, but I myself have always been a country boy and have lived around those savages, as you put it, for years."

With that said, Roger leaves the office and starts heading back to his patient. He decides if the soldier is stable and his temperature is back to normal so that he will return home this morning and check in with him in a few days. He is nearly halfway down the street when something catches his eye. He is not alone in his observation and sees General Phillip and several other soldiers turn their attention in the same direction.

He gazes up at a hill that is a good distance away. On the hill, there are two Sioux warriors. They are too far away to be recognizable in the face, but he is certain they are Sioux. They have a soldier tied to a post and have lit the ground under the post on fire. They can hear the man screaming, and he can see one of the warriors tormenting him.

"That's Steven!" he hears one of the soldiers yelling.

In a matter of moments, the entire Fort is on the street, and General Phillips is yelling out orders. Roger stands there motionless as the General is putting his men in position, and they are riding hard up the hill. He continues his gaze. Although he cannot be certain because the warriors are too far away, something in his gut tells him that it is Koawa.

"Dammit, White Horse," he says under his breath. "What are you doing?"

No sooner had he said that to himself when a flaming arrow flew over the walls of the Fort and hit a tent, igniting it on fire. Warrior calls are then heard throughout, along with an ambush of Lakota warriors being seen. Everyone scatters. Chilling screams are heard from women as Roger makes a run for cover. The sounds of gunfire and the smell of smoke are everywhere as Roger races under a wagon for protection. He can see the Indian ponies racing down the streets and the warriors igniting things on fire. He is certain that these men are Sioux. He thinks about making his presence known, as he is certain that most likely he will be recognized, but what if his gut is wrong and this is a different band of Sioux. He could be walking into his own death trap.

He remains sheltered under the wagon and scoots himself up further, where he attempts to look through the spooks of the wooden wheels for a better view. He sees a warrior whose back is turned on the other side of the street slice a man's throat and then run off. Roger nearly vomits at the sight of the near-decapitated man. He becomes alarmed when he sees the feet of a warrior from underneath the wagon. He hears him jump on the back of it. He slowly and silently removes his gun from the holster. His heart skips a few beats as he silently waits for the warrior to pounce. He wishes he knew if. Indeed, this was White Horse's band, but he quickly concludes that even if it is, the warrior would react too quick if he knew Roger was underneath here and would kill him before he knew that it was him.

Suddenly, he jumps from fright when a warrior slides underneath the wagon and grabs Roger by the leg, dragging him out. He loses his gun in the struggle but manages to hang onto his medical bag. He closes his eyes and cowers his face with his bag as he anticipates a blow at any second. He feels the warrior's presence straddling over him. He slowly opens his eyes when he realizes that nothing is happening. He looks up at a warrior holding his tomahawk in the air, straddling him. He believes it is Yellow Hawk. He can tell by the look that the warrior is giving him that he, too, is not certain if it is him and is hesitating to strike him. The warrior that was on top of the wagon jumped down. Roger sighs in relief when he sees that it is Koawa. Koawa speaks his tongue to Yellow Hawk, and in return, Yellow Hawk helps Roger to his feet. Koawa speaks his tongue again to him before addressing Roger.

"You are lucky, my friend, that he recognized you. Go with him. He will take you to White Horse."

Before Roger can say anything, he is rushed off by Yellow Hawk, who has him by the arm. He quickly has him on a horse and points to him in which direction to go. Like a bullet, Roger is off.

The fighting continues inside the Fort by the Sioux warriors when Roger races through the gate. He pushes the horse hard in the direction that he was told. He makes the ride up the hill where the warriors had Steven tied to a post. He comes across several dead soldiers lying in their own blood on the prairie grass that was ambushed by Sioux warriors as they come to the aid of Steven. He sees the lifeless, burnt body of Steven still hanging on the post. His stomach turns at the sight. He comes off his horse, grabs his medical bag, and makes his way over to the fallen soldier. One by one, he goes around to see if any of them are still alive. His hopes quickly fade when he realizes that they are all dead.

He becomes alarmed when he hears movement on the other side of the hill. He reaches to remove his gun from his holster when he remembers that he lost it when he was dragged out from under the wagon. He races to a dead soldier and removes his gun from his holster. He waits anxiously with the gun cocked to see what comes over the hill. He remembers Koawa telling him that he would take him to White Horse, but his heart is racing anyway, not being certain of what he may be facing. He releases his grip on the gun when he sees that it is indeed White Horse riding up with several other warriors following him.

"My brother," White Horse says. "What brings you here?"

"I was sending a telegram to Stella when your warriors ambushed us."

White Horse can hear the anger in Roger's voice. This is something that he has never heard before. "I can assure you, my brother, if I knew you were in there, I would have got you out before we came in."

It is at that moment that White Horse is kicking himself in the rear as he hears Prairie Dawn's words of warning Roger on what his plans are. He is so fortunate that there is not a scratch on her brother, or he would never have heard the end of it, nor would he ever be able to forgive himself if Roger had been killed.

"Why did you do it, White Horse?" Roger asks. "Why are you deliberately making it harder on your people by attacking the Fort? Do you have any idea what this going to do to you?"

It is obvious to White Horse that Roger is angry. He just barely escaped being killed, so for that reason, he remains calm and will take the brunt of Roger's anger.

"I do not expect you to understand my thinking on the choices I make, but I assure my brother I never meant any harm to you."

"There are women and children in there," Roger snaps. "Does that not bother you?"

"Does it bother your people when they kill ours?"

Roger is furious, and he is not even sure why.

"White Horse, you just need to stop all this. You are fighting a hopeless battle. There are too many of them. You are going to lose everyone you love. They will not stop until all of you are dead or on reservation land."

"Brother, if you have lived here all your life and your ancestors before you made this land what it is today, and then all of a sudden strangers come in and tell you to leave, would you not fight to keep what is yours?"

"Yes, I reckon I would," Roger admits.

"And if these strangers told you that you are not permitted to live the way that you always have and that you cannot dwell in the lodges that you were brought up in and you cannot eat what you are accustomed to eating and you are not allowed to speak the language that your ancestors spoke, would that not anger you?"

"Yes."

"How would you feel, brother, if I took away the life that you are happy with and I told you that you had to live my ways?"

"I would be angry," Roger admits.

"And would you not fight to keep that life?"

"Yes, White Horse, I probably would."

"Then why should it be any different for me?"

Roger suddenly feels very sheepish and embarrassed. "I'm sorry White Horse. I didn't think of it that way."

"Your thinking is not alone. For some reason, your men in Washington are very greedy and do not accept people who are different than them."

"There are more soldiers coming, White Horse, and I am afraid after today, you are going to be hunted down, and I worry for you when they catch you."

"Do not worry for me, my brother," White Horse smiles. "I am a born fighter."

Before another word can be spoken, a large band of Lakota warriors are seen riding up the hill with the look of victory written all over their faces.

CHAPTER TWELVE
The Sweet One

Rose steps outside to make her way to the creek when she observes a huge amount of black smoke high on the horizon. She has not been here for long and is not real familiar with the area yet, but she is certain that the smoke is coming from the Fort. Sudden fear enters her soul as she immediately thinks of her husband, who should have returned home several hours ago. She had no reason for concern, up until now, of him not returning yet, as it is not uncommon for Roger when he is tending a sick patient to be gone overnight. The blackened smoke that is filling the sky has put panic in her soul. She debates on whether she should leave and ride to the Fort to check on him or just stay put and give him a few more hours. Her anxiety of not knowing if her husband is injured or lying dead gets the best of her, and she decides to go make the ride to the Fort. She will stay on the main path in the event that she runs into Roger along the way. She quickly saddles her horse and rushes off with Max trailing behind her.

White Horse and his warriors stop somewhere on the plains to regroup and celebrate the huge victory on the Fort. There are boisterous cheers heard throughout when White Horse begins to untie the bundle of guns and ammunition that are being pulled behind a warrior's horse and distributes them around to each of his warriors.

"Take your fill of ammunition, men," he says in his tongue.

Koawa is the first to grab a handful. The other warriors follow suit. Koawa comes over to White Horse and pats him on the shoulder.

"This is a good day, my brother," he tells him. "Many scalps and guns were taken."

"Yes, we did well," White Horse agrees.

Koawa knows his brother like the back of his hand and can tell that he is not as happy as Koawa thought he should be.

"You are thinking of Roger?" he asked him.

"Yes," White Horse admits. "I have never seen him so angry."

Koawa agrees with a nod. "His people lost many today from our hands," White Horse states. "I fear that this will cause friction between us, and that pains me, as I would never want to hurt Great Healer."

"You did what you had to do for our people, and you explained to him why you did what you did. Great Healer is a wise man, and he will understand this. Maybe not today, but one day soon he will."

White Horse faintly grins at his brother, patting his shoulder before walking away. Koawa and he are extremely close, and his brother's words touch his heart. He will have to tell his wife what he did today and how close she came to losing her brother. He could keep this little mishap to himself but knows that she will find out one way or another so as not to make any further problems in the future between them; he will come clean to her. He only hopes that she will not be too angry with him for nearly causing her brother's demise.

Roger is on his way home from the Fort. He returned to the Fort shortly after White Horse and his warriors left to see if anyone needed medical attention and to see just how bad the attack really was. His heart is heavy with grief as the Fort was hit hard and virtually destroyed. Many lives were taken, including women and children who were unable to escape their burning tents. General Phillips survived the attack, only suffering a cut over his eye that he inflicted himself when his horse became spooked and ran him into a low-line tree branch. Roger is so full of rage at White Horse for organizing such a catastrophic hit, and he is certain as soon as the reinforcements arrive, that the Army's revenge will be severe. He worries about his sister and his nephew when the soldiers raid their camp, as he knows that there is little that he can do to protect her. His mind is deep in thought as he is slowly riding across the plains to his home. He fails to see a lone rider with a dog traveling towards him. It is not until his dog Max quickly bolts ahead and dashes to Roger's feet that Roger stops.

"Max," Roger says.

He is confused as to why the dog is here and can only assume that the approaching rider, who is now galloping towards him, must be his wife. Concerned that something must be wrong to bring his wife out here alone, he kicks his horse and gallops towards her.

"Roger, thank God," he hears her say.

"What is wrong, dear?" he asks her.

"I saw the smoke on the horizon coming from the Fort, and I got worried. Are you alright?"

"Yes, my dear, I am fine. White Horse and his warriors attacked the Fort. I barely escaped with my life."

Rose gasps. "Why would White Horse come after you? I thought he was our friend."

"He did not know that I was in there. I am fortunate that one of his warriors recognized me, and he and Koawa got me to safety."

"Oh, my word, Roger," Rose cries. "This is not good."

"I know, Love. I am afraid that White Horse outdid himself on this one, and I am not going to be able to talk down General Phillips on retaliating."

Rose is just beside herself with grief and worry. "I want to go home," she tells him.

Roger reaches across his horse and squeezes his wife's hand in an attempt to console her.

"Me too," he smiles.

Later that evening, Roger and Rose are finishing up their dinner. Roger reaches across the table into a bowl to pull out a biscuit. He then takes a moment to butter it before speaking.

"I met the General today. We had a nice conversation before the Fort was attacked."

"Oh?" she questions him.

"You would like him. He seems to have a very good heart."

"I wonder how good that heart is now after what happened today?"

"Yes, this is true. I saw him after the attack. He was angry, and rightly so."

"You think the Fort can be rebuilt?" she asks.

"Oh, they will rebuild it, stronger than before, I can assure you that. General Phillips is pushing that it be completed by winter so all the men that are coming in to replace the ones lost have warm quarters for the winter and will not be in tents."

"That is less than six months away. I seriously doubt that is feasible."

"I have a feeling that whatever General Phillips wants, he gets," Roger says. "Kind of like White Horse."

"I worry for them," Rose says as she takes another sip of her soup.

"Me too, especially when the Army goes in for their attack. They will kill everyone in the camp, but I think I may have a temporary solution."

"What?"

"The day I left to go to the Fort, I was studying Earl's map, and I found something. I was going to show you, but I got called away."

"What did you find?"

"You will have to see it for yourself to really understand it, but behind our fireplace is a cavern that is filled with gold."

Rose's eyes grow huge. "Gold as in the mineral?"

"Yes, and a lot of it. Anyways, this cavern is huge, and there is plenty of room and individual corridors to hide someone or ones."

"Meaning White Horse?" Rose concludes.

"Yes, just long enough until the Army scales back their search."

"Do you think White Horse will do it?"

Rose hears her husband deeply sigh before answering. "I don't know that man anymore. He has changed so much. This war has turned his heart hard."

Both Roger and Rose jump when their door is kicked in, and Koawa is seen rushing in, carrying Morning Dove in his arms. He is followed by White Horse and Prairie Dawn.

"What is wrong?" Roger excitedly says.

"Her fever is dangerously high, and she will not stop crying," Koawa says. "She keeps telling me that her stomach hurts."

"Bring her to the other room."

Roger is quick at escorting Koawa to the bedroom and orders him to lay his daughter down on the bed. Roger rushes to grab his bag and sits down on the bed beside Morning Dove.

"She was doing better when I left," he says. "When did she take a turn for the worse?"

"Early this morning," I answer.

For the first time since their arrival, Roger looks over at White Horse. No words are spoken between them, but White Horse can clearly see the anger that is still deeply seen on his brother-in-law's face. Roger quickly turns his attention back to Morning Dove.

"What have you done for her, Carrie?" he asks.

"Flying Hawk gave me an herb to bring down the fever, and he performed a cleansing on her, but it hasn't helped. Her fever and pain have gotten worse."

"As soon as we arrived back to camp, we brought her here," Koawa chimes in.

"Does she speak English?" Roger asks.

"A little," Koawa answers. "I will help you."

"Rose darling," Roger says. "Please go get me a basin filled with water."

"Certainly, dear."

"I will go with you," I tell her.

Roger begins his examination by attempting to put the thermometer in Morning Dove's mouth. She shies away, clearly not wanting Roger to touch her.

"It is alright, honey," Roger says.

He attempts again. Morning Dove whines. Koawa comes down to his daughter's side and softly speaks his tongue to her.

"It is alright, my sweet one," he tells her. "The doctor wants to make you better."

"Don't leave me, Papa," she whines.

"Never, my precious, never," he smiles.

Roger tries again and is relieved that Morning Dove gives him no further problems and he can quickly finish his assessment. He puts the thermometer in her mouth and waits for it to climb while Rose returns with the basin of water and puts it down on the table beside him. He finishes taking her pulse before removing the thermometer.

"Yes, she is very warm," he says out loud. "I need to feel her stomach. Please tell her to point to where it hurts."

Koawa translates to his daughter, and she points. Roger then places his hand on the area and gently pushes down. Mourning Dove cries in pain.

"I am so sorry, sweetheart," Roger tells her. He then turns his attention to Koawa. "I believe that her appendix is infected."

"Is that bad?" he asks.

"Yes," Roger answers.

I remember from when I was living my life as a White Woman in Willow Creek and going on calls with Roger about what the appendix is, but I am unsure as to what it means when it becomes infected.

"What do you do for it, Roger?" I ask.

"It will have to be removed."

"No," Koawa argues. "You will not cut her open."

"Koawa, I understand your concern, but if I do not remove it and it bursts, the infection could spread. Morning Dove will hemorrhage and die before I can stop it."

I see the color drain from Koawa's face. Morning Dove is his life. I come to Koawa's side and gently touch his arm.

"Roger, are you certain?" I ask him.

"I have already given her medicine that should have helped her, but it didn't. I can repeat the treatment and attempt to lower her fever, but I think it will be a waste of valuable time, as with a fever this high, I fear that it may burst at any time." Roger looks over at Koawa.

"I assure you that if there was any other way around it, I would do it, but I honestly feel that this is the only way."

"Have you ever done one?" I ask.

"No," he answers. "But I have studied about it, and I am confident that I can do it."

White Horse has been quiet during this entire time, just listening on, but he feels now that he must say something that will put his brother at ease.

"Brother," White Horse starts. Koawa looks over at him. "Great Healer is a man of many talents and has a head full of wisdom. He has brought both of us back from what should have been our deaths. If he says he can do it, then he can do it."

The air is thick as Koawa is in deep thought. He looks down at his ill daughter. He thinks of his Running Water, who his daughter greatly resembles. What would she want to do? What would she be telling him? He thinks back to the day that she died and how he wishes he could have saved her and not have been so quick to leave with the war party. He sighs deeply.

"How I wish I could have saved her mother," he begins.

I placed my hand on Koawa's shoulder to comfort him. "If only I had stayed back and made sure she got over that hill. She may be here today. I could not save her, but I can save our daughter. Go ahead."

Roger is quick at getting everything that he needs for Morning Dove. I am asked to remain with him to help. I believe this puts some relief on Koawa, knowing that I am remaining with his daughter. Rose escorts White Horse outside. Koawa remains by his daughter's side until she has fallen asleep before leaving and closing the door behind him. It is then that Roger begins.

CHAPTER THIRTEEN
A Big Dilemma

Koawa has positioned himself on the floor under the threshold of the closed bedroom door that his daughter is behind. He has remained there for nearly an hour and is refusing to leave until he receives word of how his daughter is. White Horse finds comfort in Roger's favorite chair next to the fireplace, with Max resting comfortably by his feet. Rose offers him a cup of tea. He remembers drinking the tea when he spent time with Roger last winter recovering from his accident and how much he enjoyed the sweetness of the white stuff that he put in it. His eyes light up when Rose offers him some sugar that she has in the bowl beside it.

"Roger told me how much you enjoyed the sugar when you were injured," she tells him.

"Yes, it is a taste that I have missed," White Horse admits.

"I will send you home with some. We have more than enough."

"That is very kind of you, thank you."

Rose then turns her attention to Koawa, walks over to where he is sitting, and offers him his tea. He comes out of his deep thoughts and looks up at her.

"I put some lemon in it," she says, offering him the cup.

For reasons that she herself is unclear of, she is still slightly intimated by Koawa, even though he saved her life a few months back. So, for that reason, she is very shy around him. He doesn't say a word but declines her offer by putting his hand up.

"You should try it, my brother," White Horse says, coming to his feet and making his way to Koawa. He removes the cup of tea from Rose's hand.

"You will not be disappointed," he says, grinning down at his brother.

The room is still for a few moments as Koawa looks back and forth between Rose and White Horse. Finally, he comes to his feet and takes the cup out of White Horse's hand. White Horse dips his fingers into the sugar bowl that Rose is holding on the tray and plops some sugar into Koawa's cup. Koawa puts his hand over the cup and annoyingly glares at White Horse. White Horse smiles at his brother and faintly chuckles.

"Come, my brother, and sit down," White Horse tells him.

"I told her that I would not leave her side, yet I have. I need to be here."

"Prairie Dawn is there; Morning Dove will be fine; besides, sitting by the door will not make Roger go any faster." Koawa faintly grins. White Horse knows him like the back of his hand, and they are extremely close. Not only is White Horse his brother and chief, but he is his best friend, and he is glad that he is here.

White Horse sits back down in Roger's chair, and Rose starts cutting up vegetables in the kitchen and putting them into a bowl. Koawa leans up against the unlit fireplace and gazes out into it. He takes a sip of his tea as his mind begins to wander. He thinks of his precious Morning Dove, who is so gravely ill. She means everything to him, and he would be so lost without her. He wonders if he made the right decision in allowing Roger to cut her open. He is certain he would never be able to live with himself if anything happened to her. He thinks about Running Water, who has been gone almost a year. There is not a moment in his day when she is not on his mind. He has been so lost without her, and at times, his grief is very hard to cope with. He begins to think of Prairie Dawn, who, as much as he tries to forget the love that they shared when White Horse was presumed dead, finds himself at times wondering what could have been. He can still taste her honey lips and can smell the sweetness of her hair when he holds her. He will never forget the curves of her body when he rubbed his hands up and down her thighs or how his body tingled when she pleased him with her mouth on his shaft. He thinks how close they came to lovemaking and curses the Arapaho timing of coming into camp when they did with word that White Horse was still alive. His groin aches just thinking how explosive he is certain their lovemaking would have been. It is a daily struggle for him to try to put her behind and be happy that his brother is alive and is with the woman that he is destined to be with. His thoughts are interrupted when he hears the voice of Prairie Dawn.

"Koawa," I say. All eyes turned to me, and immediately, everyone hurried over. "She is resting," I tell him. "You can go in and see her."

Koawa is quick at whisking past me and rushing into the room. Rose follows behind. I look up at White Horse.

"I need to go to the creek and wash up," I tell him.

"I will go with you."

Koawa is immediately at his daughter's side and takes her hand into his. Roger has finished washing his hands and is given a towel by Rose.

"She did really well, Koawa," Roger says, drying off his hands.

"And the sickness is gone?" Koawa asks as he strokes his sleeping daughter's hair.

"Yes. She just needs her rest. I would like to keep her here for a few days just to monitor her until she gets her strength up."

"She can rest at home," Koawa says.

"I understand you want to take her home, but I would rather you did not. She has several stitches, and there is still a chance for infection."

"But you told me that you removed the sickness."

"I did Koawa, but there is still a chance for infection from the wound. Anytime you open the body up and remove something, there is always a chance for infection, even after the sickness is gone. By keeping her still and not moving her, she will have less risk of infection setting in, and she will be in less pain from the move, making her heal faster."

Koawa is still hesitating. Roger begins again, trying to persuade Koawa to keep Morning Dove here.

"This is just like the time when White Horse was shot and you were stabbed. I would not allow either one of you to be moved until I was certain that no infection had set in. If you are worried about her being alone, you are more than welcome to stay with her. I will make up a cot next to her where you can sleep. I am only asking for a few days."

"Our medicine man would want to use the sacred medicine bundle on her, for this is custom, and I, too, will want this. She needs to go home."

"You are more than welcome to bring him here and perform whatever you want on her. I am only asking that she not be moved for a few days."

Koawa strokes his sleeping daughter's hair as he thinks. How he wishes Running Water was here and how much their daughter needs her mother right now. It pains him to know that his daughter will never have the honor of knowing her mother and witnessing what a beautiful person she was. Roger hears him sigh as he drapes the wet towel over the chair to dry.

"And Prairie Dawn or I will be allowed to stay with her the entire time she is here?" Koawa asks.

"Certainly," Roger agrees.

"Then I will allow it."

Koawa then turns his attention back to his daughter. White Horse joins me in front of the creek, sitting on a rock. I start to wash my hands in the cool water.

"I am proud of you, Prairie Dawn," he says.

"Roger did all the work. I just handed him instruments and made sure Morning Dove stayed under."

"You are always so humble," he smiles. I grin. White Horse has never been shy when it comes to complimenting me.

"I couldn't help but notice earlier some tension between you and Roger. What is going on?" I ask. White Horse smiles again.

"You are not only beautiful, but you are observant as well."

"It was not hard to see. Roger is very easy to read," I grin.

"As are you, my dear."

"So, what is going on?"

"We just don't see eye to eye on some things."

"Roger is pretty open-minded," I say. "What sort of things are you not agreeing on?"

"You are aware that we attacked the Fort," he asks.

"Yes," I answer.

"Your brother was in the Fort when we went in."

I stop what I am doing and look over at him. "Yellow Hawk recognized him, and Koawa got him out and sent him to me."

"I knew this was going to happen. If you would have warned him ahead of time like I had asked."

"Prairie Dawn, nothing happened to him. There is not a scratch on him," he argues.

"He is lucky that it was Yellow Hawk who is not as quick on his attack and that it was not someone like Night Owl or Grey Wolf who would have killed first and asked questions later."

"I know. I, too, thought of that, and I am thankful that Yellow Hawk had the foresight to question it before he struck."

White Horse watches his wife finish washing her hands as she shakes her head in disgust. He can see the emotion in her face of what could have happened and how close she came to losing her brother.

"Carrie," he calmly says.

White Horse usually always addresses me by my Indian name, but on occasion, when the conversation turns serious, he will call me by my birth name. He does this to get my attention. I shake my hands free of water as I look up into his dark, mysterious eyes.

"No, White Horse," I call out. "You messed up. You became overzealous and so thirsty for revenge that you failed to stop and think about who you are hurting."

"Oh, Carrie, come on!" he snaps. "You know why I did what I did. You, of all people, should understand. You were one of their victims."

"You are still fuming over that. When will you just let it go?"

"Never!" he barks.

"You were there when they rode into our camp when we slept. You held your dying friend in your arms when she was shot in the back, running away. You saw Running Bear floating in his own blood with a hole in his head. You wear the scars on your back from when they whipped you and left you for dead. We didn't ask for any of this. We met with them for peace, and they refused. They started this war, not us. They came onto our land. They invaded our lives. They killed our food. They took the first shot. It was our loved ones that were the first to fall. I will not be at blame for starting this bloodshed."

"But your fighting almost killed my brother," I bellow.

"And they almost killed you, and I will never forget that." He puts his hand on my shoulder. "I am sorry for putting this pain on your brother and nearly getting him killed, but sweetheart, I will never stop fighting for what I believe in, and I thought you understood that."

"I do, White Horse, but now you have made things worse, and you have put all of us in even more danger because now more soldiers will come." White Horse lifts his brow.

"Seriously, Carrie, they were coming anyway. That is why the Fort was built, to begin with. If anything, I slowed them down."

I can tell that I am fighting an endless battle, as nothing that I am going to say is going to stop White Horse from being so brutal. I know he has never gotten over my rape that was done by two Blue Coats nearly a year ago, and I cannot say that I blame him. It was extremely brutal, and their beating damned near killed me. It was shortly after my rape and Running Bear's death that I saw the change in White Horse. His eagerness to find peace with the White Man has diminished, and he is now out for blood. He used to be a chief who would keep to himself and go out of his way to be friendly to White Men, but not anymore. They are now his enemy.

"Please, White Horse," I deeply sigh. "I cannot stop you from fighting, but I beg of you, please, don't hurt Roger because of it."

White Horse cups my face into his palms and pushes his face into mine.

"I would never hurt your brother. I promise. I love you, my wife. Please do not worry your beautiful face over this. Everything is going to be alright. Your mighty and powerful chief will make certain of that." I chuckle at his humor. White Horse always has a way of cheering me up. He chuckles along with me before softly kissing me. "I love you," I say as I go into his embrace.

CHAPTER FOURTEEN
Spirit Dog

It is bright and early the next day. Last night, Flying Hawk paid Morning Dove a visit and used his medicine bundle on her. She is resting comfortably in the bed. I agreed to stay behind to take care of Morning Dove and keep her comfortable until she is well enough to go home. Although Koawa promised his daughter that he would not leave, she seems to be alright with the fact that I am staying behind in his place. He leans over her bed to kiss her cheek before heading home.

"You mind Prairie Dawn," he tells her in his tongue, "and allow the doctor to care for you."

"I will, Papa," she answers.

"Don't forget to bring me my doll when you come back."

"I won't." He flicks her nose and watches her smile before coming to his feet and making his way to the door.

"I will take good care of her, Koawa," I say. "I promise."

He faintly grins before walking out the door and getting on his horse. I walk alongside White Horse until he gets to his horse.

"We will only be gone long enough to move the camp further on. I will return in a day or two."

"You are worried about the soldiers, aren't you?"

"Yes, Roger is going to return to the Fort today and see what he can find out. Until then, I want to move our people further into the hills."

"I understand." I looped one of my fingers into his. "Are you and Roger alright?"

"We talked a little last night. We still do not agree with each other, but at least we are not enemies."

I feel for White Horse because I truly do believe that he likes Roger, and the last thing that he wants to do is quarrel with him. I know that his heart is breaking that Roger and he do not see eye to eye, but both men are stubborn, and neither man will back down. I softly pecked his cheek.

"Be safe," I tell him. "I will miss you when you are gone."

"As will I," he says.

I watch him pull himself up onto his horse and motion to Koawa and Flying Hawk that it is time to leave. Roger walks up beside me as I watch the three men ride off. Koawa and I briefly exchange a glance as he rides by me. It is a look that perplexes Roger, but he does not say a word.

We are well into the afternoon. Morning Dove is resting soundly asleep in bed. I am helping Rose in the kitchen with peeling potatoes. Roger left shortly after White Horse to go to the Fort, leaving specific instructions for me regarding

Morning Dove. He is expected to return home late this afternoon.

Further down the plains, Kikimo is nestled under some scrubs, staring out at the lone horse grazing on the prairie grass. He is mesmerized by the beauty of the stallion that is before him. He notices the saddle fastened on its great back and the reins dragging on the ground. He sneaks in closer to get a better look. The horse lifts his head and looks directly at him as Kikimo slowly advances. The horse shows no fear when Kikimo grabs his reins and starts petting its nose.

"Good boy," Kikimo tells him.

Kikimo starts to investigate the horse further. He runs his fingers across the big bulky saddle that is on its back. He wonders where the rider is. He momentarily looks around for any sign of the rider, who is perhaps injured and lying on the ground. He sees no signs or any tracks that would lead him to anyone, so he turns his attention back to the horse. He runs his fingers across the marking of the U.S. Calvary that is branded on one of the horse's hips.

"It is the horse of a Blue Coat," he says to himself.

He faintly grins, thinking to himself at what a prize this horse would be if he was to take it. He has never stolen a horse before and can't believe his luck. He thinks how proud his father will be of him and how much more respect he will gain from the other warriors when he rides into camp with a Blue

Coat horse. He smirks to himself as he visualizes the look on Eagle Scout's face when he returns to camp with a horse that once belonged to a Blue Coat.

"I will call you Spirit Dog," he says, "for you were sent to me by the Creator."

As he is petting the nose of his new horse, he thinks how jealous his mouthy friend will be and how much he will enjoy boasting to him as to how he stole it. He will make his friend believe that he fought hard for it, nearly bringing him to his death. He chuckles harder to himself as he is certain that this will shut his mouthy friend up once and for all. The temptation is too great. He must take it. He has no use for the big bulky saddle, so he removes it and places it on the prairie ground beside him. He grabs hold of the reins and leads the horse into the trees, where his own pony is waiting. He hasn't seen his mother for a few days and needs to check on his cousin, Morning Dove. His Uncle's house is not that far away, and he is so excited to show his mother what he did that he decides to ride there before he heads back to camp. He jumps on the back of his own awaiting horse and runs off, leading Spirit Dog behind him.

It is nearly dinner time when Roger arrives home. He is removing the saddle from his horse as it feeds when he sees, over a distant hill, a lone rider coming in, leading a horse behind him. He stops when he notices that the rider is Indian.

He appears of no threat to him as he is watching him ride in. It is not until the rider waves at him that he realizes it is Kikimo. Kikimo greets his uncle in his tongue when he stops in front of him.

"Leksi," he grins.

"Is everything alright at camp?" Roger asks him.

"Yes," Kikimo smiles.

"I thought your father was moving your people further away?"

"He did, but only by a half a day or so. I have come to see my mother and cousin," Kikimo says.

"I just returned myself and have not been in yet. We can go find out together," Roger smiles.

It was then that Roger noticed the horse that was trailing behind Kikimo. He recognizes the U.S. Calvary branding on the hip of the horse.

"Where did you get this horse?" Roger asks.

"I found it grazing on the Prairie."

"Kikimo, this is an Army horse."

"I know," Kikimo boasts.

He is so proud of himself that he can hardly control his excitement.

"What happened to the soldier that was on it?" Roger wonders.

"I did not see any Blue Coat, only the horse."

"Where did you find the horse grazing?"

"Close to the Fort, but there was no Blue Coat, I looked."

"What are you planning on doing with this horse?"

"Keeping it," Kikimo exclaims.

"No, son," Roger says. "You cannot keep this horse."

"Why not?"

"Because it belongs to the Army."

"They were not using it," Kikimo argues. "It was just grazing on the tall grass."

"Kikimo, you found the horse close to the Fort. It most likely fled when the soldier was taken down by one of your father's warriors during the attack on the Fort."

"If it lost its owner, then it needs a new owner."

"Kikimo, you do not understand, you cannot just take a horse without paying for it."

"One does not put a price on a horse. You simply take what you need."

"Maybe by Sioux law, but not by White Man's law. To us, it is called stealing, and horse thieves are hung."

Kikimo straightens up and presses out his chest. "No White Man will hang me, as Spirit Dog and I will run."

Roger is frustrated that he cannot make Kikimo understand the severity of his stealing this horse. He understands that it is his custom and that he will be looked up to by his peers for stealing a horse that belongs to the Army. But Kikimo could get himself and his father into so much trouble if he is seen with the horse that clearly is branded as belonging to the Army.

"Kikimo," Roger calmly says. "If you need a horse that bad, you can take mine."

"I don't want your horse," Kikimo barks.

"Why not? He is very strong. He can pull a good team. You could ride him fast and hard. He will make you proud."

"No, Spirit Dog is worth more than one horse."

Roger thinks a moment. "I have been at your camp many times, and I notice that your mother could use an iron pot. I have one that I will trade for you, as well as my horse, for Spirit Dog."

Kikimo looks down at his uncle from high on his horse. He has grown to love and admire this man and is proud to call him his uncle. His offer is tempting, as his mother could use a heavy pot to cook his favorite food. He loves his mother's cooking and is certain that with a new pot, it would taste even better. But he so much wants to smear Spirit Dog in Eagle Scout's face and shut his mouthy friend up once and for all. He is in a dilemma about what he should do.

"Alright," he finally says. "An iron pot and your horse for Spirit Dog." Roger faintly grins. "A good trade, son," he tells him.

"Uncle, what are you going to do with Spirit Dog?"

"I am going to take him back to the Fort. I will tell them that I found him grazing along the Prairie. They won't think twice about it."

"What are you going to ride if I have your horse?"

"I will use Rose's until I get another one. I am a doctor, and I am always offered livestock as payment. I will not go without for long."

Kikimo is still not thrilled that he is losing Spirit Dog, but he will get another horse in his place, and his mother will get an iron pot, so for that, he is pleased. He will still brag to Eagle Scout and stretch the truth about how he got the horse to make his friend jealous, but he will be honest with his father about how he got the iron pot. He is disappointed with losing Spirit Dog that he decides to head home and come back with his father on another day to see his mother and Morning Dove. Holding the pot in his hand and guiding his uncle's horse behind him, he heads for home.

CHAPTER FIFTEEN
Suspicions

Another day passes. Morning Dove is doing very well, and Roger is optimistic that she will be able to return home within another day or two. Morning Dove has warmed up to him tremendously and is even calling him Leksi, Uncle, even though there is no blood between them. Roger has taught her how to play checkers, and they have been playing for hours. I have highly enjoyed the time that I have spent here and have started to bond with Rose. Although she is a little too proper for my standards, we seem to be getting along very well. I am missing White Horse tremendously, and he is very strong on my mind. This is not like me, as it is not uncommon for White Horse and I to be away from each other, and I only pray that he is alright. Rose left to go to the creek to refill the bucket of water, when she sees a rider coming in. She immediately recognizes him as being Koawa. He is holding a spear in his hand and has a bag looped around his neck. She watches him as he brings his horse to a stop in front of her.

"Hello," he greets. "Hello," she greets back.

She watches him jump off his horse and walk a few steps up the hill overlooking the house. He then stabs the spear into the ground. "Leave it there," he tells her.

"Why?"

"If another tribe comes this way, they will see it and know that you are friendly to us, and they will leave you alone."

"Oh," she says.

She then watches him remove a necklace from his bag and hand it to her.

"Put this on and wear it whenever you travel. If you come across a war party, you show it to them, and you will live."

"Thank you," she says. "I have one for Great Healer as well."

"Again, thank you," she shyly says.

Koawa is no fool and can tell that Rose is still afraid of him. He has never done anything to her and risked his life to save her from the Dog Soldiers. He is uncertain as to why she is afraid of him and cannot help but wonder if it has something to do with the harsh words that they gave each other when they were running to escape. He holds no animosity towards her, as he knew how frightened she was and how fear can bring the worst out of someone. He faintly grins at her in hopes of bringing some warmth to her scared little bones.

"How is my Morning Dove doing?" he asks her.

"She is doing very well."

"I do hope that she has been behaving herself."

"Oh yes, I hardly know she is even here at times, as she is so quiet."

"Good," he smiles.

"She is inside with Roger and Carrie, go ahead and go in."

Koawa enters the house and makes his way to the room where his daughter lies. He stops at the threshold and grins at his daughter, who is sitting up in bed.

"She got you again," I laugh at Roger, as Morning Dove has now beaten him three in a row.

"You are too good at this," Roger smiles down at her.

Just then, we heard her call out. "Papa!"

We both turn around to see Koawa standing at the door. Her smile is big as Koawa comes over to her, kissing her forehead and handing her her doll that he removed from the bag looped around his neck. "You look better, my precious," he smiles.

"I feel better," she softly says in her tongue.

"Papa, when am I going to go home?"

"Very soon, my little one," he answers her. "As soon as Great Healer says that you are alright to travel."

"Koawa," I interrupt. "Why didn't White Horse come with you? Is everything alright?"

"He is fine," he answers me. "He is with Blue Thunder and Grey Wolf, cutting the trail and scouting ahead so we have a clear path when it is time to go home. He will be here later this evening."

"Good," I say, relieved.

I still cannot understand the reasoning why White Horse is so strong on my mind, and I am glad he will be here tonight. Suddenly, catching us all off guard, we hear Rose yell out for Roger. We are all quick at the door. Roger is the first out and to his wife's side and looking in the direction that she is. He, too, becomes alarmed when he sees a handful of warriors sitting on top of a nearby hill watching us. Koawa rushes forward and stands in front of Roger and Rose. For a few moments, he just stands there and watches as they stare down at us from on top of the hill. It is not until they start making their way down the hill that he speaks.

"Prairie Dawn," he says to me. "Take Rose inside and stay with Morning Dove."

I am quick at obeying and have Rose by the arm and rushing inside.

"Lakota?" Roger asks him.

"No, they are Yankton," Koawa answers. "The one in the middle is Little Crow. We are very good friends."

Roger has never heard of this tribe, nor does he have any knowledge of their demeanor. He is very glad that Koawa is here and even more thankful that they are his friends. Together, they watch as the warriors ride in. The one named Little Crow speaks his tongue to Koawa, and in return, Koawa speaks back. Roger watches on as the conversation goes back and forth for several seconds.

Suddenly, the lead warrior turns his attention to Roger and speaks his tongue to Koawa. Koawa, in exchange, answers back. Although Roger does not understand a word that they are saying, he is certain that the warrior is talking about him.

"What is he saying?" Roger asks him.

"They are looking for White Horse. Their camp was raided by Pawnee a few days ago. Many lives were destroyed, including their Chief. They were out hunting for buffalo when it happened. He is not sure as to why the Pawnee attacked because they have not had any problems with Pawnee for many years. They also heard about the attack on the Fort and how White Horse was behind it. They came to make sure that we are all alright, as well as to tell White Horse what happened. They saw the spear in the ground and my pony grazing. They saw the woman outside and were curious why my pony was here. I told them that you are a Great Healer and a friend to our tribe. He asked why I was here, and I told him that my daughter had become ill and I brought her here for help. I told him that you and your wife are good people and our friends."

"Tell them I am sorry for their losses, and if any of their loved ones need medical attention, I will be more than happy to help."

Koawa translates to Little Crow what Roger had said. Little Crow looks down at Roger from high up on his horse. He ever so slightly nods his head and speaks.

"He said thank you, but nothing more can be done."

"You can find White Horse near the Black Sands. He should be coming this way," Koawa tells him before Little Crow and his warriors turn their horses around and leave.

Evening is well upon us. Morning Dove has turned in for the night. Roger is pleased with her recovery and is confident enough that after tomorrow, she will be strong enough to go home. This is music to my ears, as much as I have enjoyed my time with my brother and forming a bond with Rose, I am anxious to get back home to Little Foot and White Horse. I am sitting on a log next to the creek, enjoying the evening air, when Koawa comes up and sits down beside me.

"Is everything alright?" he asks me.

"Yes."

"Great Healer said that Morning Dove can go home tomorrow afternoon."

"That is wonderful. I am so glad that she is alright."

"Me too," he says. "I will admit that she had me frightened. I cannot imagine what I would do if I lost her."

I console Koawa by rubbing his back. The emotion is thick on his face, just with the thought of losing his daughter. "I was scared, too. Although she is not my blood, I love her like she is." Koawa faintly smiles.

"Thank you for being here for her."

"You are welcome," I grin.

"I know you are missing your family."

"Yes, I am, but I know that Minoke and Songbird are keeping them safe and making sure that they are fed and warm."

"They can manage a few days without you," he grins.

"Little Foot and White Horse, yes, but Kikimo…" I huff. Koawa chuckles. "Roger told me about the horse. That boy, seriously," I huff. "I do not understand what has come over him."

"I would have done the same thing," he says.

"That is different, you are a warrior, he is just a boy."

"Prairie Dawn," Koawa grins. "Kikimo is not your little boy anymore. He is almost a man. Soon, he will go on his first vision quest and have a new name."

"I cannot imagine him with any other name than Kikimo."

"I remember when I had my first vision quest, and my new name was chosen, my mother had trouble letting go as well."

"I don't expect you to understand, as you have a daughter and don't have to worry about it."

"But I do understand," he says. He jokingly nudges my shoulder. "Someone does not want their little boy to grow up." I smile over at him, as he is exactly right. Before any more can be said, we both hear movement in the darkness. A figure comes into view.

"White Horse," I exclaim, rushing to my feet to give him a hug.

His eyes turn thick on Koawa, as I am embracing him. "I didn't hear you ride in," I tell him.

"Some of my men are camped out not far away. I walked here so my pony would not be seen by soldiers if they pass by."

"My husband, such a wise man," I tease.

"How is Morning Dove?" he asks Koawa.

"Better, she will be able to go home sometime tomorrow."

"That is good to hear," White Horse says.

"Did Little Crow find you?" Koawa wonders.

"Yes, it saddens me. I smoked many pipes with their Chief. He was a good man."

"Are you going to help them?"

"The Pawnee have done nothing to us in many years. I do not have the time to waste on fighting them. However, Grey Wolf and several of our younger warriors who are growing restless for a good battle will be leaving to join in the fight. You can as well if you wish."

"No, the only enemies I wish to fight right now are the ones in blue."

"I am pleased to hear that," White Horse says.

"I will take my pony and find the others. I will return shortly." White Horse only nods in agreement. Koawa briefly looks my way and then back at White Horse before walking off. Holding my husband's hand, I walk back to the log and sit down.

"You care to join me?" I ask him.

"What were you and Koawa doing?" he asks, failing to sit down next to me.

"We were just talking. Why?"

"I don't like how close you too are."

"Why, White Horse, are you jealous?" I tease.

"Maybe you don't see it, Carrie, but I do."

"See what?" I question. Finally, he decides to join me by straddling the log and coming down in front of me.

"He is in love with you."

"What?" I say in disbelief. "No, White Horse, I am sorry, but you got it all wrong. We are just good friends. That is all. I am in love with you."

"I did not say that you are in love with him, I said that he is in love with you."

He cups my hand into his and gently kisses it. "I cannot say that I do not blame him, as you are a fine woman in many ways." He deeply penetrates my eyes, and for a few moments, he is still. "I need to know the truth, Carrie," he suddenly says. "No lies, only the truth."

"I always have been honest with you."

"Sometimes I think you are afraid to tell me because you fear me."

"What is it that you think I am not telling you?"

"What exactly went on between you and Koawa after the wedding?"

"Nothing," I answer.

"You did not unite with him on the pelt?"

"No," I reassure him. "The night that we found out that you were alive was the night that we were in the wedding lodge. We were about ready to unite when Koawa heard the Arapaho coming in. As soon as we heard that you were alive, the marriage was no more, and no unity was made."

"So nothing happened?"

"Nothing happened. Honest White Horse. I couldn't even get myself to do it because I felt like I was betraying you. It was almost like my mind was telling me that you were alive and that this was wrong. But I was his wife, and I knew I had to."

I hear him deeply sigh as he lowers his head, a habit that he has when he is not sure what to believe.

"White Horse, I love you with every drop of my blood, and I would never destroy that love. You must believe me. If I had known you were alive and if Red Hawk was not swarming in, Koawa and I never would have married so soon."

"I believe you," he says, squeezing my hand. "But I do not think that Koawa is over you. I believe that he is in love with you."

"I will talk to him," I say.

"No," he argues. "You are aware of it, and now you will watch out for it. Besides, I understand that Dancing Bear is smitten with him."

"Yes, she is, but I don't trust her."

"Why? It was your idea for Koawa to take her for the walk around the lake."

"I know, but things have changed. I have been watching her, and something is just not right?"

"What do you mean?"

"She has just been acting weird, sneaking around and stuff. I can't figure it out, but something is not right with her."

"Well, I can tell you this. Her brother Crow Dog can be trusted, so I am sure she can be too."

"Are you sure?"

"Yes, I am certain." He comes to his feet, taking my hand into his. "But if my beautiful, precious wife feels something is not right with Dancing Bear, then I will have her watched. If she is up to something, I will know about it."

CHAPTER SIXTEEN
The Yellow Rock

It is early morning the next day. White Horse and I are comfortably sleeping on the floor next to the fireplace, along with Roger and Rose, not far away. Koawa is asleep in a chair in the bedroom, along with Morning Dove, when we are all jolted awake by Max's sudden obnoxious barking and scratching at the door. Roger is quick to his feet and is looking out the window.

"Shit," he curses. "

Roger!" Rose scolds. White Horse can see the panic on Roger's face and is fast at coming to him.

"Soldiers," Roger says.

"What are they doing here?" I ask.

"Hard telling," Roger answers.

Just then, Koawa comes out of the bedroom and, in his tongue, asks White Horse what is wrong. Upon hearing the response, he, too, is at the window. He looks out just as they come into view, not far from the house.

"There is no time to run," White Horse says.

"We can hide in the bedroom," I suggest.

"No," Roger says. "I do not know why they are here or how nosy they may be. I have a better idea." Roger quickly closes the drapes over the window. "Koawa, go grab Morning Dove. Rose quickly grabbed all the blankets. We must make it look like we are alone."

Koawa races to pick up Morning Dove and whisks her away in his arms. I scramble around to help Rose with the blankets. Roger peeks between the drapes to find the soldiers stopping in front of the house.

"Quickly follow me," Roger orders.

White Horse and I do as we are instructed, with Koawa right behind us. Roger leads us up the narrow stairway and into the loft. He then rushes over to a trunk and opens it up.

"Put Morning Dove in here," he tells Koawa. "The rest of you climb in that hole and be still." Koawa places his daughter inside the trunk.

"You stay very still, my precious," he tells her.

"I am scared, Papa. I want to go with you."

"The hole is not big enough for all of us. Don't worry, I will be close."

He then closes the trunk and quickly crawls in the hole behind the others. Rose answers the door just as Roger reaches the last step.

"Mrs. Briggs?" The man at the door says.

"Yes, I am Rose Briggs," Rose answers.

"Good morning, ma'am. We have not formally met. I am General Phillips."

Rose glances around at the handful of soldiers sitting on their horses and the two Indian scouts that are with them. She blushes in embarrassment when she realizes that she has her nightwear on and that her hair is in disarray. She snuggles her robe around her to cover herself more up.

"General Phillips," Roger interrupts as he comes to the door. "Is there a problem back at the Fort?"

"I reckon you could say that. First, let me apologize for the early hour. My men and I are on our way to search for the Sioux and the ones responsible for the attack. I came here to tell you that the doctor who was scheduled to come has reconsidered his position. It seems he got word of the attack on the Fort and underestimated how dangerous this area is and has withdrawn his application, at least for the moment."

"That is a shame," Roger says.

"I do hope that you will remain here for us to call on you until a replacement can be made."

"Oh certainly, if you are aware that my wife and I will remain here. That was the agreement."

"Oh, absolutely, Doctor," General Phillips states.

White Horse is sitting completely still in the dark hole, with his Prairie Dawn and Koawa closely tucked beside him. He can hear the conversation below and see through the cracks of the boards Roger and Rose standing at the door. He is aware that the Blue Coats are hot on his tail, and if he were to get caught, things could get very ugly for him and his people, but that is not what concerns him. Grey Wolf and several other of his best warriors have left to fight the Pawnee with the Yankton, leaving his camp vulnerable should, by chance, the Blue Coats find them when his best warriors are gone. He must get home so he can adequately protect his people, and he must do it quickly without being seen by any soldiers. He concentrates more on the conversation below to see if he can get any more information that may help him.

"I noticed on my way in, Doctor," the General begins, "the spear in the ground. May I ask you as to why it is there?"

"When I was a doctor in Willow Creek, a friend of the Indians told me if you put a spear with feathers on it in the ground, the Indians will see you as friendly and leave you alone," Roger answers.

"Is that so?" The General says. "And does it work?"

"I have not seen or had any problems with any Indians, sir, so I am assuming that it does."

"Hmm, very interesting. I will have to remember that," the General smiles. "Well, we have bothered you enough for one day. We will be on our way." He tips his hat to Rose.

"Ma'am," he says before turning to walk away.

"Good day, General, and safe traveling," she says.

"Oh, General," Roger says. "Do you have any idea where these Indians are that attacked the Fort?"

"No," he answers. "But I have my Indian scouts. They can track the slightest trail. It is just a matter of time." He then turns to walk away and get on his horse. Rose and Roger watch at the door, the soldiers riding away.

"That was close," Rose says.

"I say, a little too close," Roger says, closing the door.

He makes a dash up the steps. He opens the trunk to get Morning Dove out, just as Koawa is seen crawling out the hole, followed by his sister and White Horse. Koawa rushes to his daughter's side and lifts her out of the trunk.

"I stayed still, Papa," she says.

"Yes, my sweet one, and I am proud of you."

"That was good thinking, Roger, on your part, to ask them if they knew where we were." White Horse says.

"I only wish I could have found out more."

"No, you did good. They have no idea where we are at, this is good."

"But White Horse they have Indian scouts, it is just a matter of time before they find you," Roger says.

"I have dealt with scouts before, my brother. I worry not for this."

Roger is not pleased with White Horse's arrogance and wishes he would show a little more concern with the situation.

"Roger," I say. "Why is there such a big hole in your wall?"

"I need to show you all something. Rose can keep Morning Dove for a little bit."

"Certainly, dear," she says from the top of the step.

Koawa carries his daughter back to the bedroom and assures her that he will be back very shortly. He then rushes back up the stairs with Roger, who quickly goes to get his lantern.

"Follow me," Roger says.

Roger makes his way into the hole and orders everyone else to follow him. One by one, we make our way in and begin our crawl. As we are crawling, I look down through the cracks of the boards into Roger's living quarters. I pause momentarily when I see Rose walking over to the water basin. I am coaxed by Koawa, who is behind me, to continue our crawl in the darkness. Although Roger is holding a lantern in front of him, it is giving off little light to me, and I cannot see White Horse, who is directly in front of me. We take a quick turn that follows the fireplace around and then straightens out. I am no longer surrounded by the wooden walls that were part of the house. I am now surrounded by rock, which has made the space even more eerie. I hear Roger tell White Horse to watch his step before I feel White Horse touch me to bring me to a stop. I hear a creaking of something being opened. We then move again. As we got closer, I can see that the creaking that I heard was that of a door that opened from the ground. I watch White

Horse climb down the short ladder. When he hits the bottom, he then reaches up to help me down. Koawa is directly behind me. When I land on the ground beneath, my eyes widen. I have never seen such a sight.

"Lord have mercy," I mumble. White Horse and Koawa are just as amazed as I am.

"Pretty amazing, is it not?" Roger asks.

"I'll say." I gaze around at the glistening of the rocks that lighten up the dark cavern. My breath is taken away by the beauty of the place.

"What is this place?" White Horse asks.

"White Horse, you are looking at gold," Roger answers.

"Gold?" I say. "Roger, are you sure?" Roger walks a few steps to the brook that is slowly flowing through and squats down.

"Come here," he tells us. We all follow. "See how the sand sparkles. That is gold dust, and this place is filled with it. That is why Earl wanted me to stay here. This is the claim that he was talking about."

"Roger, if this is indeed gold, you are a very wealthy man," I say. "Perhaps the wealthiest in the world," he smiles.

"I do not understand how a yellow rock can give a man wealth?" White Horse says.

"I know you remember what happened in California, as it was Indian land that many crossed to get there."

"I do not need to be reminded of the trail that destroyed nature and killed many of my friends and allies," White Horse murmurs.

"Yes, this is what started it all," Roger says.

"This yellow rock, as you call it, can change a man and not always for the good."

"What are you going to do with it?" I ask him.

"I am not sure yet. I do not want another outbreak like Sutter Mills in California. If I were to tell anyone about my find, you would have a swarm of people wanting a piece of it, and your people would have no chance for peace."

"We have enough trouble as it is," I chime in.

"Yes," Roger agrees. "This cavern is filled with corridors. I have not investigated any further, so I am unsure as to how far back they go, but White Horse, there is plenty of room in here for you to hide in until the Army scales back their search for you."

"That is a very kind suggestion, my brother, and one of which I may consider when and if I am in need of doing that."

"You heard the General," Roger says. "You are being hunted down as we speak. There is no telling how long it will take until your camp is found."

"Why, Great Healer, you have lost your faith in me," White Horse smirks.

"They have scouts," Roger exclaims.

"So do I." Roger is aware of how stubborn White Horse can be. "Just consider it, please," Roger sighs.

"For you, my brother, I will." White Horse grins.

Roger knows that White Horse has no intention of taking him up on his offer and is just saying that to be nice. So, he gives up and changes the subject.

"If we continue this narrow path for a good distance, it will weave us around to another corridor. You follow it a little further, and it will take us out of here and into a remote area of the woods. The entrance is very well-hidden and very narrow. It is rather quite amazing."

"I would like to see it," White Horse comments.

As much as I wanted to see everything in the cavern, I feel it is for the best to return to Morning Dove and Koawa agrees with me, so together we climb back up the ladder and crawl back through to the inside of the house, leaving White Horse and Roger alone.

The men start to walk the cavern, exploring all the corridors. Both are quickly amazed at how large it is, and both agree that neither one has ever seen an underground cavern this large before. The place is so large that Roger has to start marking his turns with rocks on the ground so the men do not get lost, as many of the corridors turn off in more than one direction. As the men are walking and conversing, Roger stops dead in his tracks and takes a whiff of the air.

"You smell that?" he asks White Horse. White Horse takes a whiff.

"Yes, it smells like something has died."

"More like rotten eggs," Roger corrects.

Roger is determined to find the source of the smell and walks further into the corridor, holding the lantern in front of him. The smell becomes stronger. He comes to the end of the corridor and spots a small geyser spurting out fresh underground water.

"I will be damned," Roger says. "This is the source."

"Water?" White Horse questions as Roger squats down in front of the geyser.

"It is what is in the water," Roger says. "Hydrogen Sulfide."

"What is that?"

"It is a gas that comes from underground, and it is usually caused by a chemical reaction to a mineral when it comes in contact with it. With all the gold in these rocks, I am not at all surprised to find this."

"Is that bad?" White Horse wonders.

"The sulfur itself is not, but without adequate ventilation or in large amounts, it can be very harmful."

It is then that Roger looks up at the ceiling and sees a small natural opening of the rocks to the sky above. He then dips his fingers into the water in the geyser and rubs them together to see if it feels slimy.

"The gas is rising up through that crack," Roger points, "and that is why it does not feel slimy, there is no bacteria in it. This water is about as pure as it can be. It just smells bad." Roger comes to his feet and looks over at White Horse. "With this much water and enough room to move around, you put some fish in that water, and a man could live in here for a very long time."

White Horse knew what Roger was trying to do, and although he appreciated his efforts and his great concern for his safety, he had no intention of hiding from any Blue Coat.

"I think it is time you show me how to get out of here." With a grin on his face, Roger agrees to say no more and shows White Horse the exit that is in the woods.

CHAPTER SEVENTEEN
Medicine Moon

Three days pass, and Little Foot is nearby in the woods, checking his rabbit traps. He is excited to see that one of them was successful, and he has his rabbit. He thanks the rabbit for providing him with food, just like his father taught him to. He then removes it from the trap. He is petting its soft fur when he hears something moving in the trees behind him. He knows that his brother is nearby and figures it is Kikimo coming to check on him.

"I am alright, Kikimo," he says out loud before turning his attention back to the rabbit. He hears the crackling of the leaves getting closer behind him.

"I hear you Kikimo. You are not going to scare me this time."

He feels a presence behind him. He quickly turns around, expecting to see Kikimo standing in the trees nearby. His eyes grow huge, as it is not Kikimo that he is looking at. He sees in the darkness of the trees something black standing there. He backs up in fear as he wonders if it is a bear. He squints to get a better look and quickly realizes that what he sees is not a bear. It is more human-like and is standing on two legs. His heart skips a beat as the figure looks very menacing. It is in all black, and its face is covered by a cloak. He remembers hearing a story that he heard from Flying Hawk of a Dark Man, a bad spirit who lives in the woods and wanders around looking for its next vulnerable victim. He never believed in the story, as his mother said that he does not exist and that Flying Hawk was just making up a story. But now he is thinking different, maybe there is some truth to the Dark Man. He is uncertain as to what the Dark Man wants with him, as he is just standing there menacingly looking at him. He is not going to stick around and find out. He grabs his rabbit and is ready to run back to camp when he hears Kikimo call his name. He sees his brother step out of the trees beside him. He glances back over to where the Dark Man is standing to see that it is gone.

"What are you looking at?" Kikimo asks him, as he is carrying over his shoulders the dead doe that he just recently killed.

"There was someone standing there," his little voice answers.

"Probably one of our warriors checking up on you, and when he saw me coming, he left."

Little Foot is not so sure, as none of the warriors that he knows would dress like that and stare him down as if he meant to do him harm.

"Come on," Kikimo smiles. "I want to get home and give ma this doe. I found an eagle's nest hanging over the bluff, and I want to get an egg from it before Eagle Scout does."

"Why would you want to do that?" Little Foot asks him as they begin their walk home.

"It is the only thing that Eagle Scout has not done. Since I lost the Army horse to Uncle Roger, I need to figure out something to prove to everyone who the better brave is. Eagle Scout already got the honey out of the beehive without being stung, so it is foolish for me to do that. This is the only thing left since he is afraid of heights and I am not. I know he will not do this."

"Isn't that dangerous?"

"Of course it is," Kikimo smiles. "Being a warrior is being brave."

"Ma will not like this."

"Ma will never know," he says with a threatening voice. "Because you are not going to tell her." Kikimo stops in his tracks and looks down at his brother. "Right?"

"Right," Little Foot sighs.

"Good, now let's get home before Ma calls out a search party."

White Horse is sitting in the middle of camp, painting on a hide. Three days ago, he safely got Morning Dove and his Prairie Dawn home. They are both inside the lodge, safe and secure. So far, there have been no signs of any Blue Coats. He has his scouts further out, looking for any signs of Blue Coats. He is expecting Grey Wolf to return at any time with his other warriors. He is anxious for this to happen, as he worries about an attack by Blue Coats when most of his best warriors are gone. His thoughts are interrupted when he sees his boys returning to camp. They are both eager to greet him.

"Look, Father," Kikimo says, plopping the doe down on the ground next to his feet.

"Nice one, son." White Horse smiles.

"Look at me, Father. I caught a rabbit in my trap."

"Yes, my son and it is a nice big one."

Quickly, they are greeted by their mother. "Look, Mama," Little Foot says.

"Oh, son, it is a nice one."

"I am going to skin it and put its foot under my pillow."

"Okay, but be quiet if you go inside. Morning Dove is sleeping." I then turn my attention to Kikimo.

"My, my, son, what a magnificent kill."

"I was hoping you would cook it in your new iron pot tonight for dinner."

"If you skin it, I will cook it."

"Deal," Kikimo smiles.

Our conversation is brought to an end when riders are heard coming in. White Horse is quick to see who it is. Grey

Wolf and his warriors have returned. He counts the horses and the riders as they come down the hill. He immediately has a smile on his face when he sees that every one of them has returned safely.

"There will be a celebration tonight," White Horse says out loud. "As I feel that they were victorious in their defeat against the Pawnee."

One by one, we watch them come in, and one by one, White Horse greets them. He is told by Night Owl, as he is passing, that their battle was victorious and many Pawnee lives were destroyed. His brows rise when he sees Grey Wolf, who is the last to come in, carrying a rider with him. He sees that it is a woman. He is confused by this and wonders if Grey Wolf has taken a captive. He is immediately beside him as Grey Wolf brings his horse to a stop and jumps off. White Horse watches as Grey Wolf lifts the woman off his horse. He notices that she has no ties on her wrist and is covered with her own blood. He can only assume that she is injured and that Grey Wolf has somehow rescued her and brought her here to heal her. He witnesses that the woman is Cheyenne and not Pawnee, making him just that more curious as to how Grey Wolf got her. All his questions are about to be answered when Grey Wolf speaks.

"I found her in the meadow when we were returning. Somehow, she escaped the attack," Grey Wolf says. "She tried to fight me off but fell exhausted in my arms. She has been beaten, and by the cuts on her wrist, I can only assume that she was tied and held against her will. She has not said much to me except that her camp was raided by Pawnee a few months ago, and both her husband and child were killed. They kidnapped her and made her a slave. I brought her here because I thought maybe Prairie Dawn could help her."

"You did the right thing," White Horse tells him.

He looks over at the woman, who fails to make eye contact with him.

"She is frightened," White Horse says.

"Have you been able to get a name out of her?"

"She calls herself Medicine Moon," he answers.

White Horse motions for me to come to him. "Prairie Dawn," he says after I approach. "This is Medicine Moon. Take her to our lodge and clean her up and give her some fresh clothes."

"Of course." I reached my hand out to take Medicine Moon's. She quickly hides behind Grey Wolf. He coaxes her on.

"It is alright," he tells her in his tongue. "She is the Chief's wife."

"But she is white?" she says.

"Yes, but her heart is one of ours." She is still apprehensive. "Go on. I will be right here."

She finally agrees and willingly follows me to the lodge. Medicine Moon cleans up nicely and is an extremely attractive woman. She is roughly my age. She is small in stature but appears anything but weak. She has not spoken one word to me or has not even looked my way. The fear that she has of my presence is clearly seen all over her face, and I cannot help but wonder if it is due to the color of my skin. Her dress has been changed, and her old bloody one is tossed into the fire. I am speaking her tongue in the hopes of putting her more at ease as I am brushing her hair. We are interrupted when I hear White Horse outside the flap, asking me if she is presentable enough to come in.

"Yes," I answer. "Your Chief is here," I tell her before coming to a stand along with Medicine Moon.

Together, we watch the flap open, and White Horse walks in, followed by Grey Wolf. Upon seeing Grey Wolf enter, Medicine Moon rushes to his side and takes shelter behind him. Grey Wolf grabs her hand and coaxes her out. Very little is known about Grey Wolf. He is one of the youngest warriors and very quiet. I know both his parents very well. His father, Big Bull, sits on White Horse's council, and his mother, Little Doe, is a very good friend of mine. He is the youngest of three and the only sibling that is still alive. He is impressively handsome and has the longest, most beautiful hair that you can imagine. He is built very well, with his muscles well-formed, and could easily give White Horse and Koawa a run for their money with his looks.

He speaks very gently to her as he is holding her hand. He walks her over to face White Horse, assuring her that she is alright. Upon seeing her fear, White Horse greets her with a smile and orders all of us to sit down around the fire. Grey Wolf comes down beside her. This, in return, seems to calm Medicine Moon down. It is at that time that I see the trust and the bond that Medicine Moon has with Grey Wolf, who is now her keeper.

"I am Chief White Horse," White Horse begins in his tongue. "My people welcome you." Medicine Moon briefly looks up at her new Chief before quickly turning her eyes away. "You need not fear me," White Horse continues, "for you are home now, and you are one of us."

For the first time since her arrival, Medicine Moon speaks.

"Thank you," she shyly says.

"Grey Wolf will be your protector. You will serve him. We will have a lodge put up for you near his." She only nods in agreement that she understood him. "Your name is Medicine Moon, why are you called that?"

"Both my grandfather and my father were medicine men. I would gather herbs and plants for them for different remedies. I was taught many things from them both."

"So, you are a healer?" White Horse asks.

"In a matter of speaking," she answers. White Horse faintly grins.

"Small world," he tells her. "My Prairie Dawn has knowledge of it as well. Her brother, who we call Great Healer, comes around frequently. Flying Hawk, our Shaman, is getting up in years and does not go out and gather plants as much as he used to. You will be very useful to him." Medicine Moon is still not much on words and keeping her head down and is only speaking when need be. "How did you come to live with the Pawnee?"

"My camp was attacked early in the morning. I left my husband and child asleep while I left to gather plants. The Pawnee came in fast and very quietly. I saw the smoke high on the horizon. I rushed back only to find my child and husband dead inside our lodge. I was grabbed from behind by a Pawnee warrior, taken away, and brought back to their camp. One of them tried to have his way with me, but I put Vetchu in the food that I had made him earlier, which made him sleepy because I knew that he was going to try. When he woke up, he was angry, and he beat me. I pretended to be asleep so he would leave me alone. He would be gone from camp for days, and when he returned, I would put the stuff in his food again so he would fall asleep. One day, he caught me picking the leaves off the tree and putting them in my medicine pouch, and he took it away. He was trying to have his way with me and was beating me when your warriors came in and attacked the village. I quickly ran to escape. That is when Grey Wolf found me."

"Your grief must be heavy," White Horse says. "You will want time where you can grieve alone in private. Grey Wolf will see that you are treated properly, and my Prairie Dawn will help you with whatever you need. You will suffer no more."

"Thank you, my Chief," she mumbles. White Horse stands up, and he and Grey Wolf leave. It appears that White Horse has broken the ice as Medicine Moon smiles over at me. Together, we walk outside, and I introduce her to her new family.

CHAPTER EIGHTEEN
A Leap of Courage

Kikimo is heading out to the bluff where he saw the eagle nest earlier in the morning. He soon meets up with Little Foot, who comes running up beside him.

"You going to get the eagle egg?" he asks him.

"Yes, and don't you go running to mother," Kikimo scolds.

"I am not going to run and tell mother. I want to help you."

"I don't need any help."

"I am a better climber than you."

"Little Foot, you are scared of your own shadow," Kikimo cackles. "As soon as you see how high this thing is, you are going to cower. Besides, I need to do it myself, but I will let you watch me as long as you are still and don't get in my way."

The boys continue their journey, passing two scouts who are allowing their horses to graze on the prairie. In a few minutes, they made it to the bluff. Little Foot looks up at the overhang where the eagle's nest is sitting. He soon realizes that his brother was correct about how high it is and is glad that he didn't take him up on his offer.

"You are going way up there?" Little Foot asks him.

"How else am I going to get the egg?"

"How are you going to get over there?"

"See that branch hanging over the edge? I am going to sit on it and jump down, grab an egg before the mother eagle returns, and then climb back up."

"I think you are crazy in the head," Little Foot says.

Kikimo smiles down at his brother before making his way up the bluff with Little Foot right behind him. When they get to the top and reach the tree with the low-lining branch overlooking the nest, they stop. Little Foot makes the mistake of looking down. His insides curl at the enormous height and the sheer drop below.

"I do not think this is a good idea," he tells Kikimo.

"Ah," Kikimo miffs. "You worry too much. I will be fine."

Little Foot watches his brother climb the tree, slide over to the low-line branch, and jump down on the rocks below.

"Keep an eye on the mother eagle and tell me if you see her returning," Kikimo yells up to Little Foot.

"Alright." Kikimo quickly rushes to the nest to find four unhatched eggs. He grabs the closest one.

"I see her coming," he hears Little Foot yell.

He knows he has no time to waste. The mother eagle has most likely already spotted him and will have her talons out to tear him apart when she approaches. He rushes to the branch and jumps up to grab it. He immediately realizes that he cannot pull himself up with only one arm while holding the egg with the other.

"Kikimo, hurry up. She is almost here," Little Foot shouts.

"I am trying. I can't pull myself up."

Kikimo looks out into the sky to see the mother eagle quickly souring in. He knows as soon as the mother returns that, she will attack him with her sharp talons. He jumps for the branch again. He can hear the eagle squawking and knows that he has no time to waste.

"Little Foot," he hollers. "I need you to climb the tree and scoot across the branch and take the egg."

"No way," Little Foot retorts.

Kikimo looks out at the skyline at the eagle that is fast approaching.

"Little Foot, please!"

As much as Little Foot really does not want to do this, he does as he is asked and quickly scales the tree.

"Hurry! Take it!" Kikimo yells at him.

Little Foot inherited his climbing skills from his father and is scooting across the branch with ease. He leans down to grab the egg, just when the branch snaps and Little Foot falls.

"Little Foot!" Kikimo yells.

He looks down to where his brother fell to see that he landed on another overhang a few feet below him.

"Are you alright?" he yells down at him.

Little Foot is stunned by the sudden fall but alright and has managed not to break anything.

"Yes, I think so," he answers his brother.

Just then, Kikimo sees Little Foot's eyes grow big. "Kikimo, watch out!"

Kikimo quickly turns around to see the mother eagle coming to him with her talons out. He rushes to put the egg back into the nest just as the mother eagle comes in for the attack. He shields his face and starts swatting his arms around in hopes to scare the eagle off. He is prancing around on the edge of the cliff, trying to back the eagle off. He loses his footing on the edge and falls, just barely landing on another overhang that is a few feet away from his brother.

"Kikimo!" Little Foot hollers.

"I am alright," he hollers over to him.

Kikimo's ledge is very thin and narrow. He has just enough room for his own feet with his toes hanging over. He grabs tightly to the rocks and plasters himself up against them. He glances down at the sheer drop below. One wrong step, and he is done for. He gulps in fear. He is clueless as to how he is going to get out of this predicament or how he is going to rescue his brother. He glances up at the mother eagle and can see her sitting in the nest.

"You and your stupid egg!" Little Foot barks. "You always get me into trouble."

Kikimo can hear the fear in Little Foot's voice.

"I know, little brother. I have really outdone myself this time. I'm sorry, but I promise you I will get us out of this."

"How?" Little Foot whines.

This is a question that he, too, has asked himself, but he cannot allow his fear to be heard by Little Foot. He must remain calm in his thinking if he is going to get his brother and himself out of here. He can see that Little Foot's ledge is wider and that Little Foot has more room to move around.

"Little Foot, we passed two scouts on the way. They can't be far. I need you to call out for them. Do you remember how to do it?"

"Is it like the one that you used when father was chasing that scout up the falls?"

"Yes," Kikimo tells him. "Do you remember how to do it?"

"Oh yes, Father taught me."

"Good. I need you to do it. I would, but I can't let go of my grip, or I will fall."

"I can do it, Kikimo. I can."

"That's my brother. Now, be careful. Watch your footing."

He watches Little Foot step further out onto the ledge. "Careful, not too close to the edge, it may give away."

This is a thought that the little boy does not consider, and he stops dead in his tracks for fear of falling. "Right, there is good," Kikimo says. "Now call out."

Little Foot lifts his head up into the wind, and remembering everything that his father taught him, he caws out. He repeats it several times before hurrying back to the edge of the rocks, where he is more protected. Both boys are waiting anxiously in hopes that the call is heard.

"Kikimo," Little Foot says. "What if nobody comes?"

"Don't think like that, brother," Kikimo says. "They will come."

Kikimo's fingers are cramping from hanging onto the rocks. He is not sure as to how much longer he can hold on. He starts looking around for other options on how to get him and his brother off the ledge. He sees indentations in the rocks that are big enough to fit his toes in. He looks over at his brother, who is not that far away from him and is only a few feet down.

"I am going to climb over to you," he tells him.

"Why?"

"Your ledge is bigger, and I want us to be together."

"Be careful, Kikimo."

Kikimo is very good at climbing, but he has never had to scale a mountain. He says a silent prayer to himself before taking the plunge. Little Foot watches from below as his brother places his toes into the crevices of the rocks. He then watches him do it again. This time, Kikimo slips and nearly falls.

"Kikimo!" Little Foot screams.

"I'm alright, little brother," he pants.

Never has Kikimo been so scared in his life, and if it was not for his adrenaline pumping and wanting to get to his brother, he never would have considered this. He finds his strength and scales the last few feet to his brother. Little Foot watches Kikimo take his last step and jump down. He is immediately in his brother's arms.

"It is alright, little brother," he tells him as they embrace. "Now we are together."

"But we are still on top of the ledge!" Little Foot whines.

"Yes, I know, but you always complain to me that we never do anything together; well, now we are." Kikimo is trying to make light of the situation, even though he is frantic with worry as to what he is going to do if help does not arrive soon.

"This is not what I had in mind," Little Foot tells him.

"I know, brother, and I promise you when we get out of this, I will spend the entire day with you, and we will do whatever you want."

"Even collect turtle shells with me?" Little Foot asks.

Kikimo smiles over at him, although he finds collecting turtle shells boring, he will do it just to spend time with his brother.

Yes, and I will even let you use my bow, and we will go hunting."

"You promise?"

"Yes, my little brother, I promise."

The wind is picking up on the ledge, bringing a chill to the air. Little Foot tucks himself into Kikimo's side for warmth.

"They should have been here by now," he says. "I don't think they heard my call. I must have done it wrong."

"No, Little Foot, you did it right. We are just too far up, and they couldn't hear it, but not to worry, when we do not return to camp for dinner, father will come looking for us. It won't be much longer."

Just then, they hear movement from above. Kikimo looks up and yells at the top of his lungs. "Down here!"

Suddenly, the familiar face of Koawa appears. Sheer terror hits his soul when he sees both his nephews on the ledge.

"See, I told you they would hear you," Kikimo says to Little Foot.

"Are you both alright?" Koawa yells down.

"Yes, we are fine," Kikimo answers.

"How did you get down there?" Little Foot is eager to rat his brother out and chimes in.

"Kikimo thought it would be a good idea to get an eagle egg from the nest, and the mother eagle came back, and we both fell down here."

"You are not supposed to fall when you do it, Kikimo," Koawa teases.

"I did not do it on purpose."

"Hold on," Koawa says as he starts to lower a rope down.

Kikimo jumps to try to reach it, but it is just out of his reach. "I can't reach it!" he yells up.

Just then, he sees his father looking over the edge.

"Father!" Little Foot yells.

"It is alright, son. We are going to get you out of here."

White Horse yells down to Kikimo. "Put Little Foot on your shoulders and see if he can reach the rope."

Kikimo does as he is told. Little Foot is clumsy at it, but after a few attempts, he is finally able to reach it.

"Curl your legs around it and hold on," White Horse tells him.

Little Foot is then hoisted up and brought up onto flat land. Unbeknown to him, his mother is waiting anxiously nearby, as well as nearly all the warriors. Little Foot is quickly in her arms.

"What were you doing down there?" I ask him.

"I fell."

"Well, I see that silly," I tell him. "Oh, it does not matter. I am just thankful that you are alright." Little Foot crinkles up his nose as his mother is showering him with kisses.

"Ma," he whines. "Stop, you are embarrassing me."

Attention is drawn back down to Kikimo, who is still stuck on the ledge. Koawa is quick at taking action and rushes over to where the eagle nest is and scales the tree up. He takes the overhanging branch as far as he can go, up to the point where it broke off. He then jumps down on the ledge. The mother eagle extends her wings and boasts out her chest from the nest.

"It is alright, great mother," Koawa tells her in his tongue. "Your eggs are safe with me. I only want to get to the boy."

The mother eagle fixes her deep eyes on Koawa's. He continues calming her down for a few more seconds until she puts her wings down and relaxes back down in the nest. Koawa then makes his way to the edge of the ledge and looks down at Kikimo. He sizes up the situation.

"How did you get all the way over there?" he asks him.

"I scaled those rocks and jumped down here," Kikimo answers him.

"Then that is how you are getting back up."

"No, Uncle, I about never got over here. I am not doing it again."

"There is no other way, you have to."

"Maybe you can toss me the rope from there, and I can swing over."

"It will not reach. You must do it."

"I don't think I can." Koawa can tell that Kikimo is terrified.

"We all have to do things in life that we do not like but must be done."

"You do not understand, Uncle, those rocks are slippery, and I am scared of falling."

"Of course you are," he tells him. "Everyone is fearful of something. Just like the mother eagle was afraid of you taking one of her eggs, but it is what she did with her fear that made her brave."

"What do you mean?"

"She did not allow her fear to stop her from being strong and attacking you. You were her fear, just like these rocks are yours. Work through that fear, Kikimo, for that is what makes a strong and brave warrior."

Kikimo knows that his uncle is correct and that he must face his fears if he is going to get out of here. He makes his way to the first rock and pulls himself up as everyone watches on.

"That's it, Kikimo," Koawa encourages him. "I am proud of you."

Slowly, Kikimo steps to the next one and makes it across. He pauses a moment to catch his breath, as his fear of falling is wearing him out. He glances down at the sheer drop and quickly closes his eyes.

"Fight your fear, son," Koawa tells him. "You are almost there."

After several minutes at a snail's pace, Kikimo has made it to the narrow edge. Koawa yells up for White Horse to toss over the rope.

"You see it?" Koawa ask Kikimo.

"Yes," Kikimo answers.

"Can you reach it?"

"Yes, but I don't want to let go. This ledge is very narrow, and I am barely on it."

"Kikimo, grab the rope," Koawa coaxes.

Kikimo makes the mistake of looking down. He gulps in fear at how far up he is and is angry with himself that he thought this was such a great idea. He exhales deeply, finding his courage within. He quickly releases one hand from the rocks and grabs the rope.

"I got it," he yells up.

"Good," Koawa says.

"Now, hold onto it with both hands, and we will pull you up to me."

"Alright."

Kikimo does as he is told and closes his eyes as he lets go of the rocks and is swinging on the rope.

"Climb the rocks with your feet," Koawa says as Kikimo is being hoisted up from above. Inch by inch, Kikimo is climbing. When he is within the grasp of Koawa, Koawa reaches for the rope and swings him over to him. Kikimo falls exhausted on the ledge in his uncle's arms.

"You overcame your fear, son, I am proud of you," Koawa says.

"I want to go home," Kikimo whines.

Koawa chuckles as he rubs the top of Kikimo's head. Together, leaving the eagle's nest and the mother bird behind, they make their way over across the limb and down the tree to safety. He is immediately greeted by both his parents. Today is a day that Kikimo will never forget, and he will one day tell his children and grandchildren the story of how he overcame his fears. Until then, he will remember the lesson received today and will take whatever punishment his mother gives him

CHAPTER NINETEEN
The Tracks

The ordeal with the boys is behind us. Kikimo is getting nothing but static from Eagle Scout for his failure. He has received no punishment from me. I figure the humiliation he is getting from his friend and his near-death experience is punishment enough. He finished skinning the doe for me, and I am cooking the meat in the iron pot that he traded his uncle's horse for. White Horse left with him a few minutes ago to take him on a walk and have a talk with him. They will be back before sundown.

Medicine Moon is sitting beside me. I have invited her to have dinner with us. This is something that I rarely do, as a chief's wife, I have to be careful that I don't show favorites, but considering that this is her first night here and she is so distraught, I want to make her feel like this is her home and not to be so timid around me. I have also invited Grey Wolf. I thought this may help her as well. As I am stirring the meat in the pot, I glance out at the prairie and see Dancing Bear making a quick return to the camp. I am still uncertain as to why she keeps taking off. There is something about her that makes me uneasy. I have noticed that Rising Sun has taken a great liking to her and has basically blown Minoke off. This, too, has made me curious as to why the sudden change in Rising Sun, who has always shown nothing but gratitude to Minoke, who graciously took her in despite her harsh feelings towards her father, Red Hawk. My thoughts are interrupted when Morning Dove tugs on my dress.

"I am hungry," her little voice says.

I smiled down at her. I am so relieved that she has made a full recovery, with only her stitches being the only sign that anything has happened. It is nice to see her back to her normal, sweet self.

"We will eat shortly, as soon as your Chief and Kikimo return," I tell her. "Why don't you go to the stream and clean up, and then you can help me finish."

"Alright," she says before running off to the stream.

"Your daughter is beautiful." I hear Medicine Moon say in her tongue.

"Thank you, but she is not my daughter. She is my niece."

"How did you become the Chief's wife?" she asks me.

"I met him when he came to our town to trade. He later rescued me and brought me back to his village when I was attacked by a bear."

"So, you are not his captive?"

"No, I am free to come and go as I please," I tell her, "as are you."

"Tomorrow, I will leave and grieve for my husband and child. I will be gone many days."

"I am sorry for your loss. If there is anything that I can do to comfort you, please let me know."

"You have already done so much, as soon as I return, I will care for myself."

"As you wish," I tell her.

With that said, I return to my iron pot and tend to the meat, leaving her to do her own thing.

White Horse and Kikimo are walking at a leisurely pace through the woods. White Horse can tell that his son is still upset about his earlier ordeal and his failure to get the egg. He will take this time that they have alone and try to put his son at ease.

"I hear that Eagle Scout is giving you a hard time about today," he says.

"Yes, like he could have done any better," Kikimo huffs.

"I can remember when I was your age and boys teasing me as well when I failed at something."

"You failed at something?" Kikimo says, surprised.

"Oh, son, failure is a part of life. That is how you grow and become wise."

"What did you fail at?"

"I became very impatient at training a wild mare. I forgot everything that I was taught by my father, and the horse got the best of me."

"But you did eventually get it trained, right?"

"Yes, but like you, son, I had to learn the hard way."

"It is not easy to be your son. I am expected to be able to go beyond what other boys my age can do."

"Yes, this is true, but son I was trained the same way as everyone else was. I am what I am because of my father and his father. You were born into it. That is the only thing that makes you different."

"Father, do you ever get tired of being a Chief?"

"Sometimes, especially during these times when my decision can affect so many lives."

"I don't think I can do it," Kikimo says.

"No, not yet, but you will when you get older and wiser."

"But I want to be a warrior now."

"Son, the most important lesson that you need to learn is patience. The rest will come as you grow with experience."

"It is so hard when Eagle Scout smears my nose into every flaw I make."

"Eagle Scout is jealous of you," White Horse smiles. "By making you look bad, he makes himself look good. You need to not care what other people think of you, as long as you are happy with whom you are, nothing else matters."

Just then, White Horse sees something on the ground that raises his curiosity. He squats down and looks at the tracks that lay on the ground. Deep within the soil are the tracks of a huge bear.

"Mato?" Kikimo says.

"Yes," White Horse says. "But those are not," he says, pointing out. He comes to the other sets of tracks. "These are White Men tracks. See the heels of the boots?" he points.

"Yes." Kikimo watches his father come to a stand and look for more tracks

"Son, go back to camp and tell Koawa what I found. Tell him to come here."

"What is wrong, Father?"

"I am not sure yet," he answers. "Go on!" he waves him on. "Run like the wind."

Kikimo races off and heads back to camp. White Horse continues following the tracks. He starts to wonder if maybe the tracks are those of a trapper who is following the bear. It was not until he saw the tracks of the bear going off in another direction that his mind changed. He thinks perhaps they belong to a scout who is working for the Army but doubts any trained scout would leave such obvious tracks for someone like him to find.

He is concerned at how close they are to the camp and wonders if there are more White Men hiding nearby. He continues at a slow walk as he follows the tracks until he gets to a clearing. He stops and quickly bolts behind a tree for cover when, through the bushes, he sees a man sitting on a log. The man has his boot off and is tending to his blistered foot, unaware of anything around him. White Horse is deeply concentrating on the man and jumps a little when he feels Koawa tap his shoulder. White Horse points to the man. Quickly, several other warriors are approaching, and all of them take cover behind the bushes and watch the man tend to his foot.

White Horse notices the man's rifle nearby, propped up against the tree. He motions to Koawa to spot him so he can grab it. Being very light on his feet, White Horse runs a few feet and snatches the rifle. He checks to see if it is loaded. Then, on his command, all the warriors step out of the bushes and head into the clearing with White Horse in the lead with the rifle up and aimed.

The man sees the warriors and is quickly on his feet.

"Who are you, and why are you here?" White Horse growls.

The man is taken aback by White Horse's perfect English.

"I am a trapper. I was following a bear."

"Your bear went south a few hours ago."

"That damn beast has been alluring me for days," the man jokes.

White Horse is not amused and is suspicious this man is more than what he says he is.

"Have you seen any soldiers around here?" he asks him.

"No, not recently."

"How long ago?"

"Oh, I would say three, maybe four days ago."

"Which direction did they go?"

"East of here," the man says.

White Horse knows that the Fort is East of his camp and that the man probably passed it or stopped for supplies on his way here, and that is where he saw the soldiers. These are not the soldiers that White Horse is talking about.

"Do not take me as a fool," White Horse growls. "I am not talking about the soldiers inside the Fort. Have you seen any around here?"

The man is terrified of being killed. He has heard many tales of how brutal the Sioux and the Crow are to White Man. He does not want to be their next victim.

"No," the man answers.

"You will leave now, and you will not return, or we will kill you. Do you understand me?"

"Yes, of course, just as soon as I tend to my feet."

"No, you are leaving now." White Horse cocks the rifle. "Right now!"

The man gets the hint and is quick at gathering his supplies on the ground and grabbing his mule. White Horse motions for Grey Wolf and Blue Thunder to go check the trapper's supplies and make sure that he isn't working for the Army as a spy. Finding nothing but some extra food, hides, traps, and bullets, the man is cleared of any deception.

Grey Wolf grabs the bullets and the remaining food, as Blue Thunder grabs the beaver hides.

"Search him," White Horse orders Grey Wolf in his tongue.

The man is frozen with fear as Grey Wolf pats him down. He removes the knife that is in the trapper's sheath around his waist and the other one that is in his boot. When all is clear, is it then that White Horse orders the man to leave.

"This is your lucky day," White Horse growls at him, "for you live. But remember, if you tell anyone that you saw us, I will hunt you down and kill you."

"I won't tell anyone. I promise you. May I have my rifle back?"

"No!"

Fearing for his life, the man says no more and walks off with his mule. The warriors watch the man, until he disappears.

"Are you sure you want to let him walk away?" Koawa asks.

"He will not get far without any weapons or food. The wolves will pick him off, or the bear. The man will be dead by morning. Just to be certain, follow him from a distance and see where he goes. If he does anything stupid, kill him.

CHAPTER TWENTY
The Slaughtering

Koawa and a handful of warriors are making their way back to camp. They followed the trapper into the night. They turned around and headed back home when they found the man's mauled body in the grass, the apparent victim of the bear that he was pursuing. They are less than a few miles from camp and will be arriving shortly. Medicine Moon left before sunrise to begin her grieving in a remote place not far from camp. Grey Wolf is nearby to protect her if any wolves should happen to come by while she is in the middle of her ritual. Kikimo and Eagle Scout have been playing games all night and set a fire up where they slept under the stars on top of a hill overlooking the camp. The sun is just beginning to rise. White Horse is awakening when he hears the rush of a horse running in and one of his scouts yelling out. He is quick to the flap when Night Owl jumps off his pony.

"Blue Coats, coming in fast! They are less than a mile away," he says in his tongue.

"Quick, get everyone up and prepare for war!" White Horse barks. He then rushes inside his lodge to wake up his family.

"Prairie Dawn," he says, nudging me awake.

I awake from a sound sleep to White Horse pushing me.

"What is the matter?" I ask him.

"Blue Coats are coming in fast. Go hide the children. Hurry!"

I am quick at slipping on my moccasins as White Horse wakes up Little Foot and Morning Dove. When he is certain that we are all awake and heading out the flap, he then grabs his weapons and rushes off. I grab my bag with my personal belongings and wrap it around my neck before I, too, am out the flap. I grab both the hands of Little Foot and Morning Dove as we rush away to the woods and to the abandoned den, where we will hide until the Blue Coats leave. Morning Dove is still tender in her belly and is slow at her running. I pick her up and hold her as I quickly whisk Little Foot and me away. I see many of our warriors on their ponies and ready for war as we are running. I watch White Horse jump on his mare and quickly ride off with the warriors right behind him. I look up to the hill that Kikimo and Eagle Scout are on, not sure if they are aware of what is going on. There is much chaos throughout the camp as everyone is scrambling to gather whatever loved ones they can and help the elders move on.

I see Minoke pulling Rising Sun to go with her, but the girl does not want to go and is yelling at her that she must find Dancing Bear. Minoke is giving her no choice and is literally dragging Rising Sun by her arm behind her to get her to safety. Many of the elderly are slow at moving, and everyone is so busy with their own children that several are being left behind to fend for themselves. I make my way into the woods and find the den. I am quick at putting the children in there. Minoke is soon behind me with Rising Sun, who is still making a fuss. I come to Minoke's aid, and together, we force Rising Sun into the den. She spats off in her tongue.

"You hater!" Now is not the time for Rising Sun to have one of her fits.

"Shut your mouth!" I yell at her. She glares at me. "You sit yourself down, and you do not move. You understand me?"

I have never raised my voice at her, and she is completely stunned.

"But Dancing Bear," she cries out.

"Dancing Bear will find her way. Now you be still."

Just then, Songbird comes running up, cradling Jumping Badger in her arms.

"Eagle Scout," she calls out.

"I will go find them both," I tell her. "You stay here and keep the children."

"No, Prairie Dawn!" Minoke says.

"I am not staying here as long as Kikimo and Eagle Scout are out there unprotected!" I tell her. "I will be right back."

Just then, Minoke jumps up and hugs me. "Be careful," she cries.

"I will be right back." With that said, I am out the den and rushing back into camp. Along my way, I slowly see some elders approaching, as well as more women and children. I look to see if Kikimo and Eagle Scout are among them. When I fail to see them, it is then that my heart starts to race. I start to hear the gunfire and begin to smell the smoke. I continue my hasty pace into camp, not allowing my fear to overcome me.

Medicine Moon just finishes wiping her eyes when she hears the first shot a distance away. She comes to her feet and looks out at the horizon just when Grey Wolf comes charging up on his horse. He reaches down grabbing her hand and helps pull her up behind him. Together, they make the run to camp.

Kikimo and Eagle Scout jump awake when they, too, hear the shots.

"Blue Coats!" Eagle Scout yells.

"Hurry! Run!" Kikimo yells. They then begin their descent down the hill.

Dancing Bear is on her way back to camp after spending the night with her husband, Red Hawk, in an isolated area nearby. She reaches the camp just when the first shot is fired. Eagle Scout and Kikimo have made it down the hill to witness the camp under full attack. They see that many of their loved ones are still fleeing to get away. They both jump in to help. Eagle Scout takes the arm of Flying Hawk and helps him along as bullets are being shot over their heads. Kikimo runs to his lodge to make sure everyone is out and grabs one of his father's rifles that he left behind. He has never shot a man in his life, but he is confident enough to know that he could if he had to.

I made it back to camp and found myself in the middle of the battle. My heart is racing in my throat as bullets are flying everywhere. I dodge behind a lodge to hide as I see several Blue Coats on their horses igniting our lodges and firing shots at our warriors. I watch on in horror as I see one of our warriors go down.

Eagle Scout and Flying Hawk find shelter behind another lodge. Their cover is blown when a Blue Coat comes up behind it and is aiming to shoot. Kikimo sees his friend in trouble and has no time to waste. He dashes behind the soldier and shoots, killing the man. Eagle Scout is scared to death and too afraid to move.

"Run!" Kikimo yells at him.

Eagle Scout and Flying Hawk are then on their feet, making a run to the stream. I am too terrified to move. There are shots being fired all around me. The noise is deafening. The screams send shivers down my spine. I cover my ears and cower. I look out to see Dancing Bear hiding as well, behind some crates. I then see the soldier coming her way. I gulp in fear, as I know she has been seen and will be shot dead at any moment. I watch a warrior come to her rescue and bring the soldier down. My eyes widen when I see that it is Red Hawk. I deeply concentrate on his face through the thick smoke, making sure that I am not imagining things. I watch him get Dancing Bear to safety, and then, as fast as he appears, he is gone.

I turn my attention to the stream and see Kikimo running a short distance behind Eagle Scout and Flying Hawk. Sheer panic fills my soul when I see two soldiers taking aim at them. I scream out just as the shots are made, and Eagle Scout and Flying Hawk go down. Kikimo is in a full run as he is holding his father's rifle. I come out of my shelter and make a dash to him. I then watch Kikimo get shot in the back and fall to the ground. My adrenaline is pumping. My heart is pulsating as I am making my run to him. It is then that I feel an enormous amount of pain when I am shot in the arm. I bellow out as I grab it, but I keep pushing on. I make it a few more paces when I am shot again in my leg. This time it takes me down. I lay there for a few moments to catch my breath. I fix my eyes on Kikimo's lifeless body. I can hardly see him through my tears and thick smoke. I fear that Kikimo is dead. I am bound and determined to get to him. I try to come to my feet, but my wounded leg gives out, and I fall to the ground. I get to a crawl and make my way to him.

The fight is racing around me, but I hear nothing as my only focus is on getting to Kikimo. Finally, I made it to him. I turned him over to see that he is still alive but badly wounded. There are bullets flying everywhere, and I fear that at any moment, we will be shot again. I lay my body over his to shield him from any more harm. I then lay motionless in hopes that in the eyes of the soldiers, I would be dead. I listen to the slaughtering of innocent lives that are going on around me. The tears are rolling down my face. As I am lying on Kikimo, I place my hand on his wound and try to apply some pressure on it to slow the bleeding down. I can hear him struggling for air.

"Hold on, son, mama is here," I tell him.

I can feel my own blood oozing down my leg, and the pain is intense. My arm is heavy and bleeding bad. I can feel myself about ready to pass out. I fight to hold on.

Suddenly, all is quiet. I believe that the Blue Coats have left. I lift my head to look out, only to quickly place it back down when I see some soldiers nearby walking around checking the dead.

I hold my breath as I feel one coming my way. I hear Kikimo moan.

"Shh, son," I tell him, although I do not think that Kikimo is alert enough to understand. My arm and leg are pulsating, and I am growing weak by my blood loss. I fear that at any moment, one of the soldiers will check on us to see if we are dead. My golden hair catches the eye of one of the soldiers. I can hear him walking towards me. I hold my breath and pray that Kikimo does not moan as the man approaches us. At any moment, I expect him to either kick me or turn me over. I am relieved when I hear him walk away. He hesitates for a moment and turns back around to look at me. I am unclear as to what thoughts are going through his head, but I am relieved when he walks back up the hill. I lay there motionless as my blood starts to trickle faster down my arm and leg. The pain is too severe, and the blood is too great that I pass out on Kikimo's chest.

Nearly an hour would pass before White Horse is safely able to return to camp. His heart sinks, looking out at all the destruction and the many lives that were senselessly murdered, including many of his best warriors like Yellow Hawk and Night Owl. As he slowly walks from body to body, he rubs his arm, which was grazed by a bullet. He sent Grey Wolf ahead to get Roger as not everyone has perished, and his services are needed. He ordered Medicine Moon and Dancing Bear to move the women and children to a makeshift camp not far away. There, the remaining warriors will regroup, and the injured will be brought there and be tended to. He sees the shocked look on Koawa and Blue Thunder, who have just returned to camp. He watches Blue Thunder come to his knees and hug the lifeless body of a child. White Horse's heart is heavy, and his insides are fuming with rage. He gazes out at the stream, and his face turns white. Through the rays of the sunlight, he sees the golden hair of his wife draped across a body. He yells out at the top of his lungs as he is running.

"No!"

Koawa and Blue Thunder quickly look his way and take off in a run toward him. White Horse is jumping over bodies and debris to get to his wife.

"No! No! No!" he is yelling.

He makes his way to her and drops down on his knees. He turns his wife over, holding her on his lap. It is then that he sees the body of Kikimo. Koawa and Blue Thunder have made their way over to him, and Koawa is down on the ground beside him.

"Prairie Dawn, my precious Prairie Dawn, and my son," he says as he strokes his wife's hair.

"White Horse," Koawa says. "We need to get them both back to camp." With that said, White Horse comes to a stand, carrying his wife, and Koawa takes Kikimo. Together, they race to the camp.

CHAPTER TWENTY ONE
The Healers

White Horse's mind is in a blur. He is beside himself with despair. It is taking every ounce of strength that he has to keep his composure. His Prairie Dawn and Kikimo are lying motionless on their pelts, both clinging to life. He has collected the root that grows abundantly in the woods for his wife to help control her bleeding. He dips his fingers in the medicine and allows it to drip in her mouth. The bullets are still lodged in her arm and leg. He was able to remove the bullet out of Kikimo, but he will leave his wife's there until Roger arrives, for fear of his digging around to remove it would make her bleed worse.

He is going back and forth between his wife and son and taking care of them the best that he can. He fears the death of both, but it is Kikimo who he fears the most. He has now stopped moaning, and his breathing is becoming shallower. White Horse worries that, at any moment, his son will die. He is keeping his wound as clean as he can, but Kikimo is losing a lot of blood. He can only pray that by giving Grey Wolf his horse, which is known for his swiftness, he has arrived at Roger's by now and that they are on their way here. His thoughts are interrupted when Medicine Moon steps in the flap with a basket filled with remedies.

"Allow me to help them, my Chief," she says.

"Yes, please. Come in."

Medicine Moon can see the distress on her Chief's face. She does not have any doubt that he is a strong and powerful man who loves his people very much and how personal today's attack was for him. She remembers being told by Grey Wolf how Flying Hawk was like a father to him and Koawa, and she is certain that deep inside, he is grieving his loss as well. She turns her attention first to his son. She rolls him over and lifts the cloth that is placed on his wound as White Horse watches on. She reaches into her basket.

"This is a marigold plant," she tells White Horse. "I will use this to clean it."

White Horse watches her work. He knows nothing about this woman or even if she is as good as she says she is, but he says not a word and puts his trust in her. She is very quiet with her work and is very meticulous with what she does. White Horse watches on silently as Medicine Moon washes Kikimo's wound completely clean. She then reaches into her basket again and pulls out a bowl.

"This is germanium root," she says.

"Yes, I am aware of it," he says.

"I give it to my wife in a tea form because she has a condition in her blood that makes her bleed more than most people do."

"Yes, it will work that way, too, but this way is better. I will put some on his wound so it will clot."

White Horse is impressed at this woman's knowledge and watches on as Medicine Moon tends to his son. When she finishes applying the powder-like root, she reaches into her basket again. This time, White Horse steps in when he sees that she is holding a cobweb.

"What are you doing?" he asks her in his tongue.

"You put this over the wound to close it. It will help it heal faster. Trust me, my Chief. I know what I am doing."

White Horse has seen many things in his life and has spent hours with Flying Hawk picking plants and roots and listening to his stories on different ways how they are used, but he has never heard of a cobweb being used as glue. He watches on as she applies it and is amazed that it is holding. She comes to a stand.

"He is with fever. What have you been using?"

"Ground ivy?"

"Good Chief, allow me to take over and tend to your wife."

"Yes. Is there anything I can do to help?"

"Yes, ask one of your women to go to a thorn apple tree and gather as many leaves as possible."

"What is this for?"

"When your son wakes up, he will be in a great amount of pain, and this will help him. I can use it on your wife as well."

"Alright, I will see that you get some."

White Horse then briefly leaves as Medicine Moon goes to tend to his wife. She examines both wounds and quickly notices that the one in her leg is the one that causes her the most concern. The bullet is deep within the thigh and lodged very tight. She is not going to be able to remove it on her own and decides that she will wait for the Great Healer to come, which Grey Wolf says is so good. Until then, she will just cauterize around it with a burning stick to stop the bleeding. She treats the Chief's wife the same way as she does his son, with the only exception that she does not use the cobwebs. When she is confident that she has done all that she can do, she comes to a stand just as the Chief returns.

Dusk is on the land. Kikimo and Prairie Dawn are holding their own. They are both still asleep on their pelts. The blood that was oozing from Kikimo's wound has stopped. It appears so far that Medicine Moon's remedies have helped. White Horse is sitting on the bear pelt between his two loved ones. He has started his own healing ritual near the fire. He has positioned the pelts close enough together so that he can hold their hands as he prays. He has not moved from this spot all day. His mind is racing, and his anger is deep. His heart is heavy with remorse from the many losses that they suffered today. He lost over half of his warriors and many women and children, most of which were elders. He is grateful that his scouts picked up the tracks of the Blue Coats before they got to the camp. This little time frame allowed many of the women and children to get to safety. He is certain that without this time, everyone would have perished.

He starts to think of Kikimo and how he is going to react when he hears that his best friend, Eagle Scout, is dead. He thinks of Flying Hawk, who was like a father to him and Koawa, and how much they are going to miss him. His prayers are interrupted when the flap opens, and his youngest son, Little Foot, shyly steps in. He cowers near the flap as he looks over at his father and the pelts where his mother and brother lie. White Horse extends his hand out and motions for his son to come over. Little Foot rushes over to this lap and sits down. White Horse embraces him and, for a few seconds, holds on to him tightly, so thankful that he was not killed or injured, too.

"Father," Little Foot says. "You are hurt." White Horse looks over at his shoulder, which is covered with his own dry blood and the dark hole that is in it from the bullet that grazed him during the fight.

"This is nothing, son. I am alright. The question is, are you alright?"

"Yes, I stayed in the den with Morning Dove like Mama told me to until the loud booms stopped, and Minoke said that it was alright to leave."

"And I am so pleased that you did." Little Foot looks over at his brother and mother lying on their pelts.

"Are Mama and Kikimo going to die?" he asks his father.

"I hope not, son."

White Horse watches Little Foot slide over to his brother's pelt and put his little hand on top of his.

"Kikimo," his tiny voice says. "I do not care if we do not spend the day together or collect turtle shells. And I do not need to shoot your bow, my bow is fine. I just want you to wake up. Don't die, my big brother. I love you."

White Horse's heart goes soft as he watches Little Foot put his head down on his brother's chest. The tender moment is brought to an end when the flap is opened by Koawa as Roger quickly races in.

"Koawa told me what happened," Roger says.

Little Foot jumps up and races over to his uncle, taking his hand.

"You must help them," he says as he is pulling Roger over to the pelts. "You must save my Mama and brother. Please, Uncle, you must help them." Roger squeezes his nephew's shoulder. "I will do what I can," he tells him. "I promise."

White Horse is on his feet and wraps his arm around Little Foot.

"How bad are they?" Roger asks.

"Kikimo was shot in the back. I removed the bullet from him. Medicine Moon used some remedies to stop the bleeding. He is better but still has not woken up."

"And Carrie?" Roger asks as he makes his way over to Kikimo with his medical bag in his hand.

"She was shot twice. Once in the arm and then in the leg. I left the bullets in there for fear if I went to take them out, she would bleed more."

"Have you given her the root?" Roger asks.

"Yes, the best that I can."

Roger listens to Kikimo's chest. He then rolls him on his side to look at the wound. He quizzically looks up at White Horse. "Is that a cobweb?"

"Yes, Medicine Moon did that to keep it closed."

"That's different," he says to himself. "I have never heard of that."

White Horse watches on as Roger continues his exam on Kikimo. When he finishes up, he then turns his attention to his sister. He keeps his composure as he comes down beside her, touching her cold and clammy hand. He then begins to examine her. His anger for the senseless attack is fuming deep inside him as he checks her leg. After a few seconds, he comes to his feet.

"I want to see this Medicine Moon, perhaps she can help me. I am going to have to remove the bullets from Carrie."

White Horse motions for Koawa to go get her.

"This woman saved your son's life," he tells White Horse. "There is no doubt in my mind that if she had not stopped his bleeding, Kikimo would have died."

"So, he will be alright?" White Horse asks.

"He is young, and he is strong. The next few days will tell for sure. What concerns me the most is the position on where Kikimo was shot."

"What do you mean?"

"It is very close to his spinal cord. When I performed nerve tests on his feet, he failed to give any reflex. Now, there is a great deal of swelling around the wound, and that could be why. There is a good chance that it is just temporary, but I must make you aware that there is a chance that it won't be."

"Are you saying that my son may never walk again?"

"It is too soon to tell for sure, but yes, that is what I am telling you."

Roger watches White Horse go pale and turn around. For a few moments, Roger observes this mighty, strong Chief have a moment of weakness. Finally, White Horse composes himself and turns back around.

"And Carrie?" he asks. "I have to remove the bullets."

"Won't that make her bleed more?"

"Yes, but if I leave them in, she is risking infection and possibly gang green. Either way, White Horse, if I do not remove them, she will die. I have no choice."

"You are the Great Healer, and I trust you. You do whatever you have to do to make sure neither one of them dies and that my son can walk again."

"White Horse, I promise you that I will do everything that I medically know how to do for both of them."

Just then, Medicine Moon steps in through the flap along with Grey Wolf and Koawa.

"This is Medicine Moon," White Horse introduces.

"Does she speak any English?" Roger asks.

"No."

"Then you will have to translate for me. Everyone else will have to leave."

CHAPTER TWENTY TWO
The Lost Souls

Roger, with the extra hands of Medicine Moon, successfully removes the bullet from his sister. Although her bleeding was great, he got it under control, and she is resting comfortably on her pelt. A privacy blanket is hung up by White Horse in between the two pelts. This was only done because Roger and he both agreed that the shock of her seeing Kikimo so badly off may add more stress to her and hinder her recovery. Roger left with White Horse and Medicine Moon to tend to the other wounded victims and to gather more of the root that his sister will need to control her bleeding. Prairie Dawn and Kikimo are left alone in the lodge until they return. Koawa steps in, securing the flap behind him. He pauses a moment to reflect on the two pelts before making his way to Prairie Dawn and kneeling beside her. He takes her hand into his and begins to stroke her hair.

"Alright, my sweet one, it is time to wake up," he tells her. "Sleep time is over. We have more adventures to go on and more mischief to get into."

He pecks her hand and strokes her face before continuing. "That day on the rocks when I was stabbed, I heard everything you said to me. I fought to stay alive for you and for Morning Dove. Now you need to do the same for me. I will tell you now what I tried to tell you then. I love you, Carrie. I have for a long time. You are very special to me, and I do not want to lose you." He strokes her hair and takes a few moments to control his emotions before continuing. "You are one of the strongest women I have ever known. You can fight this. You understand me?" he kisses her hand again. "You fight this." He remains beside her, holding her hand with his head lowered in prayer for a few minutes. Then, before coming to his feet, he leans over her and kisses her on her dry lips.

It is well into the evening at the Lakota camp. Roger and White Horse are in the lodge. Roger is dripping water down Kikimo's throat to help keep him hydrated. He glances over at White Horse, who is staring out into the fire. Roger can see the stress on White Horse's face. He can tell that he is deep in thought. His heart goes out for him, as not only must he be worried about his wife and son but his people as well. He has lost so much today. Many of his warriors died or lie injured in their lodges. The soldiers burnt all the camp's winter food supply, and the remaining warriors are frantically hunting for food that is getting harder to find. The anger is seen deeply penetrated in White Horse's eyes, and although the soldiers were retaliating from White Horse attacking the Fort, Roger feels that this brutal slaying went overboard. He comes to his feet to sit down next to White Horse. For the first time today, he notices White Horse's shoulder.

"Why don't you let me take a look at that?" he says.

White Horse comes out of his deep thoughts and looks down at his shoulder.

"I am fine. It just grazed me," he says.

"Let me at least clean it up."

"I will go to the water and clean it up."

Roger takes no offense to White Horse's unusual rudeness and watches him come to his feet, walk over to his sister, and kiss her forehead. He hears him mumble something to her before rising to his feet and exiting the flap.

There is a bright moon reflecting through the trees that glisten over the water of the stream. White Horse squats down and cups his hands together to collect some of the cool water. He tosses it over his face and rubs it over his wounded shoulder to clean off the dried blood. His mind is fuzzy and is racing a mile a minute. Sleep is the furthest thing from his mind, no matter how bad his body is craving it. There is heaviness inside of him that is weighing him down. He feels at any moment that he will explode. He gazes out at the water and thinks of his wife and son, who are fighting for their lives. His heart grows sad with the thought that he may lose them. He then thinks of Little Foot, who is just a small child himself, and wonders just what kind of future does he have? He starts to think of his people, who depend on his judgment for survival. His guilt is heavy, as he feels that the attack on the camp is entirely his fault. His eyes start to well up, just thinking at how much he has let them down. He comes to his feet and leans up against a tree trunk. His grief is unbearable, and he cannot control himself any longer. He kicks up a rock from the ground out of frustration and anger. He thinks of his father, a man who was extremely wise and respected by everyone. How he wishes he could talk to him right now, and how much he is craving his words of wisdom. Looking up into the heavens, he says in his tongue.

"I have lost my way, Father. What do you want me to do? I am tired and weary. My heart is torn. So much has been lost. So many lives have been destroyed. I do not know which way to go anymore. Help me, Father. Help me!" He leans his head back on the tree and closes his eyes. He sees his father's face in front of him. How he wishes he could reach out and grab him. He opens his eyes when he hears the rustling of leaves. He turns around as his brother comes into view.

"Hello, my brother," Koawa greets him in his tongue.

Koawa knows White Horse like the back of his hand, and he knows that his big brother feels as if he has lost his way. White Horse has always been there for him in his darkest hours, and it is his turn now to return the favor and cheer his big brother up.

"You want to talk about it?" he asks him.

"I am the big brother here, not you," White Horse jokes.

"Yes, but I am not the one whose heart is heavy," Koawa grins.

"Not only are you a good and faithful brother, but you are wise. Yes, my heart is heavy."

"Then tell me why?"

"I have lost my way, brother. I do not know where to go from here."

"Why do you think that?"

"So much is gone. So much has been lost. My people, they are losing their confidence in me."

"No, they are not White Horse, everyone understands. All of us agree that you had no choice. You had to attack the Fort. What has happened is not your fault."

"I am certain that Songbird would not feel that way. She has lost her husband and her son. I saw her vacant look today during the burial ritual of all our loved ones; her emptiness for the loss of her husband and son is deeper than any canyon. She could not even look my way when I tried to console her. She is angry with her Chief. I have let her down. I have let everyone down."

"She is grieving my brother. She feels alone. She does not know where her life is going to take her or who will provide for her and Jumping Badger. She is not angry with you. She is angry with the Blue Coats."

"I am tired, brother. I am tired of this war, and I am tired of always having to look over my shoulders. I just don't have the strength to do this anymore."

"Sure, you do because you are a fighter. It is in your blood. Remember, White Horse, you are not alone, for I am here. I will stand right beside you every step of the way. I will be your strength. When you feel lost, you come to me, and together, we will find the right path. Together, we will always stand."

White Horse faintly grins over at his little brother. He and Koawa have been through so much together, and the bond that they share is huge.

"Thank you, my brother. I asked our father to show me the way, and he just did. He sent me you."

Koawa pats him on the shoulder. "Father always did favor me," he teases.

"He did not," White Horse barks.

"Of course he did. I was always his favorite." White Horse shakes his head and starts to chuckle. Koawa always has had a way of making him laugh. Both men are chuckling when Roger appears.

"Come, hurry," he says. "Carrie is waking up."

White Horse is quick at getting to his lodge and coming down alongside his wife.

"Carrie," he says, stroking her hair. He hears her whimper. "Shh, it is alright love. You do not need to cry. I am right here."

"She is probably in pain, and that is why she is whimpering," Roger says.

"I can give her something for pain when she is more awake."

"Medicine Moon can give her something as well, and between you two, my wife will feel no pain."

He looks back down at her, stroking her hair. "She has been through enough pain already. I do not want her to feel more."

Just then, his wife opens her eyes. He smiles widely at her. "Hello, my beautiful," he greets.

"White Horse," I faintly say. "You're alive."

"Yes, very much so," he grins.

"Little Foot?"

"Little Foot is just fine. He is sleeping in Minoke's lodge along with Morning Dove."

Roger comes down on the other side of me. "

Roger," I say.

"How are you feeling?" he asks.

"I am thirsty."

White Horse reaches for the water cup that is nearby. He then lifts my head up so I can drink.

"Slow sips," Roger says.

I have never had more of a desire to drink and welcome the cool water. I slowly take the sips of water that White Horse is giving me. It is then that I see his shoulder. I finish my sips before White Horse places my head back down.

"You are hurt," I say to him.

"I am fine, my love," he assures me with a smile.

White Horse looks like he has not slept in a week. He has thick dark circles under his eyes and looks like he has aged ten years. He is a strong man who can control his emotions well, but it is clearly seen on his face how hard this has been on him. My mind is still fuzzy, but I clearly remember the attack. I bolt up to a sit.

"Kikimo," I say as I toss the blanket off my legs.

White Horse stops me from advancing any further.

"Where is Kikimo?" I ask him as he gently lays me back down and tucks me back in.

"You need to rest, love," White Horse tells me. I know White Horse well, and there is something that he is not telling me. I immediately think about the worst.

"Oh God no, not Kikimo," I cry.

"No, not Kikimo," White Horse says.

"Then he is alive, he survived?"

"He is alive."

"I want to see him," I tell him. "I have to see for my own eyes."

"Carrie, you need to rest," Roger says. "You have lost a great amount of blood, and you are weak."

I look back and forth at both men. "What are you not telling me?" I say.

"Sweetheart, please, you need your rest," White Horse says.

"Darn it, White Horse, what are you not telling me? What is wrong with Kikimo?"

"Kikimo is resting," he calmly states.

I know by the looks on their faces that there is something that they do not want to tell me.

"Something is wrong. I just know it. Please, White Horse, tell me."

"If I tell you, do you promise me that you will rest?"

"Yes, I promise." Without looking away from me, White Horse slides the blanket over and reveals Kikimo on his pelt. I gasp.

"Oh my God!" I cry. "Is he…"

"No," White Horse reassures. "He is alive."

"How bad is he Roger?"

"He is still alive, that is a good sign."

"Stop patronizing me!" I bark while clenching my fists. "I was there. I know he was shot. I want to know what is wrong with him."

"The bullet hit close to his spinal cord," Roger says. "There is a chance that Kikimo may never walk again."

"Oh my God," I cry. "Not Kikimo, not my Kikimo."

White Horse tries to calm me down by stroking my hair. "Only a chance, my love," he says. "Kikimo is strong. He has already defeated the odds. He should have died in the grass like so many others did, but he didn't, he fought it. He will walk again."

"White Horse is right," Roger states. "Kikimo is strong and a fighter. He is lucky that Medicine Moon stopped his bleeding before I arrived, or he would have bled to death."

"So, he will live?" I questioned him.

"Like I said before, he is a fighter. Time will tell, Carrie, time will tell."

"But…" White Horse puts his finger over my lips.

"You promised me if we told you that you would rest. Now, you need to rest."

"Not until I see Medicine Moon," I say.

"Prairie Dawn," White Horse says.

"I promise you, White Horse, I will rest after I see Medicine Moon. Please send for her."

"Alright, but then you will rest."

"Yes, I promise I will rest."

Medicine Moon is brought in. I asked White Horse and Roger to leave us alone. She is standing at the edge of my pelt, holding her basket. I speak her tongue.

"Thank you for helping Kikimo. I owe you his life."

"I was glad I could help him," she says.

"I have a favor to ask you."

"Certainly," she replies.

"Great Healer and your Chief have told me about Kikimo's condition and how he may never walk again. I know you are wise with your herbs, and I want to know if there is anything that you can do that will help him?"

"Yes, I can help him."

"Then I want you to do it."

"What about Great Healer? I would not want to offend his ability."

"Great Healer is my brother. He is a very wise man and very good at what he does, but he does not know anything about herbal medicine, and that is what Kikimo is accustomed to. Allow Great Healer to do what he can, but it is your remedies that I want my son to have. Please, I ask of you this as a favor to me. Help him."

"What will my Chief think of this?"

"He would want everything possible done to help his son. You will have no problem with him. I promise you."

"Then yes, I will do what I can. I will be back shortly. I need to collect what I need."

"Thank you, Medicine Moon."

I watch her exit the lodge, and then, as I promised my husband, I lie down my head and rest. We are into the evening.

White Horse and Little Foot are sitting beside me as we watch Medicine Moon apply her basket of remedies on Kikimo. Roger is standing close by her and watching her every move. He is filled with many questions, and White Horse is doing the honors of translating for him. He took no offense that I asked Medicine Moon for help with Kikimo, and in fact, he is enjoying the lessons that he is receiving in an area of medicine he knows little about.

As the camp goes into slumber, Roger is invited into Koawa's lodge for the night. Koawa is taking the evening watch, and Morning Dove is staying with Minoke for the night, meaning Roger will have the lodge to himself. He graciously accepts the peace and quiet and is sound asleep on a pelt. The pain in my arm and leg is at a minimum, and I am sleeping comfortably. White Horse is tucked in beside me, being careful not to hit my leg when he sleeps. Little Foot in on his own pelt not far away and has been asleep for hours. I am awakened when I hear Kikimo groan. I nudge White Horse awake when I hear him groan again.

"White Horse," I say.

"Hmm," White Horse says. "Are you alright, love?"

"Kikimo is waking up."

White Horse is quick to his feet and rushes over to his son. He gazes down to see his son open his eyes.

"Your uncle is here. I will be right back," he tells him before rushing out the flap to get Roger. I am unable to apply much pressure on my leg because of the pain and all the bandages, but I am determined to get over to Kikimo's pelt, so I slide over on my rump until I get to him. I then take his hand into mine and look down at him.

"Ma," he mumbles.

"Mama is right here," I smile at him.

"You are alright," he says.

It is then that I am certain that Kikimo remembers what happened.

"Yes, I am going to be just fine."

"Little Foot?"

"He is just wonderful, as are your father and your uncle Koawa."

Our conversation is interrupted when the flap is pushed open, and Roger and White Horse rush in. Roger is quickly at Kikimo's side.

"Welcome back, son," Roger says.

"You are here," he tells Roger.

"Of course I am. Where else would I be?" he grins. "I need you to tell me, son, if you remember what happened?"

"Yes, our camp was attacked by Blue Coats. I was running behind Eagle Scout and Flying Hawk to the creek. I saw them go down. I was then shot myself. Eagle Scout, is he alright?"

I look up at White Horse. Neither one of us has ever lied to our children, no matter how painful it may be to them. I was not certain if now was the time to tell Kikimo that his best friend was dead. It was White Horse who made the decision.

"No, son, Eagle Scout was one of many who did not make it."

For a moment, Kikimo is still. Eagle Scout was like a brother to him, and I am certain that his death is going to hit him hard.

"I knew in my heart," Kikimo says. "When I saw him and Flying Hawk go down, I would never see my friend in this life form again."

"I am so sorry, son," I tell him, squeezing his hand.

"He is in the shadow world now. He is safe."

"What you need to focus on now, Kikimo, is getting well," I tell him.

"I will, Ma," he tells me. "I will do whatever I have to do. I will not allow my best friend's death to be for nothing."

I admire Kikimo's tenacity. He is so much like his father at times that it is scary. I know that he is hurting deep inside from Eagle Scout's death, and like his father, he is holding any emotion of it bottled up inside him. He is a strong boy, and I know that with the love and support that White Horse and I will give him, he will be alright.

Three days have passed. Kikimo is making an amazing recovery. After countless hours of Medicine Moon and Roger working together and Kikimo's strong will, he is up and moving around and showing no sign of any paralysis. I, too, am up and moving around with the aid of a walking stick that White Horse made me. Roger left for home yesterday, but not without receiving a rather strange warning from White Horse. He was told not to purchase any flour at the Fort for several days. When Roger asked him why, he simply smirked. I know my husband well, and I am certain that he is up to something.

Medicine Moon hands White Horse the pouch containing the poison that she made, which will be used in the flour that the supply wagon will be carrying into the Fort. It is not enough poison to kill a healthy man or a strong woman or child, but it packs enough of a punch that it will make them incredibly sick and slow them down tremendously for quite some time.

White Horse left early in the morning with his warriors to find the supply wagon that his scouts have been following. He will set up a decoy that will make the wagon stop. Then, Grey Wolf will sneak in when the soldiers are preoccupied and slip the poison in the flour. White Horse will make a point that he is seen by the soldiers and make it known to them that he is not defeated and that he is out for blood. He will make it clear that after the flour is eaten and many fall ill, he is the one who is responsible for it. They stop just on top of the hill overlooking the slow-moving supply wagon below. He then gets all his men into position. He waits for Grey Wolf to get down the hill and come up behind the wagon a safe distance behind. When he is in place, it is then that the warriors charge in.

The driver sees the Sioux coming over the hill and brings the wagon to a stop. A soldier who is riding alongside the wagon aims to fire as many other soldiers scatter to stop the advancement. One is taken down by Koawa's arrow when he detects Grey Wolf approaching the wagon. With the loud commotion all around him, Grey Wolf jumps onto the back of the wagon and finds the barrel that has the flour in it. He then opens the pouch and pours the white powder like poison in it, stirs it around, and closes it back up.

White Horse comes off his horse and is standing proud, overlooking the skirmish. He makes a point to be seen by the soldiers and fails to move when he is being shot at. The soldiers are enraged by his boldness and arrogance as White Horse stands his ground. The warriors retreat when they see Grey Wolf leave on his horse. White Horse takes one last stand before he, too, gets on his horse and rides off. The soldiers celebrate as they feel that they succeeded in scaring off the Sioux. Little are they aware of how wrong they are

CHAPTER TWENTY THREE
The Stranger in the Trees

Three days have passed. Medicine Moon and I have been spending a great deal of time together. I am growing rather fond of her and am enjoying her company tremendously. I am still at the mercy of a cane when I walk, so today, Medicine Moon is helping me carry back some water from the creek. We are on our way back to camp. I notice Koawa and Dancing Bear in a playful conversation outside his lodge. I continue my way to our lodge as I watch them joking around. There is still something about her that I do not like, and I wish that I could figure it out. My thought is turned away when Medicine Moon stops in her tracks and watches Grey Wolf riding into camp with several other warriors. I know that they have formed a bond, and although she has lost her own Cheyenne family recently, I am certain that she is growing fond of her new protector. I smile over at her and tell her in her tongue.

"Go to him," I tell her. I watch her face turn red in embarrassment. "Don't be embarrassed, I do the same thing when I see White Horse," I smile.

She smiles back. She walks the remaining way to the lodge with me and puts the water down before leaving to find Grey Wolf.

I find my husband and Kikimo whittling under a tree. Kikimo has made a remarkable recovery but is still unable to do much and does not like the idea of staying down. I come down on my knees next to White Horse.

"I was wondering if you ever were able to follow Dancing Bear?" I ask him.

"Not since the attack," he answers me before blowing away some dust.

"But you did before?"

"Yes, Blue Thunder and Koawa followed her. She went to a remote area at the river and bathed."

"That's it?" I questioned him, disappointed.

"That's it," he answers.

I deeply exhale from frustration and come to my feet.

"You seem disappointed," he says.

"I cannot explain my thinking, but something is not right with her, and I am going to figure it out."

"I know you will," he says as he grins up at me.

Further down the Plains, Roger is returning home from a very long stay at the Fort. He has been dealing with an epidemic of some strange stomach illness that has affected nearly everyone there. He has been scratching his head all day, trying to figure out what is causing everyone to get so sick. It was not until he was tending to a soldier that he overheard him talking to the General about a bizarre skirmish that had happened a few days ago with the Sioux. After listening to the details and remembering White Horse's warning about not purchasing any flour, he put two and two together and figured out why everyone was getting so sick.

He had to tell the General the reasoning of why everyone is so ill. The General guessed on how it happened and was convinced that the Sioux Chief was responsible. He now wants White Horse arrested and hung for all the havoc that he has been causing him the last few months. This has caused Roger a great deal of concern, as he knows the General will stop at nothing to see White Horse brought to justice. He must tell White Horse what he knows, and at first light, he will leave for White Horse's camp and warn him.

Back at the Lakota camp, I am in the nearby woods gathering plants for Medicine Moon that she will use on Kikimo later in the day. I am still using a walking stick, mostly just as a precaution from stumbling on uneven ground. This is becoming a cumbersome challenge the thicker I get into the trees or holding the cane and the basket as well. As I get further into the woods, I start to become uneasy, and I cannot shake the feeling that I am being watched. I look around as I continue to work, but there is nothing that is out of the ordinary. Still, I feel as if I am being preyed upon. I quickly concluded that I have enough plants in my basket and decided to head back to camp.

As I am making my way home, my skin begins to crawl, and I have a sudden urge to run. I listen more intently as I hasten my pace to home. My heart skips a beat as I feel that there is something menacing behind me. I boldly turn around, expecting to see something, but there is nothing there. I still cannot shake the feeling that I am being stalked, and at any moment, something is going to jump out and grab me.

This place is filled with bears, cougars, and wolves, and any of them could rip me apart in a matter of moments. I have had enough of wondering what it could be and dropping my basket so I can hold onto my walking stick better and run as fast as I can. My pulse is racing in my throat. I feel as if I am being chased. I am in a state of terror, as I am running as fast as I can to get away from whatever it is that I feel is behind me. I glanced back, thinking that I would see something there, but I was alone. My leg is throbbing from running, but I feel as if I cannot stop my quick pace or something is going to catch me. I let out a scream when I turn the corner and run hard into Koawa's chest.

He grabs my shoulders to calm me down. When I see that it is him, I bury my head into his chest and catch my breath. I have never been so happy in my life to see him.

"Why are you running?" he asks me.

It takes me a moment to catch my breath. "There is something back there," I tell him, winded.

"An animal?" he asks. "I do not know."

"Well, what did it look like?"

"I did not see anything. I just felt it there."

Koawa knows that I'm not frightened easily. He can see the terror in my eyes and knows something has scared me. He also knows that there is a threat of Blue Coats all around, as well as his menacing brother, Red Hawk, who hasn't been seen in months.

"Show me where?"

Together, Koawa and I walk back into the thickness of the woods. All the while, he is watching the ground for any tracks. We came to the place where I dropped my basket.

"Right here," I tell him.

Koawa combs the ground and finds nothing. He steps further into the woods and looks around. He sees nothing out of place. I gather my basket and the plants that fell out of it as Koawa continues to look around.

Huddled high up in a tree and well hidden in the branches from his dark appearance is Red Hawk. He looks down at Koawa below. He sees Prairie Dawn a short distance away. He enjoyed scaring her and watching her run for her life. He was inches away from appearing as the Dark Man, the mysterious

Sioux legend that is feared by many, but quickly held off when he saw Koawa coming. Although he wants to take his little brother down and kidnap Prairie Dawn, he will wait a little bit longer until he is ready to make his presence known. Until then, he will enjoy bringing fear and watching Prairie Dawn squirm.

"There is nothing here, Prairie Dawn," Koawa says.

"I am not crazy Koawa, there was something here. I felt it."

"I never said you were crazy," he smiles. "I just said that nothing is here right now."

"So, you believe me?"

"Of course I do," he grins. "Let me walk you back to camp."

"What are you doing out here?" I ask him as we make our short walk back.

"I was following Dancing Bear."

I am a little taken aback by it. I got the impression from White Horse that she is in the clear.

"You think she is up to something too. Don't you?" I ask him.

"Yes," he admits. "That is why I have been talking to her more. I am hoping by making her feel as if I am interested in her, I will be able to find out what she is hiding."

"What made you suspicious?"

"You."

"Me?" I say.

"Yes, you trust everyone, for you to get suspicious of someone, something is wrong."

"I wish White Horse felt that way."

"He is as well, except that he likes Crow Dog, and that is what makes him want to trust her because Crow Dog is a very loyal and honest man. But Crow Dog and Red Hawk at one time were very good friends, and that is what concerns me."

"If Red Hawk was anywhere around here, we would know about it, wouldn't we?"

Koawa does not want to worry me with his thoughts about Red Hawk, so he quickly changes the subject. He looks over at me as I am leaning on the walking stick.

"You should not have been running on your leg. Do you need me to carry you the rest of the way?"

My leg is throbbing, and I am in desperate need of getting off it, but I didn't think that White Horse would be really keen on the idea of seeing Koawa carrying me into camp.

"Thank you, but we are almost there."

"As you wish," he says.

Together, we continued our walk to camp.

Through the trees, Red Hawk silently follows Koawa and Prairie Dawn until he is forced to stop when they reach the large clearing where their camp is set up. He will return to the cave where he has been sleeping and wait for his wife, Dancing Bear, to come. He will hold her tight and whisper sweetness in her ears as he makes love to her. He will then rush her off back to camp, just as the sunset before anyone misses her.

Great darkness fills the land as another night is near a close. White Horse is stationing his men for the night, and the boys are sleeping comfortably on their pelts. I am lying on the pelt that I share with my husband, deep in thought. My mind is bothered by Dancing Bear. I know that there is something going on with her, but I just can't put my finger on it. My mind is doing circles as I try to put the pieces together. Something is missing, something is just not adding up. Why can't I figure this out? I am so deep in my concentration that I fail to see White Horse walk in. It is not until he kisses my cheek that I even acknowledge that he is there.

"Where did your mind go?" he teases. It is then that I remember something.

"Oh my Gosh, how could I be so stupid," I say.

"What are you talking about?" he smiles.

"With everything going on with the attack and Kikimo, I completely forgot," I gasp.

White Horse looks at me, confused. "What?" he questions.

"The day of the attack, I found shelter behind a lodge. Dancing Bear was behind another one a close distance away. I saw a soldier advancing on her. He was ready to kill her when a warrior brought him down." I look over at White Horse. "It was Red Hawk."

White Horse's eyes grow large. "Are you sure?"

"Yes, I am positive. He brought the soldier down and then ran off as fast as he appeared."

"And you are just now telling me this?" he huffs.

"I am sorry. With everything else going on, I didn't remember until right now. I guess what happened in the woods today got me thinking, and I remembered."

"What happened in the woods today?"

"I was gathering plants for Medicine Moon, and I felt like something or someone was watching me. I fled because I felt at any moment, something was going to get me. I ran into Koawa on the way back. He looked around for tracks but didn't see anything. I know something was there. I know there was."

"You are certain that you saw Red Hawk the day of the attack?" he asks.

"Yes, he didn't see me, but I saw him."

White Horse is very concerned, and although he wants to take his wife to their pelt and fulfill his nightly desire for her, for the moment, he has to wait. He comes to his feet.

"I will be back in a little bit," he says.

"Where are you going at this hour?" I ask him.

"I have to go take care of something. I will be back shortly, and then we will have the rest of the night together."

CHAPTER TWENTY FOUR
The Dark Man

Roger is sitting in his chair in front of the fire, reading a letter. He is very tired from his day of doctoring at the Fort, and his mind is worried about the fear of White Horse being captured. He will be turning in soon for the night so he can get a good night's sleep before making his way to White Horse's camp tomorrow. He glances up over the rim of his glasses when his wife offers him a cup of coffee.

"Thank you, dear," he tells her, taking the cup from her hand.

"You are very quiet tonight, my dear, and you hardly ate a bite of your dinner. Did you not like my roast?"

"Your roast was delicious," he says, taking her hand. "I just was not very hungry."

"What is troubling you, dear?" she asks him.

"This bounty on White Horse. I have never seen one so big on an Indian before. The General is determined to find him. I not only worry for White Horse but my sister and the others as well."

"I worry for you," she says.

"Why me?"

"You are a traitor to him, Roger, and if he ever found out that you knew White Horse and you know where he is at, it is you that will be arrested and hung right alongside White Horse."

"If I could only convince White Horse that it would be for the best of everyone if he would surrender. I know if he did, the General would go easy on him and convince a judge to only sentence him to prison and not death."

"I cannot see that ever happening," she says.

"I know. He is so stubborn and pigheaded."

"He is a proud man, Roger. There is a difference."

Roger removes his glasses and rubs his fatigued eyes. It is then that Rose sees the letter that he has been reading.

"Who is that from?" she asks him.

"Stella," he answers. "She received my earlier post about Matthew."

"And?"

"She is angry with me but has agreed to take Matthew to the Orphanage, and I will meet her there."

"Did you tell her about Blue Thunder?"

"No, I was afraid that she would run if I did. I told her that for Matthew's benefit, she needed to go to the Orphanage, and I would help her find work as a seamstress. I told her if she didn't get Matthew in a decent atmosphere soon, I would bring the law in and take Matthew away from her."

"When are you leaving?"

"She will take the first train to Cedar Brook and settle in. I will meet her there after the winter. I sent a post to Sister Ann that she should be expecting her and sent her some money to get her started." She watches Roger yawn as he places his glasses down on the table. "I reckon you should get yourself some sleep. Tomorrow, we have a long day."

"We?" he says.

"Yes, I want to go with you."

Roger faintly grins as he takes her into his arms. "I love you, Rose Briggs. I love you so much."

"Why don't you show me how much," she teases.

Roger chuckles as he comes to his feet. Taking his wife's hand into his, he leads her into the bedroom, closing the door behind him.

Red Hawk finishes his last few thrusts in his Dancing Bear before emptying himself inside her. He will enjoy what time he has left with her, as very soon, he will have to leave this cave and walk her back to camp before anyone else finds her missing. He kisses her sweet lips before rolling off her and grabbing a piece of bread that she brought to him.

"When will we be together, forever?" she asks him, laying her head down on his chest.

"We are together now forever, silly," he smiles.

"I mean when we do not have to hide, as if we are living in shame."

"Soon, my wife. I promise you very soon."

"Good, because I do not like spending any time with Koawa. It is you I want to spend my time with."

"Has he tried to kiss you?"

"No," she huffs. "I will not dishonor you like that."

"I told you that it was alright. You need to do what is necessary to earn his trust."

"But it is you that I want to kiss," she whines as she places her hand on his shaft and begins to stroke it. "It is you I want to hold."

He faintly smiles over at her, thumbing her hair. "I want this as well. I would not ask you to do this for me if it was not necessary."

"Tell me why it is necessary?"

"Koawa is very strong but weak when it comes to a beautiful woman. Prairie Dawn will be used to get to the Chief, but you will be used to get to Koawa."

"I do not understand what I have to do with this?"

"My Dancing Bear, there is so much that you do not know, but you must trust me."

"I do."

"Then ask no more and do as I wish." She strokes his shaft up and down as she gazes into his eyes. "I will do as you wish, but I will not like it," she says.

"You are a good wife," he smiles.

As he reaches for another piece of bread, he feels his wife wrapping her lips around his shaft and begin to please him. He will return the favor to her before uniting with her again and walking her back to the camp.

White Horse has returned to his own lodge. He went to Crow Dog's lodge in hopes of talking to Dancing Bear, but instead, he found her gone. He was not surprised to see that Crow Dog had not returned home from his scouting and could only assume that he was camped out nearby with the other warriors for the night. He is curious, however, as to where Dancing Bear is, and he is starting to believe that his wife's suspicions are correct about Dancing Bear and that she cannot be trusted. He is certain that Red Hawk is nearby and that his wife did indeed see him on the day of the attack. He is beginning to think that there is a connection between Red Hawk and Dancing Bear. He knows Red Hawk well and understands how twisted his mind works. He is not surprised that his half-brother has eluded him this long, as both know each other's habits and how each other thinks very well. He is confident that Red Hawk is hiding somewhere deep within a cave, and that is why he has not been seen. White Horse is determined to find him, and tomorrow, he and his men will comb the area, hit every cave that they find, and smoke the snake out. Although he only wants to talk to Red Hawk and means him no harm, he would not hesitate to kill him if provoked.

He is uniting with his Prairie Dawn as his children sleep. With the winter fast approaching, soon she will be able to stop drinking the baby tea and will be able to safely conceive and deliver when the root to control the bleeding is in full bloom. He looks forward to this time of night with his wife, even though he is aware that no baby will be made. He pushes her tight buttocks deeper onto his shaft as she rides him like a horse. They are both near their climax and soon, their lovemaking will be finished. He will then stay with her until she falls asleep. He posted Grey Wolf outside near Crow Dog's lodge to wait and see when Dancing Bear returns. If she has not returned by the time he is done, he will relieve him and wait there in the shadows himself until she returns.

Upon reaching the outskirts of the camp, Red Hawk gives his wife one final long kiss goodbye under the moonlit night. She says goodbye to him when their lips part, and she quietly sneaks into the camp. She fails to see her Chief standing in the darkness not far away. White Horse looks over in the direction in which she came and sees a figure standing there. He is too far away, and the night is too dark to make out who it is, but he is suspicious that he knows. He watches Dancing Bear running across the grass to her lodge and looking around for any movement before opening the flap and stepping inside.

He looks back over at the dark shadow and watches it disappear into the trees. He has no time to waste. He jumps on his horse that is nearby and quickly makes his way to where he last saw the dark figure. He guides his pony through the thickets, following the figure the best he can. The lack of a high moon provides him with little light as he gets thicker into the trees. A chill goes down his spine as he can feel that his nemesis is close and is most likely watching him from somewhere in the darkness. He then sees something jump out from behind a tree and run. The trees are too thick to push his pony safely on, so he quickly jumps off his horse and chases the figure on foot. By the speed of the run and the gracefulness of moving around with ease in such a rugged terrain at night, White Horse is certain that it is Red Hawk. He knows this man's speed, and he is aware of how he loves to play cat-and-mouse games. He could be anywhere. He stops and calls out into the night air.

"I know it is you!" he hollers. "Show yourself!"

There is an eerie stillness in the air as White Horse waits for a response. He squints his eyes as he looks out into the darkness for any sign of movement.

"I mean you no harm. I only want to talk to you," he yells out.

Just then, he bolts to the ground when he hears the whistling of a tomahawk being thrown through the wind. It lands hard into the tree just over his head. As White Horse is getting to his feet, he looks out and sees Red Hawk making a run and disappearing into the night. He curses under his breath as he knows that Red Hawk gave him the slip.

"Not to worry," he tells himself. "I will find you."

CHAPTER TWENTY FIVE
The Betrayal

It is early morning. White Horse has been up for hours and has gathered his warriors in the smoke lodge. Plans are being made to find Red Hawk. White Horse is certain that he must be hiding somewhere deep in a cave, so he has sent several of his warriors to smoke out every cave that they come across. Koawa and Blue Thunder are leading two separate search teams to cover more ground. White Horse gave them both strict orders that Red Hawk is not to be hurt and that they are to bring him back to camp alive. This is something that Koawa strongly disagrees with, as he wants the snake dead, but because of his loyalty to White Horse, he will put his negative feelings towards his half-brother aside and comply with White Horse's wishes.

White Horse confronted Dancing Bear about her sneaking out and he wanted to know where she has been going. She denied that she was doing anything wrong or even that she knew Red Hawk at all. White Horse is certain that she is lying but says nothing to her and walks away. Instead, he decides that he will talk to Crow Dog, who is not only Dancing Bear's brother but has been a longtime friend to Red Hawk. He is hoping he will know something about where Red Hawk may be. He finds his warrior, who has just returned from his evening of scouting, outside his lodge. He invites Crow Dog into the smoke lodge. There, they will pass the pipe back and forth a few times before White Horse will announce the reason why Crow Dog was invited into the smoke lodge in the first place.

White Horse inhales the last puff of smoke before putting the pipe down and getting to business. He speaks his tongue. "You are probably curious as to why I have asked you to join me for the passing of the pipe."

"I will admit that I am a little baffled," Crow Dog replies.

"I will get to the point then," he says. "It is about Dancing Bear."

"What has my sister done?" he asks.

"Are you aware that she is sneaking out of camp unprotected and returning in the middle of the night?"

"Yes, I am aware of this, and I have told her to stop because it is not safe, but her ears are closed, and she refuses to listen to me."

"Where is she going?" White Horse asks.

"She will not tell me."

White Horse is certain that Crow Dog knows more than he is letting on. He respects all of his warriors and usually will let them do whatever they want. But he refuses to allow any of them to lie to him.

"Have I not been good to you?" he says. "Have I not allowed you and your sister to stay at my camp? Have I not given you a pony to ride and food for your belly?"

"Yes, my Chief, you have been very good to us," Crow Dog says.

"Then why are the words that you speak to me lies?"

"I do not understand what you mean?"

"You know exactly where she is going and who she is with, and if you refuse to tell me what you know, then I will be forced to punish both you and Dancing Bear. Now, I am going to ask you again, and this time, I want the truth. Where is she going?"

For a few moments, Crow Dog is still. He admires his Chief and is very grateful to him for allowing him into his camp and for sitting as a member of his council. He loves his sister very much and would do anything to protect her, but he is tired of the lies and the deception that he is doing to a man of such great generosity and kindness.

"You are wise, my Chief, and very kind. You trusted in me, and I broke that trust, but I promise you that I will make you proud of me. Allow me to handle my sister. She will leave camp no more. I will make sure of it."

"Where is she going?" White Horse asks.

"She leaves to go see her husband."

This was not something that White Horse was expecting to hear, and he is taken completely off guard.

"Why does she not bring her husband here?" he questions. "Is she not proud of this man?"

"My Chief, she does not bring him here because she fears for his safety, as he is not welcomed here."

"Why wouldn't he be?" White Horse asks, confused. "Who is this man?"

"He is Red Hawk." Crow Dog answers.

White Horse is stunned. He is a man who is never short on words, but for a few moments, he is speechless.

"I was certain that she was meeting him, but I never thought for a moment that they were married," he finally says. "How long ago?"

"They were married the morning that my camp was attacked. That is why I was not there, and we survived."

"You have known Red Hawk for years, and you are his good friend. You are most likely aware of my history with him."

"He spoke many times about you. I am aware of how much he despises you."

"Is that why you came here? So Red Hawk could get closer to me?"

"That was the plan," Crow Dog admits. "But so much has changed, and I have grown to see your heart and realize how wrong Red Hawk is about you. Please, my Chief, allow me to go to him and talk to him. I will bring him back."

"You know where he is at?"

"Yes, I know exactly where he is."

"Then you must tell me."

"No, he will kill you if you go. Allow me to. I will convince him that he needs to return to you. Our spirits do not like what is going on. They are restless. I will bring peace to all of us. Please, Chief, let me do this for you."

"How do I know that I can trust you? You have lied to me once already. How do I know that you will not lie to me again?"

"I love my sister, and I do not want any harm to come to her. I know if I betray you, her life will be in danger. You can trust me. I will not let you down. Give me until the sun is at its highest, and I will prove to you that I am a man of my word."

White Horse reluctantly agrees. "I will give you your time, but if you betray me in any way, I will personally hunt you down."

"You come with me and wait for me by the tree that touches the sky. I will bring him there."

To make certain that Crow Dog will hold true to his word that he will return, White Horse holds Dancing Bear hostage by tying her to a post in the center of camp and placing two guards in front of her. Koawa took the honor of grabbing her and tying her up. He wanted to be the one to humiliate her and let her know that he was not fooled by her games. She will receive no food or water until Crow Dog returns. The fear is evident all over her face. Dancing Bear is scared to death, and she should be. White Horse can be brutal when need be.

Crow Dog is sitting on his pony watching on, as his sister is being tied up. She looks over his way, and through her heavy, crying eyes, she yells at him.

"How could you!" she yells at him in her tongue. Crow Dog remains stone-faced, even though he does not approve of the treatment that she is receiving. He understands why the Chief is doing it and is confident that she will only have to endure it for a few more hours.

"He trusted you!" she screams at him. "How could you!"

You could hear a pin drop as everyone is watching on. The anger of being betrayed that is on White Horse's face is obvious to everyone who is watching on. There is not one of us who dare speak a word, as we all know how White Horse can be when he is angry. When Dancing Bear is tied, and the guards are standing their watch, is it then that I see White Horse, Koawa, Blue Thunder, and Crow Dog leave.

Sitting in front of a fire deep within a winding cave, there is Red Hawk. He found himself a snake earlier in the morning and is skinning it. He has called this cave his home for several weeks. It is well hidden in the thickness of the trees and tucked between two big boulders in the ravine. He hung a string of bones throughout the cave that will rattle when walked by and will warn him of any intruders that may stumble upon him. He is heavily armed with several tomahawks, arrows, his bow, and a club in the event he needs to fight anyone off and for hunting. He is not expecting to stay here much longer, as winter is fast approaching. He is going to have to carry out his plans of killing his half-brothers and kidnapping Prairie Dawn very soon. He has been making plans on how he would do this for years. It came to him the time he was shot when his camp was raided by Blue Coats. It was the same day that he lost Running Bear and Yellow Bird. He was found by White Horse and Prairie Dawn in the canyon when they were returning home with the children who survived the attack. He was too weak to make it the rest of the way to White Horse's camp, and he was taken to a cave to recover. Prairie Dawn was left to care for him, while White Horse left to take the children back to his camp and get help. It was in that cave that he came up with an idea on how to take the Chief's wife away. He earned her trust and allowed her to teach him her language, although he already knew a fair amount of it. For a while, his plan worked until Koawa got in his way after he pushed White Horse off the falls and went missing. He was forced to leave the camp and Rising Sun behind when White Horse was found alive and remembered being pushed off the falls. His problems got worse when he stabbed Koawa nearly to death when they were wrestling on the big boulder and then again when he put a knife to Prairie Dawn's throat. He is growing tired of White Horse's incredible luck coming back from the dead and is going to put a stop to it once and for all. He is fortunate that his good friend Crow Dog convinced his Chief to allow him to come into his camp to live. He is certain, with Crow Dog's help, that this time, he will succeed at killing both of his half-brothers and kidnapping Prairie Dawn. His thoughts are interrupted when he hears one of the bones rattle. He is not expecting his Dancing Bear until this evening. The only other one who knows he is here is Crow Dog. He comes to his feet, grabs a tomahawk, and makes his way to the entrance just as Crow Dog comes into view. He greets him in his tongue at the cave entrance.

"I have not seen you for many days," Red Hawk begins. "What do you have to tell me?"

"The Chief knows everything. He is holding Dancing Bear captive until I return with you."

"You coward!" Red Hawk spats. "I told you what to tell him if he was to question you."

"He has been good to me. He is not the man that you told me that he is. He is good and kind."

"You are a fool."

"No, you are the fool," Crow Dog argues. "You are blinded by your silly revenge that happened when you were a boy that you cannot see the man that he has become. He only wants to talk to you. He wants to make things right between you two. Why can't you see that?"

"You are the one blinded. I trusted you, and you have betrayed me."

"No, I have not. I only want to help make things right. Our spirits are restless. They do not like what is going on between you two. They want peace, and so do I."

Red Hawk is furious with Crow Dog and is staring him down, but Crow Dog is not intimidated and continues. "Come with me to the great tree where the Chief and his brother are waiting. Together, we will pass the pipe, and we will make peace. You owe it to Dancing Bear, and you owe it to yourself."

"No, I will never back down to him. You gave me your word that you would help me."

"I will no longer live your lies, and neither will Dancing Bear. You are on your own."

Crow Dog then turns to walk away. Red Hawk's blood is boiling. He has come too far to give up now. He removes the tomahawk that is in his waistband and tosses it into Crow Dog's back. He watches his friend go to the ground. He makes his way over to him and rolls him over, removing the tomahawk. Red Hawk notices that Crow Dog is still alive and slowly dying.

"No one betrays me," he growls down at him before finishing him off with a blow to the head. "No one."

CHAPTER TWENTY SIX
The Warning

White Horse is standing under the great tall tree, waiting for Crow Dog to return with Red Hawk. He has been waiting for hours, and his patience is wearing thin. Koawa comes up beside him.

"He is not coming, brother. I knew this was a bad idea."

"I promised to give him until the sun is at its highest, and it is not there yet," White Horse argues.

"Brother, I know you want to believe him. He fooled me as well. We are wasting our time standing here when we should be out there looking for Red Hawk."

White Horse knows that Koawa is right and that he was fooled into believing Crow Dog. White Horse hates looking like a fool, especially in front of his warriors.

Let's go back to camp and regroup. I am going to find him if it is the last thing I do."

Red Hawk drags the body of Crow Dog into the open prairie in plain sight for White Horse to see when he is returning to his camp. He removed Crow Dog's scalp and hung it on a spear that he thrust into the ground beside his body. He did this to make a statement to his dear half-brother that he has no intention of making peace with him and that this is war. He stole Crow Dog's horse and is making his way back to the cave. There, he will pray to his spirits for guidance and plot how to rescue Dancing Bear, who he is certain White Horse will go hard on as soon as he realizes that Crow Dog is dead. White Horse and his men are on their way back to camp when they see a body lying in the tall grass with a spear in the ground beside it. Blue Thunder comes off his horse and makes his way over to the body. He rolls it over.

"It's Crow Dog," he tells White Horse in his tongue.

White Horse deeply sighs. He now understands why Crow Dog never returned to the great tall tree, and he knows who killed him. "Red Hawk," he mumbles to himself.

Blue Thunder lifts Crow Dog's body and tosses him onto the back of his pony, where he will be brought back to camp. White Horse rides up to the spear, removing it from the ground. He pauses a moment and looks at the scalp hanging off of it. He softly speaks his tongue.

"You were a good man, Crow Dog. I was proud to call you my friend. You tried to make things right, and you lost your life because of it. I promise you I will find him. Now we are at war."

I am at the stream with Medicine Moon and Songbird when I see White Horse, Koawa, and Blue Thunder returning to camp. I pick up my basket of clothes and make my way up to the lodge to greet my husband. As I get closer to the camp, I look over at our riders and see one of our warriors has died and is draped over the back of Blue Thunder's horse. I gasp when I realize it is Crow Dog. I am immediately curious as to what happened to him and stop in my tracks to watch on as the men bring their horses to a stop in front of Dancing Bear. Her attention is drawn to them when she sees Blue Thunder get off his horse and lift the body of Crow Dog off his pony.

"No!" she screams.

White Horse walks over to her as Blue Thunder places his body down on the ground in front of her.

"See what your lies have done!" White Horse spats.

"Who did this?" she cries.

"The man who you call your husband," he growls. I gasp!

I had no idea that she was married. The camp is silent, with everyone intently listening on. "You lie!" she roars. "Crow Dog was his friend. Red Hawk loved him."

I gasped again in disbelief that her husband was Red Hawk and that he was the one who killed Crow Dog. White Horse holds out Crow Dog's scalp in front of her.

"You call this love!" he roars. Dancing Bear is in tears. "Your brother is dead because of you and your lies and deceptions. It is your fault that this brave man breaths no more. This man that you love is the reason that you are tied like a dog. If you want your freedom from your bounds, then you will tell me where Red Hawk is."

"No, you will kill him," she cries.

"As you wish," he growls. "You will receive no food, water, or shelter. You will soil where you sit. Mark my words. Your husband will be found, and he will face my wrath."

We are well into the afternoon. Crow Dog's body has been prepared for his journey to the shadow world to meet his creator and has been placed high on a scaffold near the rest of our loved ones who were killed in our most recent attack. Dancing Bear is still tied to her post and has been made a mockery by everyone at the camp. The children are teasing her, the women are calling her bad names, and some are throwing rocks at her. I refuse to participate in any of it, as I remember what it feels like not to be accepted in the camp. Although I have lived with Sioux for almost eight years, I remember how I felt when I was not accepted by Minoke and Koawa when I first arrived. Fortunately for me, I was to marry their Chief, and everyone feared White Horse and what he would do to them if I was harmed by any of them. Minoke was the unlucky one to feel his wrath firsthand when she came after me with a knife to my throat. Although she and I are very close now, it took many years for us to get there. I am watching Dancing Bear curled up on the ground with her hands wrapped around the post. The fear is everywhere in her eyes. She has not been allowed any food or water, and I am certain she is starting to feel the thirst. What concerns me the most is that winter is fast approaching, and there is a significant chill in the air, especially at night. Come this evening, she is going to feel extremely cold. My thoughts are turned away when I see several of our warriors, being led by Koawa, come riding into camp with two visitors among them. I quickly see that they are Roger and Rose. I watch White Horse greet them both as Blue Thunder takes the reins of both their horses and walks off. I greet my brother with a hug when I make my way to him.

"I have missed you, my brother," I tell him.

"As have I missed you," he grins back.

I then hug Rose. I notice looping over her arm is a basket that I can only assume is filled with goodies. "I brought some more jam and a special gift for Kikimo. Roger told me what happened. I am so sorry," she says.

"Thank you," I tell her. "Kikimo is inside playing a game with Little Foot. Please come, I will take you to him."

"I need to talk to you alone, White Horse," Roger begins as he watches the women disappear into the lodge.

"Great Healer," White Horse grins. "You have made a great journey just to tell me something. I fear that is not good."

Just then, Roger sees Dancing Bear tied up. He is confused by this and asks White Horse as to what the reason is.

"What is up with the woman?" he asks.

"Pay no mind to her," White Horse says. "Let us walk together, and you can tell me what it is that has made you come so far."

The men begin their walk to the river at the edge of the camp.

"Do not leave me in suspense, my brother," White Horse says. "Tell me what is on your mind."

"There is no easy way to tell you, but you need to be aware. I was at the Fort tending to several patients who had come down with an incredible stomachache."

White Horse smirks, as he knows exactly why. "And you think I had something to do with this?" he asks.

"Did you?"

"Yes, I did," he admits. "That is why I told you not to purchase any flour. But I assure you that there was not enough poison in there to kill a strong and healthy person. I only did it to slow the Blue Coats down."

"How thoughtful of you," Roger sarcastically says. "Well, unfortunately, your last maneuver has enraged General Phillips, and he has put a bounty on your head. You are now a wanted man. He has given strict orders to his men to find you and arrest you. You will be made as an example to everyone else, given a trial, and then hanged."

"This does not surprise me, nor does it concern me, as this is not the first time your people have wanted a noose wrapped around my neck."

"You need to be concerned, White Horse, as General Phillips will stop at nothing to find you."

"My brother," White Horse sighs. "You have such little faith in me. I appreciate your concern for me, and you have come a long way to tell me this, and for that, I am thankful. Winter is fast approaching, and the white stuff will blanket the land. Soon, I will move my people further up into the hills and caves, where we will remain until spring arrives. The Blue Coats will be moving slowly, and where I am going, they will have a hard time manipulating their ponies through the deep snow. Do not fear for me, Great Healer, as I will be fine."

"I wish I was as confident as you are. I do worry for you, White Horse. I know General Phillips very well, and he is not a man you want to mess with."

"Neither am I," White Horse adds.

White Horse can see the deep concern on Roger's face, and he understands why, but White Horse has never backed down to anyone, and he knows the hills like the back of his hand. He is certain he can stay ahead of the General throughout the winter.

"Stay with us for the evening and have dinner with us and stand beside me around the fire as my warriors sing and dance.

Tonight, my brother, we will think no more of this, and we will enjoy our time together because within the next few days, we will be moving on, and we will not see each other again until spring."

"There is one more thing," Roger says.

"Then tell me."

"I received a post from Stella regarding Matthew. She is on her way to the Orphanage and will arrive before winter. I sent Sister Ann some money to get Stella started and told her that I would be there early spring to see her."

"I will make Blue Thunder aware of this and try to keep him still until after winter, but I make no guarantees to this as he is very anxious to see him."

"You need to stress to him the importance of waiting. I know Stella very well, and if I am there, things will go smoothly."

"I will tell him," White Horse says. "But I know Blue Thunder very well, too. No amount of snow would stop him from getting to his son, nor would I. I will talk to him, he usually listens to me."

"Thank you, White Horse," Roger says.

"Now, let us go home and enjoy our evening."

The evening is filled with much joy and laughter, and not once was Red Hawk or the bounty ever mentioned. Come morning, it was time to say our goodbyes. I hug my brother longer than I normally do, as I know it could be many months before I see him again. I then turn to Rose and repeat the same action.

"Do try to come," she tells me after getting on her horse.

"I will try," I smile up at her.

White Horse stands beside me as I watch both Roger and Rose leave with our scouts, who will escort them part of their way home.

"What was that all about?" White Horse asks me.

"She invited all of us to their place for Christmas."

"I am sorry, my love. I cannot make any promises."

"I know," I tell him, disappointed, before turning around and heading into our lodge.

CHAPTER TWENTY-SEVEN
A Chief's Frustration

Several days pass. This time tomorrow, we will be well on our way to our winter home. White Horse has been diligent in his pursuit of Red Hawk, and he and his warriors have been smoking out every cave and cavern that they come across. He found a cave with fresh evidence in it of Red Hawk recently being there, and by the campfire still smoldering inside it, he concludes that he has only missed Red Hawk by a few hours. This infuriates White Horse, and it deepens his thirst to find him. With the first snow only days away, White Horse is racing against the clock. He is certain if Dancing Bear is still his captive that, Red Hawk will not be far away, and it is only a matter of time until he finds him.

Slumber hits the camp. I snuggle up next to White Horse as we sleep. Outside, Dancing Bear is tied to her post. She is growing weak from her lack of food and water, but she still refuses to tell White Horse where Red Hawk is. Two warriors are always standing guard over her. Tonight, the temperature has dropped significantly. Dancing Bear squirms to try to get warm. One of the warriors who are guarding her is having to find a bush. He tells the other warrior that he will be right back. The one that is left alone rubs his hands together for warmth.

Suddenly, he is hit from behind on his head by the handle of Red Hawk's knife. He falls unconscious on the ground. Red Hawk rushes over and wakes up Dancing Bear. She gasps upon seeing him.

"Shh," he cautions. "We must hurry. The other one won't be gone long." Red Hawk cuts her hands free and helps her to her feet. She flings her arms around him.

"We do not have time for this right now," he whispers to her in his tongue. "We must hurry."

He takes her hand and quietly guides her through the camp. The warrior who had to find a bush stepped out of the trees and came face to face with Red Hawk. Dancing Bear gasps in horror. A fearless Red Hawk wastes no time charging the warrior, and after a brief wrestle with him, Red Hawk curls his arm around the warrior's neck and breaks it. The warrior falls dead to the ground. He grabs Dancing Bear's arm and rushes her off. They are near the trees when they are spotted by one of the scouts. Red Hawk knows that he has been detected and that in a few minutes, the scout will have woken up the rest of the warriors and alerted them of his presence. There will be too many for him to fight off alone.

"Run!" he tells Dancing Bear as he grabs her hand and rushes her into the darkness of the trees.

It does not take long for White Horse to become aware of the situation, and he is quickly on his feet and leading his warriors in the chase through the woods. Red Hawk does not have time to cover his tracks, as the warriors are not far behind them. Dancing Bear is weak from lack of food and water and is hindering their escape. Red Hawk only has to get her as far as his pony, which is grazing not too far away, and then he can rush them both to safety. He pulls his wife behind a cluster of bushes, keeping them low to the ground, when he hears the warriors getting closer. He can hear them talking through the trees. He can see Koawa only inches away from him. He removes his tomahawk from his waist and is ready to pounce should Koawa turn around and head his way. He hears White Horse speak in his tongue.

"Spread out, he has to be close," he tells his warriors.

Red Hawk watches the warriors scatter. He slowly comes out of the bushes and looks around. Seeing that, for the moment, the coast is clear, he motions for his wife to come. He takes her hand, and together, they make a run for it. He is almost to his horse with only a few paces left to run. He is then hit in the shoulder with an arrow. Dancing Bear screams.

"Go! Go! Go!" he yells. "Get to the pony."

His shoulder is throbbing, but he continues running as he removes the arrow from his shoulder. He helps his wife onto the horse before jumping behind her. He is then hit again with an arrow in the leg. He bellows out in agony as Dancing Bear cries in fear. Red Hawk pulls out the arrow from his leg, tossing it to the ground. He then kicks his horse hard, and they take off in a run. Another arrow is flown over his head as they make their escape. White Horse stands in the clearing of the trees, looking out onto the prairie, watching Red Hawk running off. He curses under his breath out of frustration. He was so close to capturing him.

The day arrives when we need to move on to our winter home. Kikimo is asking to see Eagle Scout's scaffold before we leave. This is the first time that he has been able to bring himself to see it since his death. Together, we make the short ride out there. I stand beside him as we look down into the valley where all the scaffolds stand up high. For many moments, Kikimo is still. There is very little expression on his face. I am unclear as to what his mind is thinking. I wrap my arm around his waist as he gazes on. Finally, he decides he has seen enough and somberly walks away. Together, we then make our ride back to camp. On our arrival, the camp is nearly packed up, and the travois with our belongings are tied behind our pack horses. I only have a few more items that I need to pack up before we leave. I have not been able to talk much to White Horse after Red Hawk got away. It weighs heavily on his mind, and it is greatly affecting his mood. I have something that I need to tell him prior to us leaving. I walk up alongside him as he is watching the camp being packed up.

"We are nearly done," I tell him.

"Good," he says, failing to look my way.

"White Horse, Rose told me that Roger offered you his cavern to stay in until the General backs off."

"Yes, he did," he speaks.

"Why didn't you accept?"

"The choices I make are not for you to question," he snaps.

In all the years that I have been married to White Horse, never has he been curt with me. I am very taken aback by this.

"I did not mean to anger you, White Horse. I am sorry if my words offend you. I am just curious as to why you would not accept such a generous offer."

"I am a Chief. The choices I make are of my own, and I do not need to consult the feeble mind of a woman."

I raise my eyebrows in disbelief at my husband's comment. I understand that he is frustrated and perhaps feeling like a fool because Red Hawk is getting the best of him, but that is no reason to insult me. I am completely blown away by this and perturbed that he even went there with me.

"Yes, my Chief," I sarcastically say as I bow to him.

White Horse towers over me.

"That's right, I am your Chief, and I have given you orders to pack up the camp and get the children ready for travel. Now go do it!"

I glare up at him. I love White Horse to death and he is one hell of a husband, but right now, I am not liking him. I know better than to push his temper any further. I bite my tongue from spatting off and adding more fuel to his fire and huff off.

White Horse watches his Prairie Dawn storm off and is immediately remorseful for his behavior towards her. Never has he been curt with her, and he is feeling like a fool that he was. His mind is so weighed down from frustration over Red Hawk that it is affecting his mood, but that is no excuse for taking it out on his wife. He will leave her alone to cool off for now. But he will make a point when they are alone tonight to apologize to her and make it up to her by showing her how much he loves her on their pelt.

Darkness falls on the Great Prairie. Soft speckles of snow are starting to dust the land. Red Hawk and Dancing Bear find shelter for the night in an abandoned den. Red Hawk is lying on a pelt, cleaning his wounds. With the help of Dancing Bear, the arrows have been completely removed from him. He had lost a great deal of blood from his leg as the arrow hit very close to an artery. Although they escaped with their lives and he embarrassed White Horse in front of his warriors on getting away, he knows that he is far from being triumphant. He is certain that White Horse will be chasing them throughout the winter, and they will always have to be on the run in order to stay one step ahead of him. They will not be able to camp anywhere near any water, as that will be the first place where White Horse will look. Hunting is going to be difficult, and game is going to be scarce. He thinks about Dancing Bear, who he just found out is four months with child, and being able to find her shelter from the harsh winter that White Horse is unaware of. His thoughts are interrupted when his wife comes down in front of him, handing him a chunk of rabbit meat that she just cooked.

"You need to eat," she tells him.

She puts the bowl down beside him when he refuses to take it.

"It is more important that you feed that child of ours," he tells her.

"I will eat later."

"I need you to keep your strength up," she tells him. "There is plenty of food here for all of us."

Red Hawk finishes cleaning his wounds while Dancing Bear eats. His shoulder is giving him little to no pain, but his leg is throbbing and continues to ooze out blood. He is applying pressure to it and will keep it covered. He is certain that it was Koawa who shot him. He knows how menacing Koawa is and what a flawless aim he has with his bow. He is certain that Koawa did not shoot to kill and was only aiming to slow him down. Unfortunately, it has worked, at least for the moment. It will be several days before Red Hawk will be able to make full use of his leg.

"The one on your leg looks deep," she tells him.

"It is," he agrees. He starts wrapping it up. "I know Koawa tips his arrows in manure. I need to keep it clean. Dancing Bear, we cannot stay here for long. White Horse is aware of this den, and it won't take long for his scouts to find it. He is moving our people higher in the hills for the winter, but he will keep his scouts close. We must keep moving."

"You cannot walk."

"I can ride. We have a pony."

"If they find you, they will kill you," she cries.

"No, if White Horse wanted me dead, Koawa would have killed me last night. He is picking me away piece by piece. White Horse loves to torture people, and he is good at it, but I am better. He will not get me, not his time."

"You two are acting like little boys instead of like strong warriors," she huffs. "You both just need to make peace."

"You saw what he did to Crow Dog," he barks. "Does that look like a man who wants to make peace?"

"He told me that you killed Crow Dog," she says.

"Why would I kill him? He was like a brother to me."

"I knew the Chief was lying. I saw him take Crow Dog alone inside the smoke lodge. I knew he found out that Crow Dog betrayed him, and he went with him to the great tree to kill him and then pin it on you."

"That's right," he lies.

Red Hawk blatantly lies to his wife about how Crow Dog died. She must never know that he was the one who killed him. He must make her despise White Horse as much as he does to keep her on his side and for his plan to work. Dancing Bear is filled with many questions and concerns, but she keeps them to herself.

"Where will we go?" she asks him.

"Do not worry about that. I know where we are going," he tells her. "Now finish eating. We will be moving soon."

The first day of our journey to our winter home has come to an end. We take shelter in a cave from the heavy snow falling outside. I have been in this cave before. We frequently stop here for night when we are moving from camp to camp in the winter and early spring. I know my way around the huge cave and the many corridors within it. It is in one of these corridors that White Horse and I will set up for the night. The children will remain with the other women and children around the central fire, where they will be warmer. There, they will eat until their bellies are full and be entertained until they fall asleep. It is not uncommon for White Horse to go off by himself in another area when we are traveling. He does this for two reasons. One is for his own protection if an enemy should sneak up on us as we sleep, and two, for him to have his time alone to pray to his spirits for guidance on our journey. It is not until the time comes for me to slumber that I will join him in the corridor. I am still perturbed by my husband's earlier attitude towards me and have been keeping my distance from him in fear of him ripping my head off if I say something wrong. I will allow him his space for tonight. I will sleep with the others and talk to him in the morning before we leave. But before I do this, I will start a fire and set his area up for the night. I am rearranging the stones when I see him coming. I fail to look his way. I feel his presence come down beside me. He softly strokes my cheek.

"You still upset with me?" he asks.

"Yes, Chief, I am," I answer him.

"This Chief asks that his beautiful wife forgive him for his foolish words. For I do not like it when we quarrel."

I tilt my head into his palm as he continues to caress my cheek. "Of course, I forgive you," I tell him. I look his way to see his grin. "I just worry for you," I begin. "My life was so hollow when I thought you died last year. I remember sitting in this very cave last winter and remembering how lonely I felt because you were not here. I do not want to ever go through that again. That is why I wished that you had taken Roger up on his offer to stay in his cavern. I want you to be safe and alive, and if that is selfish of me, then I am sorry. But I love you, White Horse, and I do not want to lose you again."

He outstretches his arm to me. "Come, my Love," he says. I go into his embrace. "I understand your concern," he says. "I truly do. I ask that you understand mine and why I will not go."

"I do, but I don't like it," I tell him.

He pulls me free from his embrace and cups my face into his palms.

"I know. I love you, my Prairie Dawn, and I promise you I will be careful because I, too, missed your touches last winter."

I have never doubted that White Horse loves me, and he has never failed at proving it to me, especially on our pelt. I chuckle to myself, as I know exactly what he missed. Our lips meet with a tender kiss, and all is forgiven. The rest of the evening, White Horse makes up for any unkind words that he said to me on our pelt. Being that we have reached the time of year when I can safely conceive and deliver, when the root to control the bleeding will be in bloom, I will not take the baby tea after our lovemaking is completed. When everyone else is in the center of the cave enjoying their evening and resting up for tomorrow's journey, White Horse and I will become one, and with the blessing of Mother Earth. Hopefully, another child will be made.

CHAPTER TWENTY EIGHT
The Cabin in the Woods

We are well into the winter, and there are several feet of snow on the ground. The hunt for Red Hawk is going strong. Several times, he has been spotted. White Horse is refusing to capture him. He is finding it more entertaining to toy with him and is making Red Hawk's life a living hell. He is always keeping Red Hawk on the run, and he is stealing the food from Red Hawk's traps before it can be collected. He is hoping by doing this, he will wear Red Hawk down, and come this spring, he will grow tired and weak and that he will give up his silly revenge and realize that he is no match to White Horse and will leave us alone.

Koawa and Blue Thunder left camp three days ago, and I have no idea where they went, but I see them returning to camp when I step outside to toss out some water. I watch White Horse come out of the smoke house and greet them. A brief conversation is made before both warriors head to their own lodges. White Horse then walks over to ours. I hold the flap open for him as he steps inside. I then come in behind him. Both the boys are sitting on their pelts playing a game. I watch White Horse come down beside them with a huge grin on his face.

"I am glad that everyone is here," he starts. "I have something to tell you all." "

What is it, Father?" Kikimo asks. "In a few weeks, we are all going to be leaving for a few days."

It is highly unusual for us to leave camp in the dead of winter. I am curious as to why. "Where are you taking us in the dead of winter?" I ask him. He smiles at me.

"Your brother's," he answers.

"Roger?" I wonder.

"Do you have another brother that I am unaware of?" he teases.

"No, you just surprised me," I tell him.

"Good."

"Why are we going to Uncle Roger's?" Kikimo asks him.

"For Christmas dinner," he answers. I gasped in surprise.

"What is Christmas?" Little Foot asks.

"Your mother can explain it better to you than I can."

"White Horse, are you sure we are safe to go?" I ask him.

"If the weather holds, we will be fine."

"What about the General?"

"Koawa and Blue Thunder have already talked to Roger. The General and most of his men will be at the Fort for the Christmas festivities. This will give us clearance to get there.

Our scouts will be watching us as we travel. Blue Thunder and Koawa will be riding with us if, by chance, we do run into a small group of soldiers on the way. Now, we will not be able to stay long, as we will need to hurry back before the General leaves with his men again after this Christmas thing is done at the Fort. Roger is going to go to the Fort a few days before we get there and see if he can find out exactly where the soldiers are. A few of my scouts will go ahead of us the day before and make a clear path for us."

I am totally beside myself with joy. When Rose invited us for Christmas at her house, I was convinced that White Horse would not take the chance of us going. His culture does not celebrate it, and he does not understand the full meaning of it to me. For him to allow this almost puts me in tears. I rush down on the pelt beside White Horse and toss my arms around him. I shower his cheek with kisses.

"Thank you, White Horse," I cry out. "Thank you."

As I am hugging White Horse, Kikimo nudges Little Foot.

"Let's go tell everyone, come on," he says.

They quickly put on their heavy buffalo robes and ran out of the flap.

"Are you certain that we will be alright?" I ask White Horse.

"Yes," he reassures. "I do not want you to worry about that. You have presents to get ready," he grins.

"I love you White Horse. I love you so much."

He curls me up in his arms and lays me down on our pelt.

"As I love you, my Prairie Dawn," he huskily says before passionately kissing me.

Somewhere on the snowy plains, Red Hawk and Dancing Bear are trudging through the snow. A few days back, Red Hawk had to kill their pony for them to eat. He was only able to save enough meat for one hearty meal as the wolves took off with the rest during the night. They are both tired and hungry. White Horse's warriors have had them moving nearly non-stop for a month. Red Hawk is desperate to find Dancing Bear adequate shelter so she and the baby that has been nurturing in her womb for six months can get some well-deserved rest and food. They have been walking all day, and Dancing Bear is exhausted. He must find her shelter quickly, as very soon, another storm will be blowing in. They come across a cabin with puffs of smoke coming out of the chimney. He sees a horse and a mule under a wooden shelter. He comes up with an idea.

"You stay here," he tells Dancing Bear in his tongue. "I will be right back."

Dancing Bear knows her husband well, and she is certain that whoever is in the cabin is going to meet her husband's wrath. "Don't do it," she pleads. "We can find something else."

"There is no place else," he says. "Now, hush! I will be right back."

She is not liking the idea of him going in on the blind and taking it on himself, but she is in no condition to help him and can only pray that he will succeed. She watches him sneak up to the cabin. Red Hawk is looking around as he sneaks up to the cabin. He hears no dog nor sees any movement at all. He peers into a window that is at the side of the house. He sees an older man sound asleep in a chair. Red Hawk smirks to himself.

"This is going to be easy," he says.

He goes to the mule and removes the rope that is keeping it restrained to the tree. He then makes his way inside. He slowly sneaks in and glances around to make sure that no one else is in there. He smells something cooking on the stove. It makes his empty stomach rumble. He comes up behind the snoring man and quickly wraps the rope around his neck. The man awakens to Red Hawk straggling him. He attempts to fight him off, but to no avail, and eventually falls to his death. Red Hawk drags the man to the door and out into the snow as Dancing Bear rushes up.

"There is something cooking inside," he tells her. "Go see what it is."

Dancing Bear is quick at obeying and goes inside. Red Hawk finishes deposing the man before joining her inside. The cabin is quickly ransacked by Red Hawk for anything that they could use. Dancing Bear stirs the pot of stew that is on the stove as Red Hawk bites into a piece of bread that is in a bowl on the table. He continues to look around while Dancing Bear finds two bowls and pours the stew into them. She places them on the table as Red Hawk gazes out the window.

"We can stay here until the storm passes," he tells her.

"Why not longer?" she asks him. "They won't think to look here."

"I cannot chance it. I know White Horse's scouts are following us."

"We have not seen them for days," she argues.

"That does not mean that they are not there. I know White Horse very well. His warriors will track us. It is just a matter of time."

He turns his attention to the stew on the table that Dancing Bear is already helping herself to. He lifts the spoon and smells it. He crinkles his nose up at the odor of it.

"It is really not that bad," Dancing Bear says.

"Right now, I do not care. I am hungry."

He finds a seat across from his wife and starts to eat.

Later that evening, Dancing Bear falls asleep on the old lumpy bed. As she sleeps, Red Hawk remains deep in thought. He begins to think of his wife, who is getting slower every day. He is concerned at just how much more she can endure. He would like to remain here in the warmth of the cabin and wait out the winter but is concerned at just how safe they are here. He knows it would not take long for White Horse's scouts to find this cabin and come snooping around. He is certain that they had not found it yet, as if they had, they would have stolen the horse and mule and most likely killed the mountain man for his food. He also thinks of the Blue Coats, who he spotted a few days ago not too far away. Either one of them could show up at any time. He then thinks of food that is in a limited supply. He himself can go without food for several days, but Dancing Bear is with child, and she needs her nourishment to feed them both. He knows he is eventually going to have to leave Dancing Bear alone to hunt. This will put him in a very vulnerable situation, not only to White Horse's scouts but to the Blue Coats as well. His eyes are heavy, and he needs sleep, but he will stay awake until sunset, protecting his wife in the event they are found. He will try to relax in front of the fire and think of his child, who will soon be born. He glances over at his wife, who is sound asleep. He faintly smiles as he thinks to himself about the future they will have together and how, once the flowers bloom on the prairie, he will have everything that he deserves.

CHAPTER TWENTY NINE
The Yuletides

The time arrives for us to leave for Roger's. With our presents securely strapped to our horses, we are on our way. The journey will take us two days. We will stop for the night in a cave. Despite the bitter cold, the sky is behaving itself by not providing us more snowfall and making our travel uneventful. By mid-afternoon the next day, the small cabin tucked in the bluff appears. We make our way up to the front door just as Roger steps out onto the porch.

"I was not sure you would all be making it," Roger says.

White Horse is the first to dismount and greet Roger. Max stops next to White Horse's feet to greet him as well.

"Our Great Creator allowed us safe travel," White Horse says.

"Good," Roger says.

Little Foot races up to hug his uncle around his waist.

"Come," Roger says to White Horse as he is hugging his nephew.

"Let us get out of this cold and next to the fire inside. Rose has some hot cider for all of us."

Except for Blue Thunder, who leaves to join the scouts nearby, we all make our way inside. We are immediately greeted by Rose, who, by the aroma that is filling the cabin, must have been cooking all day. As Rose is handing out cups of cider to everyone, Little Foot notices the bare Christmas tree standing in the corner of the room. It is obvious to me that his sweet little mind is perplexed at why there is a tree in his uncle's house. Seeing the confused look on my son's face, I come down to his level.

"Son, that is a Christmas tree," I tell him. "Remember how I told you about one a few weeks back when I explained to you what Christmas was to you."

"Yes, but where are the bright, shiny things that hang on it?" he questions.

Roger chimes in. "Rose and I were waiting for you all to arrive before we decorated it. That way, you and Kikimo can help us."

"I have never decorated a tree before," he says.

"Oh, we are going to have so much fun," Roger smiles. "But first, I hope you are all hungry because Rose has been cooking all day, and it is ready to eat."

"Yes, my brother," White Horse says. "I believe I can speak for all of us when I say that we are hungry."

Everyone gathers around the table. Roger offers White Horse the seat at the head of the table. Rose starts putting the food on the table as we all get our seats.

"Is there something I can do to help you?" I offer to Rose.

"Absolutely not, you are our guests." Roger pulls the chair out in front of me as he kisses my cheek. "Just enjoy yourself and let us do the work."

I grin over at him before taking my seat next to Kikimo. Little Foot has never eaten with White Man's utensils and is unsure of what to do. Roger sees his hesitation and is quick at coming to his aid. Kikimo, like his father, is too proud to admit that he, too, is clueless and is watching Roger as he explains.

"This is your fork. You use it to pick up your meat. This is the knife to cut it. This is your spoon. You use it when you cannot use your fork, like for your gravy and applesauce."

Little Foot smiles at him. Roger takes the seat beside him.

"Would it be an insult, Chief, if we gave thanks?"

"Not at all, Prairie Dawn gives thanks for her meals to herself all the time."

Both White Horse and Koawa have been around a dinner table and have sat through a blessing. They both knew what to do. Everyone gathers their hands, and their heads are lowered. Roger takes the honor of leading the prayer.

"Heavenly Father, thank you for gathering us all here tonight," he begins. "We ask for your guidance and protection as our guests return home. We ask that you put your hands upon them and wrap your shield around them. We thank you for the food that we are about to receive in Christ our Lord, Amen."

With the blessing made, everyone begins to eat. Roger takes the honor of cutting Little Foot's meat. This is a task that Little Foot can do himself, but he patiently waits for his uncle to finish before picking up his fork and starting to eat. The meal is delicious, and there is enough food to feed a tribe. Everyone is getting their fill, and the conversation around the table is filled with laughter. With our bellies full to their capacity, we all find seats and watch Roger and the boys decorate the tree.

Laughter is heard throughout as the little boy comes out in Roger. I am having the time of my life, and I am so glad that White Horse made it possible for us to come. Rose is finishing up the last batch of cookies and putting them on a platter. She then walks them over to the tree and lays the platter down in front of it.

"You each can have two," she tells the boys. "The rest are for Santa Claus."

"Who is that?" Little Foot says as he reaches for a cookie.

"Santa Clause is an elf from the North Pole," Roger begins. "Every Christmas Eve, he brings presents to the good little girls and boys."

"Aww, you are putting me on," Kikimo says as he is eating his cookie.

"No, I am not," Roger grins.

"How does he get inside?" Little Foot asks.

"Down the chimney."

"Why can't he just go through the front door?" Kikimo asks.

"Because he doesn't want to wake anyone up."

Kikimo is not sure that he can believe such a story and still believes that his uncle is putting him on. He looks over at his father.

"Do you believe this father?"

White Horse knows that the story is anything but true and that his brother-in-law is just telling tales, but he will go along with it because he understands that this is all part of Roger's and his wife's silly tradition.

"If your uncle says it is so, then it must be," he tells him.

That is all that Kikimo needed to hear, and he continued listening to his uncle's story.

"Now," Roger begins, "we will leave these cookies right here so Santa Clause can see them when he comes, and then he will take some with him."

"Why would he do that?" Little Foot wonders.

"Why? Because he gets hungry on such a long trip and needs something to settle his stomach until he returns home."

"I want to see him."

"No, he will only come to those who are sleeping."

"Why?"

"Because he is very shy," Roger says.

The time has come to get Roger off the hook for any more lies to Little Foot on Santa Claus, as I knew my son would keep drilling him with questions.

"Boys," I chime in, "if you want to open your presents in the morning, then I suggest that you get some sleep."

I help Rose with the setting up of the blankets. Roger offered White Horse and me his bed, and Rose and him would sleep on the floor alongside the others, but White Horse graciously refused and will be sleeping on the floor alongside the rest of us. Before too much time passed, everyone fell asleep. Roger quietly tiptoes through the house and into the kitchen, where he will pour himself a glass of milk. Careful not to make a sound and wake up his guests, he makes his way over to the Christmas tree and comes down in front of it. He placed the glass of milk on the floor next to the platter of cookies. He starts to eat one of the cookies when he hears movement behind him. He quickly turns his head around and sees that it is Little Foot.

"Those are for Santa," he says.

Roger is quick on his thinking. "I was just leaving him a glass of milk," he says.

"I see you eating a cookie," Little Foot says.

"Well, yes. Santa is getting thick around the waistline from all the boys and girls leaving him cookies. We cannot have Santa too fat now, can we, or he won't make it down the chimney."

"I guess not."

"Of course not, now you better get some sleep, or Santa won't come and leave you presents."

"Maybe Santa doesn't like our kind and won't leave us any presents."

"Oh, Little Foot," Roger says as he comes to his feet.

He takes his nephew by his hand and walks him over to his blankets. He tucks Little Foot in.

"Now, I do not want you to worry about that," he begins. "Santa loves all kinds. Now sleep, my little one, and I promise you in the morning, you will see how much he loves you."

The morning winter sun peeps through the cracks of the curtain as Christmas morning arrives. Everyone is rudely jolted awake, with Roger banging a spoon on a pan.

"It's Christmas!" he yells. "Everyone rise and shine."

"Why is it that the White Man always insists on disturbing a peaceful sleep?"

White Horse growls. I chuckled at his comment because I understood the humor behind it. Every time we have an attack on our camp, it is done early in the morning before many are awake. White Horse finds this cowardly, and it is a major pet peeve of his. Even Koawa, as he stretches, chuckles at his brother's comment.

"It is time to open presents," Roger grins.

"Oh boy!" Little Foot yells, pushing his blankets off him and racing to the tree. It does not take long for everyone to gather around the tree.

"Wow!" Little Foot says wide-eyed. "Look at all those presents."

Roger was very tired from his lack of sleep last night due to him playing Santa Claus. He and Rose were up most of the night wrapping the remaining presents and quickly sneaking out and putting them under the tree before either one of the boys woke up.

"Yes, it looks like Santa was quite busy," Rose smiles.

Roger comes down on the ground and starts handing out the presents. Little Foot was the first one to receive his gift. He looks at the gift and hesitates to open it up.

"Open it, son," White Horse coaxes.

Little Foot does as he is told as everyone watches on. He opens it to reveal wool mittens.

"Santa gave me this?" he asks Roger.

"Yes," Roger answers, "and this is from your Aunt Rose and I," he says as he hands Little Foot another gift. He opens it up to reveal a toy drum.

"Thank you," he says, rushing up to give both Roger and Rose a hug. "Now I can play my drum when the warriors are dancing around the fire."

Little Foot joins his father and me by the chair and shows off his drum while Roger reaches for another present. He hands it to Koawa.

"This is from Rose," he says. He opens it to a scarf. "I hope you like it," she tells him. "I made it myself." Koawa smiles over at her and wraps the scarf around his neck.

"It will keep my neck warm from the heavy cold. Thank you."

I can see the relief on Rose's face. Roger hands Koawa another gift. This one is wrapped in a blanket. Koawa opens it up and reveals a robe. He stands up and holds it up in front of him.

"I like it," he tells Roger. "I will wear it with great pride."

Roger grins before pulling out another gift. He hands it to White Horse.

"This is from Rose," he says. He opens it up to reveal a pipe.

"Thank you," he tells her.

Roger then slides a small crate over to White Horse. This one is from me.

"My brother, that is a big gift," White Horse says.

"You will understand why when you open it."

We all watch White Horse open the crate and move around the straw inside of it. The first thing he pulls out is a bag of sugar. I hear him chuckle.

"I missed the sweetness of this," he says. "Thank you."

"There is more, keep going," Roger says.

White Horse continues pushing the straw aside until he reaches another gift. It is a bag of tobacco. "This is a very good gift. Now I don't have to steal Koawa's," he jokes.

Everyone laughs. Roger turns his attention to the tree and pulls out another gift. He hands it to me.

"This is from Rose," he says. I open it up to reveal a bonnet.

"Oh, this is lovely," I tell her.

"Good, I was hoping that you liked it," she smiles.

I was then handed Roger's gift. Like White Horse's was, it is in a crate. I open it up and dig through the straw. The first thing I got to are two turtle doves.

"I had a hole put into each one of them," Roger states, "so a string can be put through them and worn around your neck. I will wear one, and you can wear the other, so no matter where we are at in life, we will never be too far away from each other."

"Oh Roger," I cry, "that is beautiful."

I return to the crate, dig further in under the straw, and pull out a book.

"Do you recognize it?" Roger asks me.

"Yes," I answer, teary eyes. "It is father's old journal."

"Yes," Roger answers.

"Where did you find it?"

"I found it in the attic of the Orphanage when we were moving. I have father's old rifle over the fireplace, and I wanted you to have something of his as well."

I bury the journal in my chest and fight back my tears as I thank my brother for giving it to me.

"Well, that is it," Roger says. "The tree is empty."

Kikimo lowers his eyes in disappointment.

"Ah, there is one more thing," Roger grins. "It wouldn't fit under the tree." Rose makes a quick trip to the bedroom and brings out a fishing pole.

"This is yours," she tells Kikimo. His eyes immediately light up.

"Thank you," he says. "My very own fishing pole."

"There is one more thing for you, son, but it is in the barn," Roger says. "Go out and take a look."

Kikimo was not alone in his confusion, as all of us were wondering what was in the barn.

"Go on, we will watch you from the door," Roger coaxes.

"Bundle up, son. It is cold out there," I tell him.

One by one, we all gather at the door and watch Kikimo go to the barn, within a few minutes, he returns with a huge smile on his face and leads a pony behind him.

"Spirit Dog," he says.

It is then that I understand why Kikimo is so happy. We watch him lead Spirit Dog up to the door.

"I can really have him?" he asks Roger.

"He is legally yours," he answers.

Kikimo races up to hug his uncle. "Thank you, Leski, thank you."

Roger is near tears after seeing the joy that he gave Kikimo. He tightly embraced him back. "I hate to interrupt a tender moment," I say, "but we still have our gifts to give. Kikimo, why don't you go tie Spirit Dog up with the rest of our ponies and join us again back inside."

"Alright, Ma," he says.

After Kikimo's return, it is time for us to give our gifts. Koawa goes first. He hands them out to each of them. Roger is the first to open his. It is a leather bag that is made from deer.

"Great Healer needs a great bag," he tells him.

"Thank you, Koawa. This is very beautiful, and I will use it with great pride."

It is now Rose's turn. She unwraps a pair of moccasins. She immediately started to laugh. "No more fancy boots," Koawa smiles.

She blushes as she remembers the hostility between the two of them when they were on the run from the Dog Soldiers and him breaking the heel off her imported boots. I then handed them each of our gifts.

"This is from the boys and me," I tell Roger as I hand him his first. He opens it up to reveal a bag filled with herbs and spices.

"This is great, thank you," he smiles as he gives me a hug.

Rose opened hers to reveal a dream catcher.

"You will forever be blessed with good dreams," I tell her.

White Horse comes to a stand and hands Roger his gift that he has wrapped around deer skin. Roger opens it up to reveal a pipe. White Horse is aware that Roger is not a smoker, so I am unclear as to why White Horse would give him such a gift.

"It is a pipe of brotherhood," White Horse tells him.

Roger grins and extends his hand out to White Horse to shake it. White Horse not only extends his hand to shake Roger's, but he opens his arms up and gives him a hug. Their tender moment is brought to an end when Rose announces that breakfast is done.

The time that I spent with my brother and Rose has been so gratifying, and I will never forget this day, but after our breakfast is done and everyone's bellies are full, it is time for us to go home. I say goodbye to my brother and Rose and join the others on my horse. With everyone mounted up and with our presents securely attached, we head with our scouts on home, with Kikimo trailing Spirit Dog on his lead behind us.

CHAPTER THIRTY
The Indian Scout

It is early spring, and a deep thaw has melted the land. It was a very long and hard winter for Red Hawk and his wife, Dancing Bear. They are both growing weak and tired from lack of food and always being on the move. Dancing Bear is great with the child, and her fatigue is seen throughout her face. This gives Red Hawk great concern. He allows her to rest as much as she can by moving slower and keeping on flatter terrain. This is not the safest thing for him to do, as he is wide open to being seen by any of White Horse's scouts or Army soldiers, but for the health of his unborn child and his wife, he is left with no other alternative.

He left his Dancing Bear to sleep under a tree as he went hunting. With spring in the air, the game is becoming easier to find. Red Hawk is pleased with this, as he worries about leaving his wife alone for too long to find food. He has seen little of White Horse's scouts and is certain that White Horse has moved his people on to their spring home. He, too, is heading that way. He is growing tired of his half-brother, and when he catches up to him in a few days, he will put his plan into action of kidnapping Prairie Dawn and killing both White Horse and Koawa. With a good kill draped over his shoulder, he is returning to his wife. He stops dead in his tracks when he sees a handful of soldiers and General Phillips standing over his wife with a gun to her head. He has no place to hide and no time to run. He fears his wife and his unborn child. He drops his kill and, raising his hands, he surrenders to the soldiers.

Roger is in his office when he hears a disturbance outside on the street. He steps outside on the walkway to see what it is. The walkway is filled with spectators watching General Phillips and his men bring in two Indians. Roger goes in for a closer look. He notices one is a woman who is very large with child. Although he cannot be certain, as he has only seen him once up close, he thinks the warrior is Red Hawk. The General has both his prisoners tied by their wrists and on the back of a wagon being guarded by three soldiers. Roger is immediately concerned for the woman, who looks extremely fatigued. He steps out onto the street. He rushes over to the General as he stops his men in front of a water trough. He watches one of the soldiers roughly grab Red Hawk by the arm and push him down to the ground. Another soldier grabs the woman. Roger hears her scream in fear as she is being tossed around.

"General!" Roger barks. "That woman is with child. I demand that you treat her with care."

"Unhand her soldier," the General barks. "I do not want to be accused of mishandling a woman who is with child, even though the child is Indian."

Roger comes down in front of her. He immediately can tell that the woman is dehydrated and malnourished. He grabs a canteen that is close by and gives the woman some water. Red Hawk is watching on. He is aware of who this doctor is and the connection that he has with White Horse. He could cause so much grief to this white medicine man if he wanted to, but he decides against it when he sees how much kindness Roger is giving to his wife.

"There you go," Roger tells her. "General, this woman needs food."

"She is our prisoner," the General says.

"That may be, sir, but that is no reason not to feed her."

"Very well, we will get her some food."

"Thank you, General." Roger comes to his feet. "And General, I ask that the warrior be given the same treatment."

"As you wish," the General growls. "Excellent, and when she is done eating, send one of your men to come find me. I want to examine her and make sure that her baby is alright."

Roger leaves the men but makes eye contact with Red Hawk before leaving. A soldier hastily walks up to the General, holding a sketch in his hand. He hands it to the General. The General walks over to Red Hawk and holds the sketch up next to him. He shakes his head.

"He is not the Chief," he says.

It is then that Red Hawk realizes that the General has mistaken him for White Horse. He thinks that White Horse and he look nothing alike, but to a White Man, he can see why they would make such a mistake, as to them, all Indians must look alike.

"You want the Chief?" Red Hawk huskily says. It takes the General a few seconds to comprehend what the warrior has said.

"You speak English?" the General says to him.

"Yes, and I can take you to the Chief."

"Why would you turn your own Chief in?"

"Why would you care? You want him or not?"

"Where is he?"

"I will take you to him, but only if you set my wife and me free."

The General faintly smirks. "I am not a foolish man, Indian. I smell an ambush."

"I want this man dead as well as you. He murdered my wife's brother and kept us on the run throughout the winter. You keep my wife here as your hostage and let your doctor tend to her until you have your Chief. I give you my word. He will never see you coming."

"How far away is he?" the General asks.

"Not far, you will have him in a few days."

"Alright, Indian, I will allow it."

"Pardon me, General Phillips," an officer chimes in, "I believe you are too eager to trust him."

"He has offered to leave his wife here as our prisoner. We will be heavily armed, and he will be watched carefully. I see no reason for concern," he argues.

"Men, mount up and give this Indian a horse."

Further down the plains and several days later, Red Hawk brings the General and his men to a place in the woods where they set up a makeshift camp.

"Are you sure he will be here?" The General asks Red Hawk.

"Yes, he comes here every year around this time to pick fresh herbs with his wife. He will be here."

"How do we know we have not missed him?"

"I know this man like the back of my hand," Red Hawk says. "We have not missed him."

Their camping out has paid off, and early the next morning, White Horse and Prairie Dawn are seen approaching on their ponies through the trees.

"There he is," Red Hawk whispers to the General.

White Horse is off his pony and is about ready to lift his wife down from hers when they both hear movement behind them. White Horse turns around just when the General and his men step up with guns drawn. He is quick to react and smacks the rump on his wife's pony and yells at her in his tongue to run. White Horse has no time to defend himself, as the soldiers are fast on him. He is quickly captured. His eyes turn to ice when he sees Red Hawk among them. He is certain that Red Hawk led them right to him. Red Hawk arrogantly smirks over at him. In his tongue, White Horse growls at him.

"I never thought you would give your soul to the devil." He then spits at Red Hawk. "You are dead to me."

"You are the one dead, and I will be the last face you see right before they hang you."

White Horse is livid and tries to break free from the soldier's grip to get to Red Hawk. He is quickly restrained before being bunted in the stomach with the back of a soldier's rifle. White Horse bellows out in pain.

I am racing back to our scouts as fast as my horse will take me. I quickly meet up with them. "Blue Coats have White Horse," I tell Grey Wolf in his tongue.

"Where is he?" he asks me.

"Near the meadow where we collect our annual herbs."

"Go get Koawa," he tells me. With that said, they are quickly off.

The tension is soon thick at the camp, as many of our warriors are out for blood. Koawa is trying to calm everyone down as he thinks of how to get White Horse out of there. Kikimo is involved in the debate as well and is begging his uncle to go along to help rescue his father. My heart is racing with the anxiety of the unknown of how my husband is doing. As Koawa is mounting his warriors up to leave, I begin pleading with him to go along. I understand that it is not likely that he will agree, as never is a woman allowed in a war, especially a Chief's wife, but I had to try.

"Please, Koawa, I promise when the fighting begins that I will not get in the way. Please, Koawa, let me go."

"You will go," he calmly says.

I will admit I was surprised at how quickly he gave in.

"Thank you," I tell him.

"Prairie Dawn, the only reason that I am allowing you to go is because I am not certain how they found him."

"What do you mean?" I wonder.

"I find it odd that they knew exactly where he was and did not even try to attack the camp. It makes me believe that Red Hawk is involved in this. With White Horse out of the picture, you will be easier for him to get to. That is why you are not going to leave my eyesight. Now go grab your pony, we leave now."

Attention is drawn to the streets when the General and his men, along with the Indian scout, are seen bringing in the Chief, who is responsible for all the havoc that has been going on. Spectators are watching on as the Chief is forced to walk behind a horse. White Horse considers himself very physically fit and can endure a great deal of torture, but his legs are giving in from the many miles that he has been forced to walk with no break and no water. Despite his fatigue, he holds his head up proudly and looks forward, ignoring all around him.

Roger and Rose are both at the Fort today to do some shopping and for him to check on Dancing Bear when they hear the commotion on the street. They both try to get a better look at the street to see what is going on. They observe an Indian being led in behind a horse. Roger looks at the Indian scout that is riding with them. He turns pale when he notices that it is Red Hawk. He was curious as to why he was not being held with his wife, who was locked up in a corral next to the stables like a horse, and found it odd when he asked one of the soldiers that was guarding her where he was, and he refused to tell him. It has now all become perfectly clear to him when he notices that the Indian being forced in is White Horse. He hears Rose gasp.

"Roger, look," she says.

"The son of a bitch turned him in," she hears him mumble.

"Roger, this is not good; we have to do something."

The crowd around them is getting large so as not to be overheard by everyone, Roger takes his wife's hand and leads her away so he can talk to her in private.

"What do we do?" she cries to him.

"I am not sure, but we have to do something because very soon, we are going to have a lot of pissed-off Lakota warriors out for blood."

"They are probably heading this way right now."

"I am certain of it." Roger pauses to think for a moment. "Do you remember how to get to their camp?"

"Yes," she answers.

"Alright, start making your way there. I am suspicious that you will run into them on your way. I am certain Koawa will be with them. Tell him to meet me on the hill where I met them on the day the Fort was attacked. He will know the place."

"What about White Horse?" she asks him. "I will think of something. Now go, love, and hurry."

CHAPTER THIRTY ONE
The Diversion

White Horse is held in a stall in the stable. His hands and feet are bound by ropes. He has not been treated well and has suffered several blows by soldiers to his face and stomach. He can taste the blood from his cut lip trickling down his throat and the pain in his ribs every time he takes a breath. He was offered some bread on a plate from a soldier, which he is certain contains the poisoned flour. Although it has been months since he poisoned the flour, he does not trust that the General would not hang onto a bag and keep it for later use on such an occasion as this.

He starts to think about how he is going to get out of here. He has been playing with the ropes around his wrist for hours and has rubbed them raw. He nearly has himself free. After a few more attempts, he has one hand released. He keeps a careful watch on the door for any sudden arrivals as he frees his other hand. He then unties his ankles. He makes a short crawl to the edge of the stall and peers out through the cracks of the wood. He tries to figure out the best escape. He can see soldiers all around and is certain that they are standing right outside the barn door. He looks up at the hayloft and then comes up with an escape. He reaches the ladder when he hears the barn door open. He quickly races back to where he is sitting, loosely ties himself back up, and pretends that he is asleep. He feels the presence of the soldier standing in front of him.

"Hey," he hears him say. White Horse fails to move. He feels the soldier kick him.

"Hey, Chief, wake up." White Horse remains motionless. "Filthy Indian," the soldier says.

The soldier reaches down to grab the plate of bread, but before he comes to a stand, White Horse has him in a death hold around his neck. He remains tightly gripped and watches the soldier struggle to free himself until he falls limp and dies. White Horse then comes to his feet. He drags the soldier's dead body behind some bales of straw and then makes his escape up to the hayloft. He rubs his aching ribs as he starts to climb the ladder. He pushes the hay loft window open and peers out. He observes several tall buildings not that far from him. He reaches for the rope that is dangling from outside of the loft and swings himself to the ground below. He crouches down behind some crates next to the corral. He sizes up the situation as he plans an escape. He thinks about stealing a horse and making a run for it, but the Fort is heavily guarded, and he knows he will not get far. He looks up at the tall buildings that line evenly down the street. The only escape that he can see is on the rooftops. He comes down on all fours to better cover himself as he crawls as fast as he can to the closest building. He stops along the way and dodges underneath a wagon when he hears two women approaching, conversing amongst themselves.

He watches from under the wagon as the women walk by. Seeing that the coast is clear, he continues. He reaches the first building. He sees a woman with her back turned, sweeping the walkway. He sneaks up behind her and makes his way into the alley. He finds a way to climb up to the roof. Keeping himself low, he scales four rooftops. He can see the open prairie behind the wall. His freedom is only a few yards away. He cannot go any further on the rooftops and is forced to jump down. He looks around and sees nothing. He is at the back of the Fort in an area that is not heavily guarded. He has a clear run to the prairie. He runs past the last home. He stops in his tracks when he is spotted by a woman hanging up her clothes behind her home. She gasps when she sees him. White Horse is just as surprised to see her. She lets out a scream.

"Indian!"

White Horse is in a panic that her scream will be heard by someone. He is so close to getting out of here. He leaves her be and makes a run. He hears her scream again. He is inches from scaling the perimeter wall of the Fort to his freedom when he hears numerous rifles being cocked behind him. He knows he has been caught. Before he can react, he is struck from behind and knocked out.

Rose met up with Prairie Dawn, Koawa, and the Lakota war party on her way to the Fort. They made it to the hill that Roger told her to wait on. Roger is talking to the General and trying to make a deal with him on White Horse when he gets word of White Horse's near escape. He is on his way to the stables where White Horse was drug back to. The soldiers have ganged up on White Horse, and he has been beaten. The General is adamant that the Chief remains alive so he can be sent back to the main Fort and held accountable for what he has done.

"Men!" he scolds as he steps into the barn. "You lay another hand on that prisoner, and it is you that will be beaten."

The young, overzealous soldiers do as they are told and leave White Horse where he lies. The General stands over White Horse. He is amazed that he is conscious.

"He is a tough one, I will give him that," he says.

"Aw, General," one of the soldiers says, "you should just let us kill him. He is not worth the aggravation."

"No soldier," he argues. "We do things here the proper way. He will be put on a train tomorrow morning and headed to Fort Laramie, where he will be tried and hanged."

"That is if he makes it," the soldier laughs.

The General is a very serious man and does everything by the book. He does not find the soldier's comment to be funny at all.

"Go find Doctor Briggs," he says.

"I am right here," Roger says as he steps inside the barn.

He takes one look at White Horse. "You promised me that no unnecessary harm would come to him."

"He tried to escape," the General argues.

"If your men had properly restrained him, he never would have escaped," Roger snaps.

"My men were only trying to detain him."

Roger wants nothing to do with the General's lies and is furious that he allowed his men to let it go on as long as it did.

"You will leave me alone with my patient," he snaps to the General.

"Doctor, I cannot allow that. This man is dangerous. He has already killed one of my soldiers. I found his body behind the bales of straw."

"This man is in no condition to fight anyone, thanks to you and your men. I insist that you leave me alone to tend to him in private. If I need any assistance, I will let you know."

"As you wish, but do not say I did not warn you."

After the barn door closes, Roger turns his attention to White Horse. He has his back turned to him and is lying in a fetal position.

"White Horse," Roger says as he comes to White Horse's side. "It is me, Roger."

He hears White Horse moan. He gently turns him over to lay him on his back. He immediately observes the severe beating that his brother-in-law endured and is amazed that he is even conscious.

"Oh my heavens, look at you," Roger says.

"They are nothing but cowards," White Horse moans. "Tie me up so I cannot defend myself."

"I am amazed that you are even able to talk."

"I covered my face, so at least they couldn't break my jaw."

It is then that White Horse tries to sit up. He is in agony when he moves, and his breathing is labored, but being the warrior that he is, he refuses to let it hinder him.

"Easy White Horse," Roger cautions. "I am certain you have broken some ribs."

"My brother, you need to do me a favor and get Koawa. He will get me out of here."

"He will never make it. Your attempt to escape has heightened security. The General anticipates an attack by your warriors. There are soldiers everywhere, and they are heavily armed."

"Koawa will not let that stop him. He will come."

"I have a better idea," Roger says.

"What?"

"Did you eat any of that bread?"

"No, I do not trust that it is not poisoned."

"I believe that it is. I overheard some soldiers talking about it."

"What does this have to do with me getting out of here?"

Roger opens his medical bag to get some antiseptics. It is then that he sees the bottle of Ether. His eyes light up as the idea of how to get White Horse out of there comes to him.

"I got it," he says. "White Horse, I know how to get you out of here."

"How?"

"I am going to have to leave for a little bit. If someone comes in, I want you to lay motionless and not open your eyes. I will be back soon."

I have been sitting on the hilltop with Koawa and the warriors for hours with no sign of Roger. I can tell that Koawa is getting anxious, as well as the other warriors. The anger that their Chief was captured by the General and that Red Hawk was the one who turned him in has made every one of these warriors out for blood. I am not certain as to how much more patience Koawa has before he takes matters into his own hands.

"Rose," I say, breaking the silence. "Are you sure that Roger said to wait for him here?"

"Yes, but I thought he would have been here by now."

"Something went wrong," Koawa says. "I knew we should not have waited." Koawa is ready to get on his horse when I see someone coming in a wagon.

"Koawa, wait," I say. "Look!"

"It's Roger," Rose smiles.

Everyone looks out onto the prairie and watches Roger riding up. We are all anxious to hear what he has to say as we watch him bring the wagon to a stop and jump off. Koawa is quick at wanting answers.

"How is White Horse?" he asks Roger. "The soldiers caught him when he tried to escape. He has been beaten badly."

"Oh my God!" I cry out.

Upon seeing my reaction to Roger and my near tears, Blue Thunder wants to know what the Great Healer is saying and asks Koawa for a translation. Upon hearing the news, the hill is filled with many boisterous outcries by our warriors. Many of them are irate and are getting on their ponies to take off to the Fort. Koawa is quick at taking charge of the situation. Grey Wolf is the most vocalist and the hardest for Koawa to control.

"I understand how you want to go in," Koawa tells him in his tongue. "But let us hear Great Healer out before we act."

Grey Wolf calms down enough that Koawa can return to Roger.

"How bad is he?" he asks him. "White Horse is strong. He will be sore for a while, but he will be alright," Roger says.

He comes over to my side and takes my hand. "He is scheduled to be transported by train tomorrow to Fort Laramie. There, he will be tried, most likely convicted, and then hanged."

The tears are starting to roll down my face. Blue Thunder, who is like a brother to me, comes up beside me, places his hand on my shoulder, and gently squeezes it.

"We have wasted enough time," Koawa barks. "We go in now!"

"No, Koawa, wait," Roger says. "I have an idea how to get White Horse out of there."

"How?"

"I can put him in a deep sleep. To the soldiers, it will appear as if White Horse died from his beating. I will then tell them to allow me to take his body back to his people to be buried. I believe the General will go along with it."

"What if the General wants to see his body?" I ask.

"When I put him in the deep sleep, it will make his breathing very shallow. If I place a blanket over his chest, no one will be able to detect his chest moving."

"And this will not hurt White Horse?" Koawa wonders.

"No, I will only give him enough to keep him asleep for a short time. I will have to work quickly to get him out of there before he wakes up."

Everyone is still, as Koawa translates to the rest of the warriors on Roger's idea. A brief conversation is made before the decision is made to allow Roger to go ahead with his plan. Rose comes up to her husband just as Roger steps up onto the wagon.

"Are you sure this is going to work?" Rose asks him.

"I sure hope so, dear. If not, we will have a war on our hands and a sister who is really going to need me."

I watch Roger kiss his wife's hand before looking my way.

"Wait here," he tells me. "Carrie, I will bring him back alive." I dry my tears as Roger rides off. Koawa is quickly at my side and has me in an embrace when Roger disappears over the hill.

CHAPTER THIRTY TWO
The Fabricated Plan

Roger returns to White Horse. He sees him completely still, appearing to be asleep. He is relieved to see that the General kept true to his word and has left White Horse alone.

"White Horse, it's me, Roger," he says.

He sees White Horse open his eyes and hold his ribs as he sits up against the stall. His breathing is labored, and he is in excruciating pain. His tunic is torn open, and his chest is scratched up and starting to bruise. Roger is so thankful that White Horse was able to think of covering his head as he was being beaten, for if he hadn't, he is certain that his injuries would have been worse.

"How is Carrie?" he asks.

"Worried, she is with Koawa and the rest of the warriors not far from here. I told them my plan on how to get you out of here. Koawa went along with it for now, but if we don't hurry and he doesn't see you soon, I am certain he will come in."

"So, what is your plan?"

"You are going to have to die."

"How can I die and return here?" White Horse wonders.

"Not literally die, White Horse," Roger grins. "I am going to put you in a deep sleep so you appear dead to them. I will then request that your body be taken back to your people to be buried. I will then ride you out on the back of my wagon and take you to Koawa and your freedom."

"And how am I suddenly going to die?"

"Your beating was so bad that you suffered internal bleeding. When I came back to check on you, you were dead."

"You have a very mischievous mind," White Horse says.

Roger chuckles to himself. "You ready?" he asks White Horse.

"As ready as I can be."

Roger is seen by the General coming out of the barn. "Is my prisoner well enough to transport?" he asks Roger.

"Your prisoner is dead," Roger answers.

"Dead?" the General says, bewildered. "But how could that be? He was fine a few hours ago."

"Your soldiers beat him so bad that they broke all his ribs, and it pierced his lungs. He could not survive his internal injuries."

The General is not happy with this, as he wanted the Chief alive so he could be transported to Fort Laramie and the Sioux to be out of his hands for good. He is certain that this will cause an outbreak with the Sioux as soon as they find out that their Chief is dead. Roger hears the General deeply sigh.

"News of his death will bring gratitude to many Generals, and some may say that the Chief deserved what he got, but I am a Christian man, Doctor. I do not enjoy killing Indians, but it is my job, and I take it very seriously."

"Be the Christian man that you claim to be, and allow me to take the Chief to his people so he can be properly buried."

"This is going to start a war," the General says.

"General, I have been friends with the Sioux for years. I met them when I was a doctor in Willow Creek. They came to me for help. They are decent people who want their freedom. They fight because they have to. I can explain to them how it happened and return their Chief to them. I cannot guarantee what they will do when they see the beating that he received, but by returning him to them, you are showing them some respect, and that goes a long way with them."

"So, you know where their camp is?"

"I am not going to their camp. There are about a hundred of them stationed about four miles from here. They are ready to attack. I asked them to hold back until I could talk to you. They agree that they will stop any future attacks on the Fort or anywhere else if you release their Chief. They are unaware of his death. Give me his body, and I will return him to them and just pray that they don't back out on their word."

"You think they will stop?" the General asks.

"I think it is worth a try. At least you are putting in an effort to work with them and not against them."

The General thinks for a moment. He respects the doctor and knows that he is a good Christian man, but he is a little concerned as to just how friendly he is with the Sioux? He remembers being told about what happened in Willow Creek and how a small band of Lakota Sioux came to the rescue of the town when it was being attacked by renegade Indians seeking revenge on their sheriff. He was also told that their Chief took off with the doctor's sister as payment. He wonders if this is the same band and if it is the same Chief. He decides to keep his suspicions to himself but will be keeping an eye on the doctor in the future.

"Alright, take the body," he says.

"Thank you, General."

"But Doctor, I will be waiting for your return if you double-cross me in any way."

"I won't," Roger interrupts.

"Men," the General calls out. "Help the Doctor move the Chief into the back of his wagon."

I am sitting on the hill overlooking the prairie. Time is dragging on, and my anxiety of not knowing what is going on with White Horse is at an ultimate high. Terrible thoughts keep stirring in my head, as well as seeing visions of White Horse hanging from a noose. It is taking all my strength to keep myself from losing control. Koawa is nervous as well but is having better luck at keeping his composure than I am. He sent Grey Wolf and a few other warriors to scout ahead and watch for any signs of White Horse. He comes down beside me, and together, we keep looking out at the prairie in hopes of seeing Roger returning with White Horse.

"How are you holding up?" he asks me. "

The not knowing is the hardest. It is like the time when White Horse fell off the falls, and I was waiting for you to find him."

I couldn't control myself any longer, and I burst into tears. "Oh God, Koawa, what if Roger cannot get him out of there?"

Then we will go in and get him."

"What if it is too late?"

"You heard your brother," Koawa begins. "He is alive, and he will stay alive. If I have to burn that Fort again and kill everyone in there to get to him, then I will. He will come back to us."

I faintly grin over at him through my tears. He gently whips away the ones that are on my cheek.

"Have I let you down yet?" he asks me.

"No," I answer.

"And I never will. I promise you I will get White Horse out of there."

"You are so good to me," I grin.

Before he can respond, we hear Blue Thunder say. "Here he comes."

Koawa and I both come to stand and see our scouts coming in with a wagon behind them. I am too anxious to wait and start to run down the hill. I am joined by Koawa and the rest of the warriors. Rose, with her high-heeled boots, begins a leisurely walk down the hill.

Roger stops the wagon just as I get to the bottom of the hill. I immediately climbed into the back of the wagon, followed by Blue Thunder and Koawa. I see White Horse sitting up in the corner. I am quickly on my knees and have him in my arms.

"Oh, thank you, Jesus," I cry out.

I showered him with kisses. It is obvious to everyone the severity of the beating that White Horse received. He has cuts and bruises all over him. His tunic is ripped open, revealing the dark red and black bruises around his ribs. Apart from his cut lip and a bump on his head, his handsome face is untouched.

White Horse is greeted by his brother and Blue Thunder. While he is getting a warm welcome, he notices me wiping my tears.

"Do not cry, Prairie Dawn," he says. "I am alright."

"I was so worried about you."

"So was I," he comments. He looks up at Koawa. "Red Hawk brought the soldiers right to me."

"Prairie Dawn told me that she saw him when she was running off," Koawa says. "I brought her with me because I did not know where Red Hawk was, and I feared he may try to get her with you gone."

"I thought of that as well," White Horse agrees.

He reaches across and squeezes my hand. "I am so thankful that he didn't. My patience with him is gone," White Horse growls. "I will find him, and when I do, I will kill him."

"And we will all be standing right beside you, brother, when you do it."

Rose has made it down the hill and comes up to the side of the wagon next to White Horse.

"It is good to see you," she smiles. "You had us worried."

"Thank you," he says.

He looks over at Roger, who is beside Rose. "Once again, my brother, I owe you my life."

"I am just glad it worked," he says.

"Will you be alright if I leave?"

"Is there a problem, Roger?" I ask him.

"In order to make this lie believable, I need to return to the Fort. General Phillips is already suspicious of me, and I don't want to make it worse."

"What do you mean?" White Horse asks.

"When I asked him if he would release your body to me so I could take it back to your people, he asked me if I knew where your camp was. I told him I wasn't taking you back to the camp, that there was a Sioux war party waiting, and if I didn't return with their Chief, they would come in. He agreed to let you go because I lied to him and told him that if he released you, the Sioux would agree not to attack the Fort or the surrounding areas."

"Brother, you should not have done that," White Horse says.

"I know, and I am sorry White Horse, but I was running out of time, and I had to convince the General by any means that it was in his best interest to release your body to me. I am worried about it, White Horse, because he is aware of my history in Willow Creek and how I am friends with the Sioux. If he was to find out just how involved I am, it is I who will be hanging from a noose."

"We never should have involved you in this war," I say.

"I am involved in it because you are my family, and I do not approve of what the politicians are doing to you all."

"You are a good man, Roger," White Horse says, "and yes, I will be fine if you leave."

"I will see to it that Medicine Moon tends to him," I tell Roger.

"I will come and see you when I can." Koawa comes off the wagon and extends his hand out to Roger. "Go in peace, Great Healer, and thank you for everything," he says.

"You are welcome." With the assistance of a few warriors, White Horse is helped off the wagon and painfully gets on a horse. "Good luck to you, White Horse," Roger says. "I will see you soon."

CHAPTER THIRTY THREE
The Closure

Two weeks have passed. White Horse is in his lodge getting dressed for the day. He is feeling better, thanks to the remedies of Medicine Moon. He stops briefly from putting on his tunic to rub the muscle in his shoulder that still aches him and reminds him of the beating he received a few weeks ago. The search for Red Hawk is in full gear. Although there has been no sign of him yet, White Horse is confident that he will be found. He grabs his wife's hand when he feels her come up behind him with an embrace. He turns to face her, returning the hug.

"It feels so good to have you in my arms," I tell him.

"It always feels good when you are wrapped around me," he smiles down at me.

"Are you going riding today?" I ask him.

"Yes, I have not been able to ride freely for some time."

"Just do not push yourself, dear," I caution.

"Koawa will be with me," he grins.

I watch my husband attach his tomahawk to his waist belt and finish putting the last touches of his attire on for the day.

"White Horse, I am worried about Roger," I say.

"He is fine. He is just staying low for a while. He will return when he feels it is safe to leave."

"I would feel better if you would send some of your scouts to check on him."

"Prairie Dawn, if I thought he was in any sort of danger, I would be there immediately. Silence your worry. He is fine."

"Yes, I reckon you are correct. I will try to stop worrying about him."

"Good." He leans in and kisses me. "Remember," he warns, "you stay close to camp when I am gone."

"I am only going to the meadow with Medicine Moon to gather herbs."

"Alright, but you go no further than the meadow. I will not be far from you."

"Now, who is worrying?" I tease.

"Prairie Dawn, I do not know for certain where Red Hawk is, and until my scouts find him, I will not chance you leaving on your own or straying too far."

He comes over to me and strokes my cheek. "I bear to think what would come over me if I ever lost you."

"I understand."

"Good," he smiles. He leans in and kisses me goodbye. "I will be back soon."

"I love you," I tell him as he opens the flap and steps out.

Medicine Moon and I are in the meadow gathering herbs. We are sharing many tales, and much laughter is being heard. Medicine Moon and I have become very close, and I consider her as my sister. Rarely are we ever seen apart. On one of the occasions when we were it was when she took off with Grey Wolf. That was the day I accidentally stumbled upon them when I was returning from the creek and caught them in a tender kiss through the trees. We are taking our time gathering what we need. The day is beautiful, and neither one of us is in a hurry to return to camp.

Further down the Plains, White Horse and Koawa are sitting on the Prairie grass, conversing as they allow their horses to graze. They both saw Medicine Moon and Prairie Dawn in the meadow a few moments ago when they rode through. They are only a few minutes from them, and White Horse is confident that his wife is alright.

Back in the meadow, Medicine Moon and I have our baskets full and are sitting under a shaded tree. We are enjoying each other's company. We abruptly stop our conversation when Grey Wolf is seen riding through the meadow towards us.

"Go to him," I tell her.

She blushes and is quickly off to greet him. From under the shaded tree, I watch Grey Wolf get off his pony and reach for Medicine Moon's hand. I am too far away to make out what they are saying, but I can tell by Medicine Moon's stance that she is enjoying the conversation. I smile to myself as I remember back to the time when I was courting with White Horse, and we would secretly meet in the meadow. I, too, had a similar stance when White Horse would take my hand. I continue on my watch when I hear movement behind me. I turn around, thinking it is probably White Horse. I become stunned when I see that it is Dancing Bear. She is heavy with a child, and her face and clothes are dirty. She looks as if she has been crying.

"Dancing Bear," I say in her tongue.

"Help me," she cries.

"What is wrong?" I ask her.

"I am so frightened. I do not know what to do."

"Why are you frightened?"

"It is Red Hawk. He has gone mad. He is evil."

"Why don't you come back to camp and let me get you cleaned up. You can talk to White Horse, and he will help you."

"No!" she snaps. "That will be the first place he will look for me."

"Are you running from him?"

"Yes, we got into a huge argument, and I ran off. I know now that he has been lying to me and that he was the one who killed my brother Crow Dog and not the Chief."

"Dancing Bear, come with me back to camp. You will be safe there. I promise Red Hawk will not come near you. I can see that the time to have your child is near. You need to rest, and you need proper nourishment. Let me help you."

"Alright, I am camped out not far from here. Let me grab my stuff."

"No need," I tell her. "I will provide you with everything you need."

"No, I need my stuff. It is all I have," she pleads.

"Alright, let me help you. Just let me tell Medicine Moon where I am going."

"No," she argues. "There is no time. I fear Red Hawk is near."

My heart is going out to Dancing Bear, and I truly want to help her. I know she loves Red Hawk and her heart must be crushed when his true colors finally come out.

"Alright, I will go with you."

Medicine Moon turns her head to look at the tree where she last saw Prairie Dawn.

"She is gone," she says.

"Our Chief is just over the other side of the hill, he probably came and got her," Grey Wolf says.

"She would have said something."

Grey Wolf is more interested in Medicine Moon and her beauty and is certain that the Chief has his wife. He strokes her cheek in hopes of getting her mind off it.

"No, something is wrong," Medicine Moon says. "I can feel it.

" It is then that Medicine Moon makes a dash over to the tree and into the woods.

"Grey Wolf, something is wrong. Please trust me on this. Prairie Dawn is aware that she is not allowed to leave alone."

Grey Wolf can see the anxious look on the beautiful Medicine Moon and grows concerned as well.

"I am going to go get the Chief. You stay here," he tells her.

"No, I am going to go find her."

Before Grey Wolf can stop her, Medicine Moon is gone.

"We are almost there," Dancing Bear says. "Just right over here."

She stops us under a cluster of trees. I watch her grow still and step back. It is then that my skin begins to crawl, and I realize I have walked into a trap. Before I can make a run for it, I am snatched from behind by Red Hawk.

"Prairie Dawn!" Medicine Moon calls out.

She is frantically searching for any sign of her dear friend. Her skin begins to crawl as she can sense that something is wrong and that Prairie Dawn is in danger.

"Prairie Dawn!" she shouts out again before disappearing into the trees.

Red Hawk has me in a stronghold around my waist and is carrying me out into the woods. I am trying to wrestle him off as I am screaming for help. He quickly has me gagged and my hands tied together and on his pony. Dancing Bear has already mounted another one that Red Hawk stole from a rancher a few weeks back. He jumps on behind me, and in a flash, we are off.

Medicine Moon heard my scream, as did White Horse, Grey Wolf, and Koawa, who are all racing on their ponies to where they heard it. They split in directions, and each takes a different route into the woods.

I am frantic as we are galloping through the trees. I desperately need to get off this horse and somehow free myself. As much as I knew this was going to hurt, I lean over and deliberately fall off the horse. I land hard on the ground, and for a few seconds, I am dazed. I can feel the stinging in my ankle, and I am certain that it is either sprained or broken. The gag in my mouth came free when I fell and I can scream. Red Hawk has his pony stopped and is on the ground beside me. I attempt to fight Red Hawk off me with my good foot, but he is incredibly strong, and I am quickly losing my strength. I am in tears from fear of what Red Hawk is going to do with me and am screaming for him to let me go. It is then I see White Horse jump over a log and onto Red Hawk's back.

I hobble to my feet, come to a pointed rock, and start to rub my hands up and down it in an attempt to free myself. I watch anxiously as White Horse and Red Hawk are fighting. I look over at Dancing Bear, who is off her pony and is intensely watching the fight going on in front of her. I glance over at White Horse, who is giving the fight of his life. We are not far from camp, and I knew Koawa or Grey Wolf had to be close. I cup my mouth and give out the best war call I can in hopes of getting a warrior's attention.

Upon hearing this, Dancing Bear is angered. I see her grab a rock and rush my way. I hobble to my feet and run as fast as I can. Red Hawk is swinging a war bear claw at White Horse. White Horse dodges to the side to not get hit. He makes a bold move upon seeing the opportunity rise and kicks the claw out of Red Hawk's hand. He then takes his knife out and lunges at him. The men are wrestling with the knife. Each of their strengths is being tested, and neither one has the upper hand on the other.

I am being chased by Dancing Bear. My ankle is throbbing and is slowing me down. As large as this woman is with a child, she has incredible speed and is quickly catching up to me. I ran between two trees. My ankle gives away, and I fall. I stagger to get back up, only to realize that my dress is snagged on a branch. I attempt to pull it free and quickly give it up to shield my head when I see Dancing Bear right on top of me and ready to strike. As my head is covered, I hear a war cry. I open my eyes just as Medicine Moon comes up behind Dancing Bear and hits her on the back of the head with the bear club. I watch Dancing Bear fall to her death.

"Your timing is wonderful," I tell her.

"I saw you making a run for it and Dancing Bear chasing you. I saw the bear club on the ground and grabbed it. Are you alright?" she asks me.

"I think so," I tell her.

"Can you walk?"

"I think so."

Medicine Moon tears my dress free and helps me to my feet. I look over at the lifeless body of Dancing Bear.

"She didn't deserve this," I say. "She was just another one of his victims trapped in his web." I then gasped. "Medicine Moon, look," I say, pointing down at Dancing Bear.

Dancing Bear's stomach is moving. "The baby," I tell her.

"We have to get it out," she says.

"We must hurry. It will not last long inside her without its mother to keep it alive."

White Horse and Red Hawk are still going strong. Punches are landing hard, and knives have been drawn. Finally, after several intense minutes of fighting, White Horse is getting the upper hand and has Red Hawk up against a tree. Both men are wrestling with the knife. Suddenly, White Horse has Red Hawk pinned. He towers over Red Hawk and stares him down. He sees Red Hawk sneer. His boyhood life and years of torment that were given to him by this man flash through his head. Then, without so much as a blink, he jabs the knife into Red Hawk's heart. White Horse watches Red Hawk go pale and start gurgling for air. Never removing his eyes from Red Hawk, White Horse takes the knife and slices it up into Red Hawk's heart, giving him a quick death. He watches him fall dead to the ground.

Koawa has reached his brother, comes up alongside White Horse, and looks down at a dead Red Hawk. He sees White Horse holding the bloody knife. He pats him on the shoulder. "Now it is done," he says.

He hears White Horse deeply sigh. He knows his brother very well, and he understands how this was not the outcome that White Horse wanted.

"He gave you no choice. His heart was too cold," he tells him.

"I know," he hears White Horse mumble. "Nevertheless, he will be given a proper burial, and his scaffold will stand high."

Further into the woods, Medicine Moon and Prairie Dawn are attempting the delivery of a dead Dancing Bear's baby.

"Almost," Medicine Moon says.

I watch on as Medicine Moon pulls the baby free from its womb.

"It is a boy," I hear her say.

Just then, Grey Wolf appears. He looks down at the dead body of Dancing Bear and then at the baby that Medicine Moon just delivered. He comes off his horse and squats down in front of Medicine Moon.

"She was coming after Prairie Dawn," she tells him. "I had no choice; I had to kill her."

He gently strokes her hair. "Take the baby back to camp. Songbird has milk to feed him."

"I woke him up to be delivered. We will call him Sleeping Bear."

Grey Wolf softly smiles at her. He then looks over at me. "Can you walk?" he asks me.

"I think so," I answer him.

"Grey Wolf, White Horse needs help."

"Koawa found him. I left them to go further on to find you both."

"And White Horse?" I ask him.

"I will take you to him."

We head our way to find White Horse. Grey Wolf lifts Dancing Bear's body and lays it across his pony. He then gives me the lead, so I have the support of the horse when walking.

He walks alongside Medicine Moon, who is cradling Sleeping Bear in her arms. My heart is racing as I worry for White Horse, who last I saw was in a brutal fight with Red Hawk. Some relief comes over me knowing that Koawa is with him, as I know Koawa would give his life to save White Horse's.

We see the warriors walking our way. I see Red Hawk's body draped over White Horse's horse. I see the look of despair on his face. I know this was not the outcome that he wanted. The warriors stop when they see us approaching. White Horse is leading his pony behind him and stops in front of me.

"You are hurt," he says as he looks down at my ankle.

"I am alright," I answer him. "How are you?"

"I did not want it to end like this. But now our spirits will rest, there will be peace in our lives once again." He looks over at the baby.

"It is Dancing Bear's," I tell him. "Medicine Moon delivered him after Dancing Bear died."

He smiles down at the baby. "Red Hawk lives on through him."

"Medicine Moon saved my life, White Horse. Dancing Bear would have smashed my head with that rock if Medicine Moon had not shown up when she did."

He looks over at Medicine Moon. "I thank you. Once again, you have proven yourself. In your old life, you were given the name of Medicine Moon because you are a great healer. But you will be known to the Lakota as Night Eagle because of your wisdom and your ability to fight like a warrior."

I am certain that Medicine Moon is honored, and she should be.

"Thank you, Chief," she tells him.

"We will all go home now," he tells us, "And prepare the bodies for their journey into the Shadow World."

The moods are somber as everyone walks back to the camp, leading our horses behind us.

EPILOGUE

Over the hills, the grand home of the Orphanage comes into view. I can see Roger's wagon parked out in front and a small stream that flows behind it. This is the moment that Blue Thunder has been waiting on for many months. I stop my horse alongside my husband, Blue Thunder, Koawa, Grey Wolf, and Night Eagle. I look across to Blue Thunder.

"Are you ready to meet your son?" I ask him in his tongue.

Blue Thunder is a man of few words and even fewer expressions, but he has a heart of gold. Although he would never admit it, I am certain his insides are turning with anxiety about what is about to occur.

"Yes," he says. "I am ready."

I smile over at White Horse. He extends his hand out to take mine.

"You ready, my Love?" he asks me. I widely smile.

"I could not be more than ready to not only finally be able to see Matthew and Stella but to tell Roger that he is going to be an uncle again."

"Our spirits are at peace, and for that, they have blessed us again." He kisses my hand before giving the signal to the others to start moving down the hill. Our future may appear uncertain, and no one can predict where our lives will take us. But one thing I am certain of is that as long as I have my husband by my side, there is nothing I cannot do, for I am a Lakota.

366

The End

Join White Horse and the Lakota band in the 5th book of the Prairie Dawn series, Native Warrior. White Horse becomes a target that will make him question the loyalty of one of his own. A beautiful woman will capture the heart of Koawa, which will lead him on an adventure to save her life. Kikimo will come of age, and when he announces to White Horse that he will marry, it will cause friction between them that will end in tragedy. Roger will suffer a severe loss, which will result in his capture and arrest for Treason. A cavern filled with gold will become a sanctuary and a curse. Native Warrior is a must-read, action-packed page-turner with many twists and turns until the end.

About the Author

Karen Dee Musson is the author of the Prairie Dawn series. Karen continues her love and admiration of the Native American culture in her 5th book, Native Warrior. Karen lived most of her life in a small town in Northern Illinois and spent twenty-five years in Southern Arizona, where her knowledge and respect grew for the Native American culture. Karen currently resides in Northern Texas with her family.